These TWO
HEARTS

Kenna White

Bella
BOOKS
2015

Bella Books, Inc.
P.O. Box 10543
Tallahassee, FL 32302

First Bella Books Edition 2015

Editor: Cath Walker
Cover Designer: Linda Callaghan

ISBN: 978-1-59493-451-3

Other Bella Books by Kenna White

Acknowledgments

A big hug and thank you to Dr. Marvita McGuire for her expertise and her patience with me as I learned the ins and outs of laboratory science, knowledge she shared so generously while she fights an incredibly difficult and painful battle with cancer.

My prayers, admiration and my unending love are with you.

And a big hug and thank you to Mary Hettel for graciously sharing the details of her life with diabetes with me. I can't even imagine the struggles this entails. She is the kindest and most knowledgeable reference an author could have.

Both of them are true friends, or as they say, BFFs.

About the Author

Award-winning author, Kenna White resides in Southwest Missouri and enjoys traveling, creating dollhouse miniatures, her family, and writing with a good cup of coffee by her side. After living from the Rocky Mountains to New England, she is once again back where bare feet, faded jeans and lazy streams fill her life.

Dedication

This book is dedicated to Trevor,
a truly sweet, kind and energetic young man,
taken far too soon.

CHAPTER ONE

Sara Patterson snaked her way through the cafeteria tables to the one in the alcove reserved for hospital employees. It had been a long, stressful morning. The outlets on the microscope bench weren't working, the printer was in one of its contrary funks and she had just reported test results showing a young mother with acute lymphocytic leukemia.

Sara had only been working in the hospital laboratory for a few weeks, but wasn't sure she'd ever get used to heartbreaking results. Her previous job as an assistant in a research lab meant her day was spent pipetting serum samples and recording test results. Not interacting with actual patients.

She needed this lunch break and looked forward to it if only for a chance to sit down and relax. With luck she'd have thirty minutes of friendly conversation with co-workers to recharge her batteries. And with a little more luck the woman from Physical Therapy wouldn't keep hitting on her. A nice enough person probably, but Sara didn't have time for that. She had one last class to finish her master's degree in medical laboratory science and a student loan from hell to pay. At thirty-four years old, she had the job she had always dreamed of and was in the prime of her life. But since her last relationship hadn't worked out, dating wasn't very high on her priority list. She wasn't ready to plunge back into that dating pool. Not yet. Sure, she had those little urges from time to time. Who didn't? That's why God invented batteries. Right now she wanted to enjoy her egg salad sandwich and a cup of fresh, non-reheated coffee.

"Hello," she said, setting her lunch sack at an available space. "What's the cafeteria special today?" She studied the trays, wondering if she'd rather forego her sandwich for something cooked with melted cheese on it.

"Cardboard tartare," offered a gray-haired woman in Hello Kitty scrubs, her sneer speaking volumes. "It must be a new recipe."

"Oh, *ew*." Sara pulled a ceramic coffee cup from her sack and went to fill it, a perk offered to hospital employees who supplied their own cup. By the time she returned, three others had joined the table.

"Hey, Sara. Did you sign up for the cruise?" a stocky woman with bushy eyebrows asked with an expectant smile. "The deadline is Friday. We need five more to get the free shuttle and happy hour discount."

"I can't, but thanks for asking. I don't have any vacation time yet."

"That is so stupid. They should give you two weeks when you start. Not after six months."

Sara unwrapped her sandwich and took a bite. She was tired of egg salad. And she was tired of being asked every day if she was going on the cruise. Even if she had vacation time she wasn't sure she'd spend it on a cruise. She was probably the only person at the table who hadn't been on a cruise somewhere. Ilwaco, Washington, sat at the mouth of the Columbia River on the northern shore across from Astoria, Oregon. As part of Washington's Long Beach Peninsula, home to nearly five thousand residents and a popular tourist destination, Ilwaco was one of several towns along the shore. Cruising was a way of life, or at least it seemed to be. West to the Hawaiian Islands, north to Alaska and the Inside Passage or just up the Columbia River for a lazy weekend. As a voracious reader, Sara would rather spend her spare time curled up with a good book or walking the shores of Long Beach. Quiet, peaceful, stress-free in unobtrusive solitude.

"Did you ever consider she didn't sign up because she doesn't like cruises?" A thin woman slid her tray in next to Sara. "Hi. I don't think we've met," she said, smiling down at Sara. She wore a light gray pantsuit and navy blouse over small breasts. "I'm Margie Snow. Patient Accounts. Welcome to the tribe."

"Hello. I'm Sara…" she said behind her hand as she hurriedly chewed.

"Patterson. Yes, I passed you in the hall outside the lab Monday afternoon. I was going to introduce myself then, but you looked like you were in a hurry. You were carrying one of those trays of tubes."

"Phlebotomy tray. Yes, I was on my way to ER." Sara offered a handshake. "Nice to meet you, Margie. And you're right. Cruises aren't my favorite thing."

"It's okay. When the spirit moves you you'll sign up for one. I finally did and loved every minute of it. At least I did until we left the dock. Do yourself a favor. Buy a fifty-gallon drum of Dramamine before you go."

"Thank you. I'll remember that."

"You're going to scare her off, Margie," Hello Kitty scrubs whined. "We're trying to break her out of her shell. Not send her running for the hills."

"Is that true? Are you lacking a daring spirit, Sara?" Margie stirred her fork through her salad, picking out bites of tomato.

"She's cautious."

"I'm practical," Sara replied.

"Don't look now, Ms. Practical, but here comes your boss."

Everyone at the table looked at the white-haired man entering the cafeteria. Dr. Irving Lesterbrook had been laboratory director for more years than most employees had worked at Ocean Side Hospital. He wore dark trousers, and a white dress shirt and tie. That was his attire, every day, year round, rain or shine, regardless of the season, and topped with his ubiquitous plain white lab coat. Somewhere in his late sixties, it was assumed he was approaching retirement although he never discussed it. As far as anyone knew, his life revolved around his job at the hospital. He was a no-nonsense boss with an almost military demand for efficiency. He was also an expert on microbiology. Sara admired that in spite of his authoritative attitude.

"I have a feeling my lunch break is about to end," Sara muttered as Dr. Lesterbrook crossed the room with purposeful strides.

"Sara, we're jammed up. Edie is covering ER and Trevor is in the ward. I need you to come take care of a couple walk-ins. It shouldn't take long. Sorry to interrupt your lunch." He didn't sound sorry. He sounded impatient.

"Sure. I'll be right there."

Sara took a quick bite then dropped the sandwich in the sack and headed for the lab. Seniority-wise, she was low person on the totem pole. This wasn't the first lunch or coffee break she had been asked to give up. Working at a small regional hospital with staffing and budget constraints, she knew it wouldn't be the last either. She considered it a rite of passage. Demonstrate she was worthy of his trust. Demonstrate she was a team player. Demonstrate she could grin and bear it.

Sara stopped at the laboratory receptionist to collect the orders. Dr. Lesterbrook was right. The waiting room for walk-in patients needing laboratory tests was indeed jammed up. A gentleman with a two-day-old beard occupied the first chair just inside the door, his eyes staring off into space as if lost in thought. A thirty-something woman with a sleeping toddler on her lap sat across from him. Another child a year or two older stood on the chair next to her, playing with the woman's jacket zipper. Another woman Sara guessed to be in her mid-twenties sat in the corner chair. She wore faded jeans, a green army jacket and had her legs crossed. Not the typical crossed at the ankle or at the knees but a full-fledged, foot-perched-on-the-opposite-knee leg cross. In spite of her rough-edged attire and brazen posture, she had an anxious look about her.

"Hello. My name is Sara and I'll be taking care of you today. I'm not sure who was first."

"Take them," the woman in the army jacket said, pointing to the mother and the two small children.

The man by the door nodded in agreement in spite of his vacant stare.

"Marietta Lattimore?" Sara read from the computer printout. "That must be this little gal." She stroked her hand over the toddler's curly hair. "Mrs. Lattimore, would you like to come with me?"

The woman turned to the child standing in the chair and scowled.

"Loretta, you sit down and don't touch anything. Do you hear me?"

The child slid down onto her bottom and began swinging her legs. Sara had no children of her own but recognized a mischievous just-wait-until-you're-gone look.

"Ma'am, why don't you bring them both? We've got plenty of room for her."

There wasn't. The drawing station was a cubicle large enough to accommodate a phlebotomy chair, a small cabinet and room for the technician to draw blood. But Sara thought leaving an energetic child unsupervised in a waiting room with strangers seemed overly presumptuous.

The woman followed Sara to the drawing station, one child sleeping against her shoulder, the other scanning the room as if searching for something to grab as she was pulled along by the hand.

"Mrs. Lattimore, you can have a seat here and Loretta, is it?" Sara smiled down at the child, diverting her hand as she was about to grab the tray of test tubes. "I have something for you." She opened the cupboard and took out a plastic box of small toys and miscellaneous gadgets left by sales reps. "Would you like to play with these? I think there's an Etch A Sketch in there somewhere. And a few Legos." The child immediately sat down on the floor and began digging through the goodies.

Sara quickly collected what she needed for the tests, including a swaddling blanket with Velcro straps. As gentle and kind as she would try to be, there was no way to draw blood from children without them screaming and fighting the procedure.

"The doctor has ordered a throat culture and a CBC on Marietta. Why don't we do the throat swab first?" She unwrapped a sterile swab while the mother situated the groggy child on her lap. "Marietta, can you open your mouth for me and say ahhhh, sweetheart?" she asked, cupping her free hand under the little girl's chin. "It won't hurt, sweetie. I just want to touch the back of your tongue."

The child wiggled and tried to pull away, barking a raspy cough.

"Hold still, Marietta," the mother coaxed. "The lady said it won't hurt. Open your mouth." She kissed her cheek then helped hold her head. Finally she opened her mouth wide enough for Sara to quickly swab the back of her throat.

"That was great. You are so brave. Thank you, Marietta." Sara placed the swab in a tube, labeled it and set it aside. That was the easy part. "Marietta, can I see your arm, sweetie?"

Sara was willing to try to do the stick without wrapping the child in a protective restraint, but she wasn't expecting that a two-year-old would cooperate enough for that. She was right. The minute Sara tried to straighten her arm she began to squirm and whine.

"Shh." The mother tried to soothe the unhappy child. "Hold still."

"Mrs. Lattimore, why don't you bring her up here? Let's wrap her in this blanket." Sara cleared the counter and spread the blanket. "I know it seems harsh but this way she won't thrash around and hurt herself."

"No wonder the doctor's office didn't want to do it."

"It'll just take a minute. I know it isn't what she wants but it'll be over before she knows it." Sara handed the toddler a ping-pong ball with a smiley face on it as they went about wrapping her in the blanket, leaving one arm free. "How you doing down there, Loretta?" she asked, checking to make sure she hadn't wandered off into the lab. She was busy with the contents of the box. "Mom, I need you to hold Marietta's head against your body, just like this. Put your other hand on her shoulder."

Sara quickly secured a rubber tourniquet around the child's arm and traced her fingertip downward, searching for a vein. When she found what she was looking for she cleaned the area with an alcohol wipe, affixed a small-gauge needle to a syringe and pulled the child's arm down straight.

"You're doing so well, Marietta." Sara held tight to her arm as she slipped the needle in the vein and released the tourniquet. Just as she expected, the girl let out a blood-curdling scream and tried to pull away. "One more second, sweetie. Almost done." She quickly drew the three cc's she'd need. She covered the puncture site with a gauze square as she removed the needle. "There. All done." She applied a Band-Aid to the gauze then helped unwrap the child, hoping it would soothe her screaming. It didn't. Sara could hear it all the way down the hall and until they were out the door into the parking lot. Poor thing, she thought. Children, especially sick ones, shouldn't have to endure things like that.

Sara transferred the blood in the syringe into a labeled tube. Normally she would place the tube in the rotator and she would culture the swab onto an agar plate. But she had additional patients waiting. She set the samples in the refrigerator to be processed later and went back to the waiting room for the next patient.

"He's next," the woman in the corner said as Sara came through the door.

"Okay. Mr. Yates would you like to come with me and we'll get your pro time drawn? I'm sorry you had to wait."

"I didn't mind. Got to take a little nap." He smiled and looked her up and down. "You're new, aren't you?"

"Yes sir."

She followed him to the drawing station. According to the lab orders, Mr. Yates was a regular. He was taking a blood thinner and stopped in once a month to have his clotting checked. He was an old hand at having his blood drawn. He sat down, rolled up his sleeve and extended his arm. Sara collected his sample and labeled the tube.

"See you next month, Mr. Yates," she said, escorting him to the door, inserting the tube into the centrifuge as she passed the table.

"You're a good poker," he announced with a kind nod. "Didn't feel a thing."

"I'm glad. You take care."

One patient left. The woman in the army jacket in for routine blood counts, a pregnancy test and a BRCA test to detect the gene mutations responsible for many breast and ovarian cancers. Sara couldn't help but wonder whether someone in the woman's family had succumbed to breast cancer, raising her doctor's concern that she too might be at risk, or already have breast cancer herself.

"Jessica Singer?" Sara read from the printout.

"Jessie Singer," the woman replied, still sitting cross-legged, her arm draped over the back of a chair. "It's not Jessica. Just Jessie." She rolled her eyes up to Sara.

"Oh, I'm sorry. Jessie Singer." She smiled, lingering a moment in the woman's big brown eyes full of apprehension. "Are you ready?"

"Sure. I guess so." She took a deep breath then stood. The color in her cheeks faded slightly.

"How are you today, Ms. Singer?" Sara used small talk to allay the woman's fear, as she tried to do with all the patients she had to stick.

"I'm fine. Is this going to take a lot of blood?"

"No, just two tubes." She stopped at the laboratory restroom and handed Jessie a specimen cup. "Could you also provide a urine sample for me?"

"Why do I need that?" She looked down at the cup but didn't take it. "I thought this was a blood test."

"The BRCA and CBC are blood tests. This is for the HCG test."

"Which is?"

"The pregnancy test."

"I'm not taking that." Jessie chuckled sarcastically.

"Your doctor ordered it. It's just routine."

"I'm not taking a pregnancy test. I'm not pregnant."

"The test measures the HCG hormone in your body and can tell if you are pregnant even before you miss your first period."

"Look, Miss Patterson," she said, staring at Sara's name badge. "I'm not taking a freaking pregnancy test. I'm not pregnant. There is absolutely no way I'm pregnant. I don't sleep with men and I don't believe in immaculate conception. I'm gay." She took the cup from Sara's hand and placed it back on the shelf. "Any questions?"

"Nope. Not a one." Sara led the way into the drawing station trying to hide a smile. She wasn't all that surprised Ms. Singer was gay, but she was surprised at her blatant admission to it. In spite of the orders, Sara had to agree with her. If Sara's doctor ordered a pregnancy test she would decline as well and for the same reason.

Jessie pulled off her jacket and took a seat.

"Which arm do you want?" she asked, exposing both.

"Let's see what they look like." Sara sat down on the stool and rolled herself up close. She wrapped a tourniquet around the woman's well-proportioned bicep and palpated for a good vein. "This feels promising." She tested the spot with her fingertip. As she cleaned the area with an alcohol wipe she noticed Jessie take a deep breath and look away. "Alcohol is a little cold, huh?"

"Little."

"So, what do you do, Ms. Singer?" she offered as a distraction. But it seemed to fall on deaf ears. "You're doing fine. You'll feel a little stick now," she said as she slipped the needle in the vein and released the tourniquet.

Jessie sucked air between her teeth and stiffened as blood filled the first tube.

"You've got great veins." Sara held the needle in place as she changed tubes. "How are you doing?"

"You're sure taking a lot."

"Different tests require different tubes." She lowered Jessie's forearm, coaxing the second tube's worth.

"What's the difference?"

"The purple-topped tube has anticoagulant in it. That's for the CBC. Red-top tube doesn't. That's for the BRCA."

"Like I know what that means." She kept her eyes on the wall as she offered a feeble chuckle.

Sara covered the needle entry with gauze as she slipped it out then applied pressure.

"The CBC is a complete blood count. It measures hemoglobin, hematocrit, white cell count, things like that. It detects anemia or an infection. There. All done. Would you like to hold this for a minute?"

Jessie placed a fingertip on it.

"Press down." Sara covered her hand. "Helps stop the bleeding."

"Masochist."

"I beg your pardon." Sara snickered.

"First you stab me then you want me to poke it. What are you? A vampire?"

"How did you know?" She turned on the stool and rolled across the alcove to the counter. She returned with a Barbie doll Band-Aid.

"Wait! You're not putting that on me, are you? That's for little kids."

"You need to keep the puncture site clean and covered until it clots. And these are the only Band-Aids we have right now."

"But Barbie? How about plain tape?"

"I can do that." She pulled a roll of tape from the drawer and secured a strip over the gauze. "How's that?"

"Much better." Jessie flexed her arm then pulled on her jacket as if dismissing the pain.

"I'll walk you out." Sara followed her through the waiting room. "I hope I didn't hurt you too bad."

Jessie stopped in the doorway and looked back.

"I probably should apologize."

"For what?"

"Being a stubborn mule about the pregnancy test. I should have just done it and not said anything."

"No. You are always within your rights to refuse any test or treatment a doctor orders. I understand why you said no."

"I don't usually do that."

"Refuse pregnancy tests?"

"Out myself to strangers. You're the first."

"Thank you for that. And by the way, I'm not judgmental. I have no problem with it." Sara stopped short of admitting she too was a lesbian. Her family and friends knew. It wasn't a huge secret although she didn't advertise it. It was just who she was.

"Thank you, Ms. Patterson. You were very gentle." Jessie extended her hand.

"You're welcome. I hope you have a lovely day." Sara took Jessie's hand, the warm caress of it strangely comforting. Not at all what she expected.

"How long will it take for the test results?"

"The CBC will be finished today. The BRCA has to be sent off. It takes a little longer."

"I guess I can wait." She heaved a sigh then shoved her hands in her jacket pockets and started up the hall.

"Ms. Singer?" Sara called. "Try not to worry."

Jessie looked back with a frown.

"Tell my stomach that." She continued up the hall with long deliberate strides.

"I don't blame you," Sara muttered to herself. "I'd have an upset stomach too."

"Sara, are you going to shut off the centrifuge or let it keep beeping?" Dr. Lesterbrook declared as he walked past.

CHAPTER TWO

Dr. Lesterbrook stood in the doorway to his office with a cordless phone pressed to his chest.

"Sara, where are the HCG results on J. Singer? Dr. Simon's office didn't receive it. It should have gone out with the CBC four days ago."

"The patient didn't offer a urine sample." Sara was busy refilling the Coulter counter with diluent and hoped that would be sufficient explanation. "She chose not to take the test."

"You should have given her a glass of water and waited." He held the phone to his ear and said, "Sorry. We'll have to redo that one. We'll test on our sample."

Sara waited until Dr. Lesterbrook finished the call then stepped into his office and closed the door.

"I doubt Ms. Singer will return for that test. She was very adamant she didn't want to take it."

"Did you tell her pregnancy can be detected before she has missed a period? Let me know when she gets here. I'll take care of it." He gave Sara a patronizing nod and sat down at his desk.

"Dr. Lesterbrook, the woman said there is absolutely no way she's pregnant. None."

"Oh. A virgin?"

"No. She's a lesbian." Sara crossed her arms, wondering if she was going to have to defend the woman's choice not to be tested. "I find it strange that test was ordered in the first place."

"Maybe the doctor doesn't know." Dr. Lesterbrook raised a suspicious eyebrow.

"She confessed it to me and I'm a stranger."

"And I don't need to remind you her admission to you is privileged and confidential information. It can't leave this lab."

"Yes sir. Absolutely. And I'm sorry but we don't have the rest of her blood sample anyway. I bumped the top of the tube and cracked it when I slid the tray into the refrigerator. I'm not sure I'd trust it."

Dr. Lesterbrook glared up at Sara, his nostrils flared.

"Well then I'll let Dr. Simon's office know the remainder of the blood sample was compromised and we can't run the test," he said flatly then turned back to his computer. "Let them deal with it."

Sara hated what she just did. Yes, they still had Jessie Singer's blood sample in the fridge. It was standard procedure to keep it for at least a couple weeks for retesting and she knew how to handle test tubes. And yes, they could run a beta HCG test to suggest pregnancy. But for some unknown reason, Sara felt compelled to protect the woman. If the woman said she wasn't pregnant and didn't want to be tested, that decision should be honored. Sara went back to work, mad at herself for lying and mad at Dr. Lesterbrook for forcing her to do it.

"Sara," Edie called from the doorway that led out into the hall. Her attention was on something on the floor. "Come see this."

"What is it?" Sara slipped two tubes onto the rotator and turned it on.

"I think we have a visitor."

"Who is it," she asked as she stepped through the door and into the hall. A small beagle sat obediently against the wall, her body trembling. A blue "Therapy Dog" vest was slung sideways around her belly, one of the straps dragging along behind. "Gypsy? What are you doing out here, baby?" Sara squatted next to the dog, cupping her hands under her muzzle. "Where's Lucille?" she said frantically. She stroked the dog's head lovingly as it moved closer.

A large woman in her fifties burst through the door at the end of the hall, the one that led to the employees' parking lot. She looked panic-stricken. She had a dog leash in one hand and her purse in the other.

"Oh, thank God. There she is." The woman gasped breathlessly, clutching the leash to her bosom as she hurried toward them. "I was so worried."

"Lucille, what happened? Why is Gypsy here?" Sara glared up at her as she continued to pet the dog. "She's scared to death."

"So am I. Believe me, so am I." She wiped perspiration from her upper lip. "I haven't run like that since junior high." She braced her hand against the wall as she tried to catch her breath. "We were at the nursing home, waiting for them to buzz us in the door and she took off. I had my arms full and I couldn't catch her. She was galloping across the parking lot before I could turn around."

"Did you have the leash on her?" Sara straightened the vest and adjusted the straps.

"No," she replied sheepishly. "But she walked right beside me from the car to the porch, just like she always does. Then this truck started backing up and she took off. You know how they have that obnoxious beeping sound. It must have scared her. I'm so sorry, Sara." She looked down at Gypsy and added, "I'm sorry, sweetie. But you're supposed to stay with Auntie Lucille when we go visiting. Remember, we talked about this."

"Lucille, she's a therapy dog. Not a guide dog. She isn't trained to stay at your side. If she hears loud noises she gets scared. That's why the leash." Sara took the leash from her hand and attached it to Gypsy's collar.

Edie knelt on the floor and pet the dog lovingly.

"Is this your dog, Sara? She's so cute." Edie scratched her nails under the pup's chin. "Yes you are." She kissed the dog's head then let her lick her face. Edie's long bangs, a curious shade of hot pink, dangled over Gypsy's muzzle.

"I hope you plan to wash your face and hands, Edie," Dr. Lesterbrook said as he came out the door and headed up the hall. "Don't you ladies have work to do?"

"Here you go, Lucille. Please keep the leash on her, okay?" Gypsy was on her feet, tail wagging enthusiastically.

"Absolutely. We won't forget, will we?" She smiled down at the dog as they headed for the door. "Tell Mommy bye-bye."

Sara rolled her eyes.

"You have a therapy dog?" Edie asked.

"Yes, and I hope this wasn't a bad idea." They headed back into the lab.

"Okay, I have to ask. Why do you have a therapy dog but you work in the lab? And what is that woman doing with her?"

"Gypsy used to belong to my neighbor. Pauline trained her as a therapy dog from the time she was a puppy. She'd take her to visit nursing homes and assisted living facilities all the time. Gypsy has a wonderfully gentle temperament and loves people. When Pauline passed away last year her family was going to give Gypsy up to the humane society. No one wanted to take her, so I did. Lucille is a social worker. She convinced me to let her continue using Gypsy at the local hospice and nursing homes. It's amazing to watch her bond with people. She seems to know when it's okay to move closer or give a little nudge. Lucille is good with her, normally. She's also my doggie daycare when I need a babysitter. She loves Gypsy and loves having her visit."

"How did Gypsy know how to find you? The nursing home is on the complete other end of the parking lot."

"Good question." Sara hated the thought of her dog running loose, frightened and desperate. It was an image she had trouble getting out of her head.

* * *

Sara sat staring through the microscope, counting cells, oblivious to her surroundings. The gentle rain against the window provided the perfect white noise for the time-consuming urinalysis. It had been three days since Dr. Lesterbrook reported Jessie Singer's pregnancy test wouldn't be run. Sara half expected a lecture about protecting the integrity of specimens but nothing else was said about it. Subject closed, at least for now.

"Excuse me," someone said from across the laboratory.

Sara's first thought, what was an unescorted patient doing in the lab?

"One minute, please," she said then looked up, her concentration gone.

Jessie Singer stood in the open doorway, her hair damp and matted against her forehead. She had a backpack slung over one shoulder.

"Hello, again." Sara spun around on the stool. "Let me guess. It's raining in Washington."

"Yeah. Just a dab." She pulled a quick though apprehensive smile.

"If you're back for the pregnancy test, you don't have to take it. The doctor's office can't make you. Don't let them bully you into any test you're not comfortable taking."

"That's not why I'm here." Jessie rotated her keys around her finger nervously. "Have you got them?"

"Got what?"

"The test results. The ones you said had to be sent off. Are they back? It's been over a week." She swallowed hard.

"Test results? Oh, right. BRCA. No, I'm sorry. I don't have them. Those results will be sent directly to your doctor from the lab. It'll take a couple weeks, sometimes longer."

"A couple weeks?" Jessie groaned. "My doctor didn't say it would take that long."

"I'm really sorry, but even if I had the test results I couldn't give them to you. That information has to come from your doctor."

Jessie mouthed a curse word.

"Sorry," Sara offered sympathetically.

"What's the name of the laboratory where you sent them?"

"Ms. Singer, I'm going to do you a favor and not tell you. They wouldn't give you the results either. It's all part of the HIPAA privacy act. And if you call and bug them you'll probably just delay the process."

Jessie heaved a frustrated sigh and looked away.

"Do you have any idea how hard it is waiting?" she said with quiet desperation. "My doctor said it's possible I have a genetic pre…" She scowled as if searching for the word.

"Genetic predisposition?" Sara offered, then took Jessie's arm and led her into the empty waiting room. "Let's sit down a minute." She waited for Jessie to take a seat then pulled a chair around and sat facing her. "I'm sure it's very difficult, Ms. Singer. Waiting out any test is difficult."

"They might have to cut off my breasts." Jessie slowly raised her eyes to meet Sara's. "I could have cancer." There was a subtle but clear catch in her voice.

"I really wish someone would explain this to patients before they send them off for testing. This test does not mean you have cancer." She folded her hands over Jessie's. "That's not what this test shows. Genetic testing is meant to show vulnerabilities to inherited diseases. Not their presence. The test can't determine whether or not a person will develop the disease, just the likelihood of it."

"You're saying just because my cousin died from breast cancer when she was twenty-eight doesn't mean I'll get it too."

"Was she tested?"

"I don't know, but I doubt it. She hated doctors and hospitals. They said she refused chemotherapy of any kind. Something to do with her religion."

"Has anyone else in your family had breast cancer?"

Jessie lowered her eyes.

"My mother. She died when I was three. Her doctor wasn't sure if it was breast cancer or meta-something lung cancer. She was a heavy smoker."

"Metastatic carcinoma," Sara said softly and squeezed her hands. "I'm so sorry for your loss, Ms. Singer."

"I don't even remember her, but the doctor said those two mean I'm at greater risk."

"That may not necessarily be sufficient lineage." Sara knew it could be, but it wasn't her job to tell her. And there was no reason to add to Jessie's already heightened anxiety.

Jessie looked down at her chest.

"I don't have much but what I've got I'd like to keep."

"Look, I don't have a crystal ball, Ms Singer. But I do know you're going to make yourself sick if you spend every waking moment expecting the worst. Relax. Take a deep breath." She patted Jessie's hands and demonstrated. "Come on. You try it."

"I really don't think a deep breath is going to ward off breast cancer."

"Neither will worrying. Remember, the odds are in your favor."

"You're the first person to say that. Mostly people just look at me like I'm a leper when they hear I'm having tests for breast cancer. They assume I'm already sick."

"Ignore them. You're not sick. How old are you?"

"Twenty-seven."

"You're a healthy twenty-seven-year-old with a long life ahead of you. Don't let your imagination run away with you. Stay positive. Assume it's just the doctor eliminating a needle in a haystack."

"I wish it was that easy."

"What do you do for a living, Ms Singer, if you don't mind me asking?"

"Pool." She was obviously still wrestling with the possibilities and paid little attention to Sara's question.

"Oh. Do you clean pools or install them?"

"It's not that kind of pool. It's billiards."

"So you play pool for a living."

"Yeah, when I'm not waiting for test results that could change my life."

Sara closed her eyes tight and tilted her face upward as she clutched Jessie's hands to her chest.

"What are you doing? Having a séance?"

"No. Just reporting my wishes and expectations to the powers that be."

"I feel like an idiot. How many of your patients act like jerks?" Jessie finally pulled away and ruffled her hand through her damp hair.

"You're not a jerk or an idiot. Your anxiety is a direct and understandable result of the lack of counseling you received. But you didn't hear that from me." Sara stood, sinking her hands into the pockets of her lab coat. "Try not to worry. I'm afraid I really need to get back to work. Is there anything else I can help you with?"

Jessie started for the door.

"Actually, yes, there is. Do you think I could put something on the bulletin board?" She pointed across the hall.

"It's not up to me and it probably depends on what it is."

"It's an ad." Jessie pulled a sheet of paper from her backpack and handed it to Sara.

"You're selling a motorcycle?"

"Motor scooter."

"What's the difference?" Sara handed it back.

"There's a big difference. A scooter has a step-through frame and a floorboard for your feet. They also have smaller wheels and engines."

Jessie was pointing at the picture as she explained, but Sara's attention was drawn to her long fingers and neatly trimmed fingernails. She had noticed them when Jessie came in for her blood tests. Dirty nails were a breeding ground for germs. Jessie's had no polish, but they were clean and nicely rounded with no dangling cuticles, not something Sara would have associated with a green army jacket.

"So, I can put it up? I brought my own thumbtacks." Jessie fished two from the front pocket of the backpack.

"Sure. Why not?" Sara followed her into the hall. The bulletin board was covered with business cards, group meeting notices and sale flyers. She watched as Jessie adjusted the other postings to make room. "Tell you what." Sara yanked down a card advertising Regina's Humidor. "That one has been up long enough. I don't think we need to support a cigar store."

"Are you sure I don't need permission from someone? No one needs to initial it or anything?" She pressed the tacks in snug.

"You're right. It should be approved." Sara took a pen from her lab coat pocket and initialed the corner of the ad. "There. It's official now."

"SEP. What's the E for?" Jessie asked, studying the initials.

"Elise."

"Sara Elise Patterson. Pretty. I like it."

Dr. Lesterbrook rounded the corner and hurried down the hall toward the lab.

"They're performing a spinal tap on a sixteen-year-old in the ER," he said. "They need a CSF, stat."

"I'm on my way." Sara turned to Jessie. "I've got to go, but please try not to worry."

"Thank you," Jessie said, with a nod of appreciation.

"You're welcome."

Sara headed into the lab to retrieve a collection tray before going to the Emergency Room. Spinal taps took precedence over everything else in the lab, especially when looking for meningitis. The teenager's life might depend on it. Jessie Singer's anxiety would have to wait.

CHAPTER THREE

"Does anyone know who belongs to this?" Dr. Lesterbrook asked from the door to the waiting room. He held up a navy blue backpack with a red carbineer dangling from the strap. "It's been in the waiting room since yesterday."

"Nope, don't know," Edie said, looking up from her seat at the computer. She popped her gum loud enough to be heard above the whir of the centrifuge.

Sara was busy at the microscope and didn't look up until she had finished.

"What's been in the waiting room since yesterday?" It took a moment for her eyes to focus across the room.

"This backpack. Do you know who it belongs to?"

"Look inside. Maybe it has a name in it or something." She went back to the microscope. Then it hit her. Jessie Singer had a backpack when she came in but not when she left.

"I'm taking it to lost and found. Let them deal with it." Dr. Lesterbrook turned to leave.

"Wait a minute," Sara said, crossing to him.

"Do you know who it belongs to?"

"Maybe. Does it have advertisements for a motor scooter inside?"

"I have no idea. Here. You take care of it." He thrust the bag at Sara then disappeared out the door as if escaping any responsibility for it or its return to the owner.

Sara unzipped it and sure enough, there were several more flyers like the one Jessie had pinned to the bulletin board. The information on the ad read "Contact Jessie Singer, Batch's Bar and Grill" and a phone number. Sara studied the flyer, wondering why a cell phone number wasn't included. Surely she had one. She rummaged in the bottom of the bag, hoping to find an address or phone number for someplace other than a bar, someplace she could call and be assured Jessie would get the message. She found an application for some kind of tournament, several road maps, a cell phone charger and a letter in an envelope, unsealed. Sara didn't open it. That would be an invasion of privacy.

"Find anything?" Edie asked, flipping her bangs out of her eyes.

"Yes. Remember that woman yesterday, the one who posted the flyer on the bulletin board?"

"Oh, yeah. The cute one with the brown eyes."

"Yes, well, her name is Jessie Singer and this is hers."

"Isn't she the one who refused to take the pregnancy test? Said she was gay."

"Edie!" Sara gave her a disapproving frown. "How did you know that?"

"I was in the storeroom loading the autoclave and she wasn't exactly quiet about it. I know, I know. Privacy rules. I haven't told anybody else. But she had an incredible body. Tight little buns you just want to squeeze," she said through clenched teeth as she pantomimed that action. "I love it when cute people out themselves. Kind of like Christmas all year." Edie didn't try to hide it. She was an out lesbian and didn't seem to care who knew.

Sara headed into the office to use the phone.

"Hey, you should ask her about her motor scooter. Cute bike. I had one of those. Great gas mileage."

"You had a motorcycle?"

"Motor scooter. Fifty cc. It got ninety miles per gallon. Saved a ton on gas. Of course the top speed was only thirty, but hey, around town, back and forth to work, who cares?"

"Ninety miles per gallon? Wow. Wish my car got that much. Gas prices are killing my budget."

"Buy it. Be a scooter hooter."

"Yeah, right. Me on a motor scooter. I think not."

"If you can ride a bike you can ride a scooter. You just sit there and steer."

"I don't think so. I've never even ridden on one."

"They're lots of fun," Edie said with a childish lilt.

"I'm sure they're great fun in the rain too."

"So when it rains you drive your car. Come on, Sara. Live a little. I have yet to hear you do anything for fun. Crawl out of your shell and do something daring. Buy a scooter. It's cheaper than that cruise everyone is talking about."

"Will you go back to work so I can call Ms. Singer and tell her I have her backpack?"

"Actually, no. I'm taking my break. Thought I'd let you know." She waved playfully and sashayed away. "Be back in fifteen."

"Hello. Is Jessie Singer there, please?"

"Nope," a man said. He sounded like he was chewing something crunchy.

"When do you expect her?"

"Da-know."

Sara heard laughter in the background.

"Okay, thank you. I'll call again."

"Try Friday night," the man offered.

"What time?" Sara asked, but he had already hung up. "I just love people with articulate communication skills." She'd deal with Jessie Singer's abandoned backpack later. Perhaps she'd remember where she left it and return to claim it. If not, there was always Friday.

Sara tried the phone number again on Wednesday and got a different though equally uncooperative individual. She was told Jessie worked on Friday but little else.

"You need to turn that backpack into Lost-and-Found," Dr. Lesterbrook said, pointing to the shelf by the door.

"I know who it belongs to and it goes back tomorrow." Sara didn't elaborate. Dr. Lesterbrook was a black and white kind of person. Tests are run in a timely manner. The lab was kept orderly and functioning efficiently. And left items should be turned in to the powers that be. Period. "It's all taken care of." Small exaggeration.

Sara looked up the address for Batch's Bar and Grill and planned to stop by after dinner Friday evening. As much as she tried to ignore her curiosity, she wanted to ask about the motor scooter. A few weeks ago she never would have considered it. But something childishly wicked had her wondering if Edie was right. She knew how to ride a bicycle and assumed the skills were transferable. *Could* she ride a scooter and save on gas? Might it truly be fun zipping around town with a helmet strapped securely under her chin and the wind in her face? Assuming there was no rain and little traffic, of course. It was a crazy idea but one she couldn't get out of her head. And with a motor scooter for town driving she might be able to coax a few more years out of her aging car.

* * *

It was after seven when Sara pulled into the small parking lot next to Batch's Bar and Grill. It was a prime location, a corner building across from the bank. She had driven past it many times but hadn't paid it much attention. She guessed it was the flashing beer sign in the window that kept her away. She envisioned spittoons on the floor and loose women plying their trade to intoxicated men. She wasn't the bar type. She was more of a Starbucks type. She would give it five minutes. Either Jessie Singer was there or she wasn't. If she was, she would hand over the backpack, ask a couple quick questions about the scooter and be out the door before the smell of smoke and liquor permeated her clothes.

She stepped into the dimly lit bar, a firm grip on the backpack strap slung over her shoulder. The smell of french fries and

Febreze flowed over her as she waited for her eyes to adjust. Surprisingly, there was no smoke. Two televisions mounted on the wall behind the bar silently showed a basketball game while the jukebox quietly played country music. The wide-planked wooden floorboards, polished mahogany bar and brick walls provided a cozy atmosphere somewhere between turn-of-the-century rustic and urban chic. She scanned the room looking for Jessie. She expected her to be a waitress or perhaps playing pool in the back. The bar wasn't overly crowded, but the randomly-spaced tables had enough customers to be successfully busy.

"Hello," Jessie called from behind the bar. She was wearing a forest-green polo shirt with the name Batch's B&G embroidered above the pocket and a matching narrow apron over black jeans. She was filling a tall glass from a beer tap. "What brings you to my little corner of paradise?" She had a welcoming smile, very unlike the worried look she had when she had come seeking test results.

"I thought you said you were a professional pool player."

"That's the plan." Jessie wiped a puddle of beer foam off the bar with one efficient stroke of a bar towel. "Bartending is just a means to an end. What brings you to Batch's, Ms. Patterson?" Her expression suddenly turned serious. "Oh, damn. You've got my test results."

"No. I told you. They'll go directly to your doctor."

"Whew, I was afraid you were here to tell me I'm pregnant." Jessie had a devilish twinkle in her eye.

"Actually, I am playing the stork, but I'm delivering something a little less life-altering." She pulled the backpack off her shoulder and placed it on the bar. "I believe this is yours."

"Oh, crap. Did I leave that at the hospital the other day?"

"Yes. I'm sorry I didn't get it back to you sooner."

"How did you know where to bring it?"

"The motor scooter ad you posted. Your name and this place were listed as the contact information."

"Oh, yeah." She placed the backpack under the bar, seemingly unconcerned about it or its contents.

"By the way, don't you have a cell phone? It would have been helpful if the number was printed on the flyer."

"I know. Sorry about that. I didn't want people seeing my cell number and filling my voice mail with a bunch of jerk calls. Bad choice, huh?"

"Can we get two more?" a man in a sport coat called from across the room, waving an empty bottle.

"Hold your horses. They're coming." Jessie pulled two beer bottles from a stainless steel tank behind the bar. "Thanks for bringing it back but you could have called. I would have come to get it. I just didn't remember where I left it. That was a crazy day."

"I called and they said you worked on Friday. It wasn't a problem." Sara hadn't yet summoned the courage to ask about the scooter but she was working on it.

"I can guess what they said." Jessie gave a cynical snort. "Can I offer you something to drink? Glass of wine? Beer? Pop? It's on me."

"Thank you, but no." She cleared her throat nervously. "By the way, the motor scooter in your ad," she started hesitantly. She wasn't sure exactly what to ask. She knew nothing about them. If Edie were here, she'd know.

"Could you do me a huge favor and set this on that table over there?" Jessie set the glass of beer on the mat between two chrome railings. She went back to mixing rum and coke with one hand while popping the caps off the beer bottles with the other.

"I beg your pardon."

"This glass needs to go to the guy with the mustache sitting at the table under the neon Budweiser sign. I'm being slammed. Just set the glass on the table, please."

Not what Sara expected to be asked but she delivered the glass. Just as she was about to set it down she slopped a dollop of foam on the table.

"Oops, sorry." She quickly swept it off with her hand.

"Here you go, honey," the man said, holding up a five-dollar bill between two fingers. He did a quick scan of Sara's body then smiled and added, "Keep the change."

"Oh, okay." Sara didn't expect to be the cashier either, but took the money and headed back to the bar, convinced she had been doing a good deed. Perhaps this wasn't a good time to discuss the scooter.

"Could you bring us some napkins, miss?" a woman asked, grabbing Sara's arm as she passed.

"Um, just a minute." Sara slithered between the chairs, trying not to bump the customers. Jessie must have heard because a stack of napkins was waiting on the bar. Sara placed the money next to them. "The man with the mustache said keep the change."

Jessie looked up from mixing a drink and smiled brightly. "Your first tip. These go to table six, next to the jukebox." She nodded to the two longneck beer bottles waiting on the mat.

"Don't you have waitresses for this?" Sara scanned the room, looking for whoever's job she was being asked to do.

"I did, but Charlene is out sick and Steven quit. His boyfriend didn't approve of him getting pinched. And the other bartender took the night off."

"You're a little busy so I'll come back another time. I just wanted to ask about the motor scooter but it's not important."

"We need another pitcher back here, Jessie," a woman shouted from her perch on a tall stool near one of the pool tables in the back of the room.

"Coming right up, Bonnie." She set a pitcher under the spigot and flipped the handle then went back to mixing a drink. "Thanks for returning my backpack, Ms. Patterson. I appreciate it."

"You're welcome. And you can call me Sara." She headed for the door, but stepped aside as four young women streamed in, laughing and smiling.

"I'm having nachos this time. They looked awesome," one of them said, as they claimed the first available table.

"Where's my beer?" the man called from the table by the jukebox.

Sara didn't frequent bars and never pictured herself working in one. She spent years going to college so she wouldn't have to. But she felt sorry for Jessie. Jessie was right. She was being slammed and trying to do a Herculean task alone. Sara took a deep breath, released the door handle and walked back down the bar to the chrome railings and the puzzled look on Jessie's face.

"Fifteen minutes. That's all I can give you. Fifteen minutes." Sara snatched up the napkins and took them to the woman then delivered the two beer bottles. "Sorry about the delay sir." She smiled cordially, the way she did for patients waiting for their blood to be drawn.

"Two for one, right honey?" the man asked, holding out a twenty-dollar bill.

"Um, I guess so." Sara had no idea, but took the money. She hurried back to the bar and slid the bill across to Jessie. "He said they are two for one. Is that right?"

"The hell they are. Longnecks are three and he knows it. Drafts are two."

Sara delivered the pitcher to the woman by the pool table and returned to the bar.

"She didn't pay for that," she said, leaning in.

"Bonnie has a tab. I run one for some of the regulars." She scribbled something on a pad under the bar then slid a mug of beer down the bar. It stopped in front of a bearded man on a barstool wearing a ball cap. "Last one, TJ. Your tab is full."

"I paid last week, Jessie," he argued.

"Eight bucks on a fifty-dollar tab won't cut it," she said sternly. "I'm not your banker." She looked up at Sara and said, "Thanks, by the way."

"You're welcome." She looked over at the table of young women. "Are those girls old enough to be in here?"

"To drink, probably not. To order food, yes." Jessie dumped a shot of vodka into a tall glass and filled it with orange juice while she talked, all without spilling a drop.

"Should I ask for their IDs?"

"If they order booze, yes. And check all of them. I don't want them sharing with anyone underage. But I doubt they'll try. They're college girls. I think they're part of the volleyball team from Concord College. We get a lot of college kids in here. I hear the campus food is lousy."

"What do I do if they order food?"

Jessie set an order pad and pen on the bar.

"Write it down and take it to the window." She nodded to the framed opening in the wall. "Jimmy's back there."

"And you trust me to know what I'm doing?" she mumbled, as she gathered up the pad and pen and headed to the table.

"Just remember, they're more scared of you than you are of them." Jessie chuckled.

"Hello, ladies. Can I take your order?"

"Can we have a pitcher of Diet Pepsi and a pitcher of Dr. Pepper?" one of the women said then looked at her friends for approval.

"Diet Pepsi and Dr. Pepper." Sara wrote it down, relieved she didn't have to ask for ID.

"I want nachos," another said, tossing her long hair out of the way with a nod of her head. "With extra salsa."

"With extra salsa," Sara repeated as she wrote then turned to the next woman.

"I want a cheeseburger with grilled onions but no ketchup. Do you have onion rings?"

"My God, Gracie. You're going to fart up a storm all the way home."

"Okay. No onion rings. Just the cheeseburger."

"Cheeseburger, grilled onions, no ketchup." Sara meticulously spelled out every word. "And you?"

The last two were huddled together, reading the menu card.

"How big is the pizza?"

"Um. Just a second." Sara hurried over to the bar. "How big is the pizza and do you have onion rings?"

"Pizza is ten inch. Two toppings included. Dollar each for extras. Yes, onion rings," Jessie said without looking up as she loaded beer bottles into the cooler. "Pizza takes twenty minutes."

Sara hurried back to the table. "The pizza is ten inches and takes about twenty minutes. It comes with two toppings but you can add more for only a dollar each. And yes, we have onion rings."

"We want sausage, pepperoni, olive," one of them started.

"And mushrooms," the other added, drawing her finger down the list. "And an order of poppers."

"Poppers?" Sara looked down at the card. "What are poppers?"

"Fried jalapeños. Can we have extra ranch dip?"

"Extra ranch dip," she wrote, assuming they knew what they were talking about. "Anything else, ladies?"

"Are you a regular waitress?"

"No. I'm just filling in."

"We thought so. You're better than that guy who used to work here. If you didn't order right away he'd get this huge attitude and walk away."

Sara took the order ticket to the window and leaned her head through the opening.

"Hello? Jimmy?"

"Hi." A middle-aged woman in a stained white apron appeared on the other side. She set a red plastic basket containing a large mound of french fries on the windowsill and slipped the ticket under the corner.

"Hi. Jessie said to give you this." She handed her the order and stood waiting for instructions.

Jimmy read the ticket, snickering as she moved down the page.

"What? Did I spell something wrong?"

"Nope. You definitely spelled everything right." She looked up and smiled. "Next time, c b is cheeseburger, g o is grilled onions and p z is pizza."

"Oh." She wanted to say there wasn't going to be a next time.

"Could you take this to table two?" Jimmy nudged the basket of fries. "It's up front under the picture of Mount Saint Helens. "Put the ticket on the table but watch out they don't walk it. I know those guys. The large order is six bucks."

"Okay." She carried the food to the front and set it on the table. "Here you go, gentlemen. Large fries. Do you want me to go ahead and take care of that check for you while I'm here?" They both looked up at her as if they had been caught with their hand in the cookie jar. "Save me a trip," she added with a sweet smile.

"Okay," one said, and pulled out his wallet. He handed her a ten and said, "Keep the change."

"Thank you. Enjoy."

"Order up," Jessie called, filling a round tray with a mixed drink, two longnecks and a draft. "Table nine. Redhead in the yellow tank top." She nodded in that direction. "They've got a tab running. Could you bring back some dead soldiers?"

"Dead soldiers?"

"Empty beer bottles. And any empty glasses you see. Cuts down on breakage. If anyone needs more popcorn, it's back here." She looked over at the commercial-sized popcorn popper.

"I've heard about that. You supply free popcorn, loaded with salt so the customers keep ordering drinks. Right?"

Jessie just smiled.

Sara delivered drinks and food, refilled popcorn baskets, cleared away empties and took food orders nearly nonstop for over an hour before she realized how long she had been at it. But Jessie was still struggling to keep up. The bar was full. Most were couples and groups watching the game while they ate and enjoyed pleasant conversation. As soon as the two men with the large french fry order left, another couple took their place.

"I forgot to give you this. Those guys at table two gave me ten dollars for the six-dollar french fries. Here." She dug in her apron pocket for the money, something Jessie convinced her to wear so she didn't dirty her clothes.

"That was nice of them. But they hadn't paid for the pitcher of beer." Jessie laughed and shook her head. "No problem. I'll get them next time."

"I didn't know. I'm sorry."

"It's not your problem. It's like a game with those two." Jessie looked up when an argument in the back escalated into a shoving match. "Would you stand back here and don't let anyone behind the bar," she said as she wiped her hands on her apron. She headed toward the ruckus with long strides and a scowl on her face. "Okay, that's it guys. You're not fighting in here.

Take your sorry asses out or I call the cops. Right now. You've got five seconds to be out the door." The two men were both taller and heavier than Jessie but she didn't seem intimidated. She stepped between them, holding them apart. "OUT!" She pushed them toward the front and continued until both were out the door and on the sidewalk. "Beat it," she added angrily then returned to the bar. The other customers went back to their conversations as if nothing had happened.

"Those guys were actually going to fight, weren't they?" Sara gasped.

"It happens. Thanks for watching the store."

"Weren't you afraid one of them would hit you?"

"Naw. They know I'd press charges. They were drunk, not stupid. Although sometimes it's hard to tell the difference. Those two argue all the time." She looked up at Sara. "Were you scared?"

"Yes. A little. We don't get drunks fighting in the lab very often."

"You can't let them see fear. If they think they can intimidate you, they will. I have to take the upper hand before it gets out of control."

"You're lucky you've never been decked by someone with too much to drink."

"I didn't say I haven't." She laughed. "Been there, done that. Several times. Worse black eye I ever got was from a sixty-year-old woman with a vicious right hook."

"Did you hit her back?" Sara was surprised she had asked. She didn't approve of such things. Violence was never an answer.

Jessie pulled a crooked smile.

"Nope. Did one better. Charged her with assault and she did a couple months in county." She looked across the room. "Table four is waving. You want to get that? Those gals are good tippers."

"Order up, Sara," Jimmy called from the window. "Table three."

Sara delivered the food, collected payment then took table four's order. Jessie was right. They each tipped generously. Sara also felt their eyes undressing her as she walked away.

"Do your feet hurt yet?" Jessie asked, setting four glasses of draft on a tray.

"How did you know?"

"Dress shoes don't have arch support."

"If I'd known I was going to be waiting tables I would have worn my duty shoes." She delivered the drinks, removed the empty glasses and swept the popcorn crumbs onto the tray. She collected empty beer bottles as she made her way back to the bar.

"Duty shoes? Sounds like military shoes."

"It's an old term. It means shoes hospital employees wear while on duty. Flat bottoms and good support. Meant to be worn all day."

As the evening wore on business finally began to dwindle. The kitchen closed at nine o'clock and by ten the crowd had thinned to a manageable size. Sara cleared the last of the empty food baskets and glasses. As customers left she wiped the tables and straightened the chairs.

"What do I do with these?" She held up a jacket and a ball cap. "Do you have a place for lost and found?"

"Yep." Jessie dried her hands on a towel then opened a cupboard. "Lots of lost and found." She pulled out two tubs full of forgotten jackets, hats, gloves and the like.

"How can someone forget their belt at a bar?" Sara dropped the items on top and mashed them down.

"You'd be surprised what people leave behind when they're drunk. I think there's a jock strap in there and a couple bras."

"*Ew.*" Sara stepped back with a smirk. "Why do you keep that stuff?"

"I don't. I just haven't had time to donate it. After a couple weeks I give it to the thrift store down the street. They sell what they can and toss out the rest. And no, I probably won't give them the jock strap."

"Do you run Batch's all by yourself?"

"No," she chuckled. "Batch Singer is my grandfather, but he's out of town. His brother had a heart attack and he went to visit. I work for him. My dad helps out once in a while." She looked away in disgust. "Once in a great while."

"Wow. Three generations. That's wonderful. You don't see that very often."

"Like my dad. We don't see him very often either." Jessie ran her finger down the pad she had been scribbling on then began counting out money from the drawer.

"I think I better get going. My dog is going to wonder where I am."

"Wait a second," she said then went back to counting. "Here you go. One forty-five." She handed the money to Sara. "I really appreciate your help."

"What's that for?" She looked down at the stack of bills.

"Your tips plus salary. I've been keeping track."

"You're kidding. I didn't stay for the money. I did it because I thought you needed the help."

"I did. And you got tipped for your service. Not bad for your first day. If you'd wiggle your butt and let them pinch it you'd get more." She grinned and placed the money in Sara's hand. "Seriously, I really do appreciate your help. We're always looking for good-looking waitresses. If you ever get tired of working in a hospital, come look us up."

"Thank you, but I don't think this is a career move I'm likely to make."

"What was it you wanted to know about the scooter?"

"To be perfectly honest, right now, I can't even remember. I'm too tired to care. Another time maybe."

"Another time." Jessie draped her arm over one of the chrome railings and smiled. "Take care, Sara." She touched two fingers to her forehead as if saluting.

Sara headed for the door. She could feel Jessie's eyes on her, watching her every step until she was outside. She wanted to look back, but couldn't find the courage to do that either. It was enough to know she had done the right thing. And Edie was right. There was one incredible pair of buns behind that bar.

CHAPTER FOUR

Jessie leaned over the table, her T-shirt and small breasts just inches above the green felt as she lined up the easy bank shot. Kiss the eight ball and let it roll into the corner pocket. Run the cue ball up the table for a shot at the nine. She always thought at least two shots ahead. She learned that at an early age, back when she had to stand on an overturned milk crate and use a short cue stick. Raised by her grandparents, she spent many after-school hours at the bar, washing dishes, taking out trash and waiting for permission to play at one of the pool tables. Where's the cue ball going to end up, her grandfather would ask. And what's your next shot going to be? She could have played softball or volleyball in high school. She was strong and athletic. But she found team sports tedious and boring. There was always someone too lazy or too slow to keep up. Someone more interested in their hair or makeup than in the game. For Jessie, playing the game, any game, especially pool, meant one hundred percent devotion and concentration. She didn't play for fun. She played to win. Practicing hours a day with a cue in her hand was the means to that end. What better way to put the anxiety of waiting for the test results out of her mind?

She pocketed the eight ball and chalked her cue as the white ball caromed off the rail and came to rest in perfect alignment for a shot at the nine.

"Hey, Kid," a man shouted from behind the bar. He had a deeply wrinkled face and a neatly trimmed goatee. The hair on his chin, like that on his head, was salt-and-pepper gray. "How long are you going to waste time doing that?"

"All day," she said, as she settled over the shot.

"The old man needs you to run the delivery invoice. The truck will be here by two." He slid a clipboard down the bar.

"Not me. I'm off today. That's your job." She circled the table, pulling balls from the pockets.

"It's not my job. You're the bookkeeper. Get your ass out there and count the damn boxes."

"Nope. You wanted to work today so you get to handle the delivery. That's the rule. Be sure you count the Heineken. They shorted us last week. And check the expiration date on that crap from Mountain Valley Brewery. Don't accept anything under four months."

She positioned the cluster of balls over the foot spot and pressed them snug against the rack then leaned over, ready to break. Before she shot the clipboard landed on the middle of the table.

"Do your damn job," he demanded and returned to the bar.

Jessie ricocheted the cue ball off the rail, sending it around the clipboard and striking the one-ball. She snatched up the clipboard and tossed it on a nearby stool as the balls scattered around the table.

"What was it you said to Batch? Oh, yeah. I remember." She lined up a shot. "Let me work Thursday and Friday," she said with a brusque, mocking tone. "I didn't come back to be Jessie's barmaid. I've always worked Thursday and Friday. Those are my days." She took another shot, blasting two balls into pockets. "You owe it to me, Dad." She waited for the cue ball to stop spinning and sunk another before looking up at him.

"I know why you talked him into letting you work Thursday and Friday. That's your buddies' paydays. You figure to grab a couple hundred in tips before you disappear again."

"You're full of crap."

Jessie didn't have to look up to know he was sneering at her. The only time he didn't was when he wanted something from her.

"I may be, but I'm still not doing your work when I'm not on the clock. You wanted to work today. You have to work the delivery."

"Those pool tables are for paying customers you know."

Jessie chuckled and held up the glass of iced tea she had been nursing.

"Did you pay for it?"

"Did you pay for the Coke you keep squirting into your glass?" She squatted to line up a long shot down the table.

"Hey, Jessie. I thought I saw your truck out there," a man said as he came through the door. He was wearing a blue and white striped uniform shirt advertising an air conditioning company, a pager clipped to his belt. "How about a quick game? Best two out of three."

"Sure. Nine ball?" she asked, raking the balls to the side of the table with her cue.

"Yep. Fifty bucks? But if my boss calls, I'm out of here."

"She's got work to do, Chuck," the man behind the bar said.

"No, you've got work to do." She went about racking balls as Chuck selected a cue from the rack mounted on the wall.

"Are you two arguing again?" a gray-haired man asked as he came out of the small office in the back corner of the room. At sixty-eight, Batch Singer was a husky man and he had a noticeable limp, the result of an arthritic knee he was too stubborn to have replaced. His bushy eyebrows flared upward like white feathers caught in a breeze. Like Jessie's, his green polo shirt had Batch's B&G embroidered over the pocket.

"We're not arguing again," Jessie muttered under her breath. "We're arguing still."

Batch noticed the clipboard on the stool.

"Good. I'm glad you're taking care of the delivery," he said, hesitating next to the pool table. "The truck should be here any time now."

"I'm not working the delivery. I'm off today. Remember? Dad is on the clock so he's the one receiving the delivery." Jessie saw the optimistic look in her grandfather's eyes change to disappointment. "It's always been that way. The person working the bar processes the liquor delivery."

Batch looked over at his son then back at Jessie and swallowed nervously. Like the rule that no one drank alcohol while working, Batch made the rules and expected everyone to live by them. But when it came to Ron Singer, his only son, Batch made exceptions. It had always been that way.

"Hey, Kid," Batch said softly. "Could you do this for me? It won't take long. Twenty minutes, tops."

"Why do you coddle him?" Jessie asked.

"Come on," he begged. "One time. You know Ron can't do it by himself."

Ron stood behind the bar with his arms crossed, a disgustingly smug confidence on his face.

Jessie wanted to say no and remind him it was a two-hour task. Not twenty minutes. But she couldn't do it. She couldn't disappoint her grandfather. This was his livelihood. Processing the delivery correctly was too important. Batch was right. If Ron was forced into it, he would inevitably screw it up. His best effort wasn't ever good enough.

"Okay. One time." Jessie tossed the cue on the table. "Sorry, Chuck. Next time." She grabbed the clipboard and headed to the storeroom to make room for the dozens of liquor boxes and beer kegs about to be delivered.

It was a big order, bigger than usual because of the upcoming Washington–Washington State basketball game airing on the big-screen televisions. It would hopefully bring out the locals to cheer the Washington Huskies. It was after five when she finally finished counting and sorting boxes.

"All done," she said, dropping the clipboard on Batch's desk. "They shorted us a case of Johnny Walker Red but I think we've got enough until next week."

"Second damn time they did that. Last week it was Seagram's." Batch shook his head disgustedly. "They keep it up and I'm going to Brenner's Distributing."

"I told him that."

Batch leaned back in his chair and looked up at Jessie.

"Thanks, Kid. I know when you handle it, things get done right."

"No problem." Jessie patted him on the shoulder. She knew complaining about her father's undependability wouldn't help matters. Batch would do what he always did. Offer excuses and promise he'd talk to him about it. The more she and her father argued and bickered, the more Batch defended him.

"Ron's working Saturday night. You want to work the floor?"

"I'm bartending Saturday night. It's on the schedule." She pointed the sheet on the wall. "Saturdays are mine."

"I'm giving you the night off. He'll cover for you."

"I don't need a night off. I need to work my schedule. He already has my Thursday and Friday."

"Sorry, Kid." He shrugged as if it was out of his hands. "Waitresses do damn good those nights. You'll probably do better than bartending."

"Hey, which gin do you want in the well tonight?" Ron asked, sticking his head in the office door.

"Gilbey's and Barton, same as always," Jessie offered. She suspected her father's appearance in the office was more paranoid curiosity than anything else.

Ron looked over at Batch as if seeking his approval instead of accepting Jessie's advice. Batch nodded in agreement.

"You're waitressing for me this evening, right?" he asked.

"No, I'm not. Charlotte's working tonight."

"We're going to be busy. I need more than one waitress."

"Make do. I have." Jessie could have reminded them she was left high and dry with no waitress and had it not been for Sara Patterson's generous offer to stay and help, she could have lost customers, perhaps permanently. But it wasn't worth the argument. She pushed her way past before Batch could commandeer her. Ron had talked Batch out of her shift. He wasn't going to talk her out of her night off. Jessie had a date and she wanted to keep it. She stopped in the storeroom, selected a nice bottle of wine, dropped a twenty-dollar bill next to the register and headed home to shower.

"Son of a…" she grumbled, pulling to a stop as the railroad crossing arms lowered. She wasn't mad at the passing freight train. She was mad at her father. And mad at herself. Why did she let him get to her like that? He wasn't worth it. Ron Singer could waltz into Ilwaco every few months with a sob story of how the world had mistreated him and he needed a job and BAM, just like that, Batch turned everyone's world upside down to provide one. Then he'd be gone again, following some can't-fail scheme that promised untold riches. But now, he was back. And like always, Jessie drew the short end of the stick.

Jessie pulled up to her garage apartment not remembering how she got there. Her mind had been elsewhere. She sat drumming her fingers on the steering wheel and staring off into space as she willed the frustrating images from her mind. She didn't want them to accompany her inside. Blocking out bad thoughts, thoughts that robbed her of her serenity and focus, was a skill she had learned as a teenager when being gay in a small town kept her isolated and insecure. She had better things to think about, or at least different things to think about. Darlene. Cute. Sexy. Deliciously femme. All the things Jessie liked in a woman. Not as mature or personable as someone like Sara Patterson, but acceptable. They had been dating a few weeks and Darlene was already suggesting co-habitation. And that scared Jessie. She wasn't ready to co-hab with Darlene. She wasn't ready to co-hab with anyone. Tonight they would sip a nice piñot noir, listen to music and if Jessie played her cards right, taste Darlene's wonderfulness.

CHAPTER FIVE

Sara walked through the waiting room to the sound of her stomach growling. It had been a busy morning. Her coffee break had been missed and she was hungry. She had been called to ER twice to collect blood from suspected heart attack victims as well as the usual tests ordered after the doctors' morning rounds. She'd have just enough time to gobble down a fruit salad, a baggie of wheat crackers and the last half of a brownie before getting back to the centrifuge.

"Hello, Ms. Patterson." Jessie smiled over the top of a magazine from the chair just inside the waiting room door.

"Ms. Singer! How long have you been waiting? Let me get your lab orders from the receptionist. She should have told me you were here."

"I'm not here for tests." She tossed the magazine on the table and stood, smoothing her hands down the legs of her jeans. "I'm here to answer your questions. Have you got a minute?"

"Actually, I'm on my way to a quick lunch," she replied, holding up her insulated lunch tote. "What questions are you talking about?" She started down the hall with Jessie at her side.

"Last week at the bar you wanted to ask something about the scooter but couldn't remember what. You helped me out so the least I could do was come by and answer your questions."

"I have to plead complete ignorance. I have no idea what I was going to ask. I'm sure it wasn't much. I know absolutely nothing about them. It was a ludicrous idea anyway."

"That's okay. It's parked right outside if you want to see it." She pointed to the door at the end of the hall. "I didn't know where you lived so I brought it here. Did you know there are three S. Pattersons in the Long Beach area?"

Sara gave a quick dismissive glance out the glass door, her stomach once again grumbling. "I appreciate your bringing it by for me to see, but maybe we should do this another time."

"Come on." Jessie took her arm and guided her outside. "It'll just take a minute."

Sara didn't go willingly.

To her surprise, the photocopied picture on the flyer didn't do the scooter justice. The red and chrome machine was sparkling clean and polished to a brilliant shine. It looked like a toy awaiting a Christmas tree. All that was missing was the bow. At that moment, with the sun glinting off the handlebars, Sara thought if this was a woman she'd be described as perky, vibrant, even intriguing.

"Cute, isn't it?" Jessie must have seen Sara's wide-eyed surprise. "Not a scratch on her. Tires are new. Twenty miles on the oil change. Brakes are in great shape. Gets great mileage. The tank holds a little over two gallons." She opened the matching storage bin behind the seat. "You can store your helmet in here or use it for groceries. There's storage under the seat too. They both lock."

"Yes, it's very cute."

"Sit on her." Jessie took the lunch tote from her hand and nudged her closer.

Sara reluctantly perched on the seat but kept one foot on the ground for good measure.

"I used the center stand so you can put both feet up." She lifted Sara's leg onto the platform, her fingers gently cupped under Sara's thigh. "It's very stable. You could stand on the seat and it wouldn't tip over."

"Yes, I can tell." Sara wanted off. Just the thought that it could roar away with her on it made her heart skip a beat. She dropped her foot and moved to dismount but Jessie blocked her way.

"Why don't you take it for a spin around the parking lot? Get a feel for it." She pushed her back on the seat and put the key in the ignition.

"No, no," Sara insisted and climbed off the other side. "Not today." She reclaimed her lunch. "It's very cute and clean, and I'm sure it's energy efficient and all that, but I don't think so." This might as well be a tandem tractor-trailer rig with umpteen gears and an impossibly high seat. She'd be just as comfortable driving it as this zippy red rocket.

"I thought you were interested? How are you going to know if you like it if you don't try it?" Jessie gave a worried scowl. "It's easy to ride. Very responsive."

"Thanks for bringing it around, but I'm really not interested in buying a motor scooter right now."

"If it's the price, it's below book value. You can check. But I could take another fifty off, if that helps."

"Thanks, but I'm just not ready to be a motorcycle owner."

"Motor scooter," Jessie corrected, her eyes drifting down Sara's body.

"Semantics, Ms. Singer. It's still a two-wheeled motorized missile. And I'm not ready to own one."

"But you said you were interested. I came all the way over here just so you could see it, and now you're telling me I spent my morning washing and polishing it for nothing?"

"I didn't ask you to do that. You should have called first and asked."

"I was being nice."

"You're being pushy. You sound like a used car salesman. Read my lips. I don't want to buy your scooter."

"Fine." Jessie tossed her an angry frown then climbed on the scooter and sped away, leaving Sara in the parking lot, clutching her lunch tote.

"What does that woman want from me?" she muttered, then spun on her heels and went inside.

Sara headed for the cafeteria but stopped at the ladies' room to wash her hands. And to settle her nerves. Jessie Singer just added to her already stressful morning.

"Hello," she said to the woman at the sink.

Her eyes were closed and her head was lowered. She nodded slightly.

"Margie, isn't it? You're in Patient Accounts?" Sara asked, studying the woman.

Margie nodded again. She looked exhausted and pale.

"Are you okay?" Sara asked.

"Actually, I'm not sure." Margie washed her hands then fumbled a zipper pouch from her purse and opened it.

Sara instantly recognized the contents of the pouch.

"Are you diabetic, Margie?"

"Uh-huh." Her speech was slurred behind a lethargic expression.

"Can I help?" Sara offered after watching her struggle with the meter. Margie nodded as if too tired to reply. Sara pulled the lancet pen from the kit and cocked it. "When did you last test?"

"Before breakfast," she mumbled and held out a finger.

Sara loaded a test strip in the end of the meter then applied the tip of the pen to her finger and snapped the button. Margie didn't flinch, suggesting she was well used to being stuck. Sara gently squeezed to produce a droplet of blood and touched the test strip to it.

"Pretty high. Five fourteen, Margie," Sara read from the meter. She noticed there was no insulin or syringes in the pouch. "Do you have your insulin with you?"

Margie raised the side of her sweater to reveal an insulin pump clipped to her waistband with tubing leading to her abdomen. Sara checked the screen on the pump. It was on and seemed to be functioning correctly.

"Let's get you down to the lab. You need to sit down, and the ladies' room isn't the best place for that." She zipped the test supplies into the pouch and took Margie by the arm. "What did you have to eat today?"

"Pancakes for breakfast with orange juice. I stopped at the Pancake Kitchen downtown."

"Anything else?"

"Our supervisor brought in doughnuts. It's somebody's birthday. I had a maple glaze. But it was small."

"Did you program a boost for those carbs?"

"I did for the pancakes. But not for the doughnut. I was going to include it with my lunch later."

Sara helped Margie into a chair then motioned for Edie to find Dr. Lesterbrook.

"Do you mind if I test you again with our meter?"

"Okay, but I just put new batteries in mine," she said faintly.

By the time Sara returned with a test kit Dr. Lesterbrook was hurrying across the laboratory with a concerned look on his face.

"What's up?"

"Margie is wearing an insulin pump but I think she's testing high. Five fourteen a few minutes ago. I want to test her again with our unit just to confirm," Sara said as she prepared the meter. "Five sixteen," she said, holding up the new meter reading.

"Be right back." Dr. Lesterbrook disappeared out the door. He returned a minute later. "Dr. Green is on the way."

"The ER doctor? That's overkill. I just need to program a little boost." Margie groaned, but seemed too tired and confused to resolve her insulin needs.

"What do we have?" A tall woman strode through the door. She had a stethoscope draped around her neck and the name Dr. Asia Green embroidered on her lab coat. "Well, hi, Margie. What's going on with your new pump? More problems?"

The doctor took the pump from Margie's waistband and traced the line to Margie's belly. She did a quick inspection of the infusion site then checked the settings.

"Glucose is five sixteen," Sara offered.

"What have you had to eat today?"

"Uh." Margie leaned her head back against the wall and closed her eyes as if trying to remember.

"She told me she had pancakes, orange juice and a doughnut," Sara offered.

"I programmed for the pancakes, I think," Margie said softly.

"We'll get you fixed up here. Your base rate is set a little low."

Dr. Lesterbrook retrieved a bottle of water from the break room. He opened it and handed it to Margie while Dr. Green reprogrammed the pump, tapping in new readings.

"I'll be back in a few minutes to check on her. Let's give it twenty minutes then test her again," she said in Sara's direction.

"That's way overkill," Margie argued, then sipped at the water. "All I need is a couple units' boost. How high was the reading again?"

"I've already programmed a new bolus. I want you to sit here, drink the water and relax. Give it twenty minutes, okay? The hospital can't have an employee roaming around with a five hundred glucose reading. Rules, Margie."

"I'll be okay. I've had a five hundred reading before."

"And if you continue to run high you're running the risk of ketoacidosis. You know better."

"Do you want us to run a UA?" Sara asked.

Dr. Green leaned in and sniffed Margie's breath.

"No, I don't think so. Not this time. Now sit, Margie," she said sternly.

Margie heaved a sigh and nodded.

"Can you let my boss know where I am?"

"Already done," Dr. Lesterbrook offered. "He said take all the time you need. Let him know if you need to take the rest of the day off."

"Heavens, no. I've got high blood sugar. Not a stroke." She looked over at Sara. "And to think I trusted you with my pancreatic deficiency."

Sara laughed and said, "I'm glad I was there to help."

"I'll be back." Dr. Green headed out the door but paused and said, "Don't let her leave."

"How are you feeling?" Sara asked, nudging Margie to take another drink.

"If you really want to know, I'm feeling silly." She sipped again. "Sorry I created all the fuss. I'm type 1. I'm used to glucose spikes. It's nothing new. The only thing that is new is this bleeping pump. You have to be a rocket scientist to program the thing." She heaved a sigh. "I don't feel like I'm in control. At least not like I was when I was injecting. But, hey, if this is supposed to make my life easier, I'll try it. Bring on the bells and whistles." She leaned her head back against the wall again. "By the way, thanks. I appreciate your help. I'm not sure I could have gotten an accurate reading, not the way I was feeling. I probably would have just programmed a quick boost. I knew I was high."

"No problem." Sara waited a few minutes then checked her watch. "Shall we test and see how you're doing?" It had been nearly fifteen minutes. Sara expected her count to have dropped at least a hundred points, hopefully two hundred. Not to goal but a good start. Sara stuck Margie's finger, collected the droplet and waited for the meter to show a reading. "I'll be right back, Margie. Don't move." Sara hurried out the door and headed to ER. Dr. Green was standing at the nurses station, reading an x-ray. "Dr. Green," she said quietly then extended the meter for her to see. "It's been almost twenty minutes."

"Hmmm. Ms. Cole, have you got an insulin pump infusion set in the cabinet?" Dr. Green asked the woman behind the desk. She retrieved a sealed packet and handed it over. By the time they returned to the lab, Margie was asleep in the chair. "Hey, girl. Can I see your infusion site?"

Margie roused but had trouble lifting her sweater. Dr. Green disconnected the tubing from the pump. A dribble of liquid ran out, leaving a wet spot on her lab coat. She removed the tape around the cannula then gently pulled it out of her skin and inspected it.

"Margie, when did you change your infusion set? How long has this been in?"

"Two days ago," she said, her speech even more slurred.

"I think we've found your problem. You're not getting the dose you've programmed. You need a new one."

"I might need some help."

"I'm going to do it. Don't worry." Dr. Green had already begun cleaning a fresh spot on her belly. "Here we go," she said, then snapped the button to insert the needle. Once the tiny tube was under the surface of the skin she removed the needle. She attached the tubing and watched for a flow of insulin. "I think we'll see an improvement pretty quick," she said in Sara's direction. "She wasn't getting anything. The cannula was bent."

Dr. Green pulled up a nearby chair and sat, holding the pump in her hand as it dispensed the dose. Within a few minutes, color had returned to Margie's cheeks, and she slowly came to life. Dr. Green nodded to Sara to check her glucose. Just as she predicted, it had dropped to four hundred. When it reached three hundred Dr. Green was confident enough to return to the ER and her patients.

"Call me if you need me."

Within thirty minutes Margie was alert and coherent. Her blood sugar was down, well on its way to a normal reading.

"Okay, what was it? How high? Five twenty. Five twenty-five," Margie asked, attaching the pump to her waistband.

"Five thirty-eight. How did you know it went up?"

"I've been a diabetic long enough to know when my count is out of whack. And if it was down you wouldn't have rushed out of here like that. Thank you for taking care of me, Sara." She squeezed Sara's hand. "You are my hero."

"I know the theoretical part of people with diabetes. I test them all the time but I don't always see the results of uncontrolled blood sugar levels. I have to admit, you scared me."

"I'll try not to do that again." Margie started out the door then looked back and rolled her eyes. "Oh, Mother flowers. Now I have to eat lunch. More carbs." She laughed and headed up the hall.

"Oh, yeah. Lunch." Sara looked over at her insulated tote. Between Jessie's interruption and Margie's medical emergency, lunchtime had come and gone over an hour ago. She wasn't hungry anymore. Anger mixed with adrenaline had squashed her appetite.

CHAPTER SIX

The first glimmers of sunlight were peeking over the horizon as Sara pedaled at a leisurely pace. It had been two weeks since Jessie Singer brought the motor scooter to the hospital and tried to convince her to buy it. As much as Sara tried to put it out of her mind, she couldn't. She didn't want to buy it. The thought of riding one scared her. But she was ashamed of the way she handled it. Jessie was right. She was just being nice. She took the time to bring it by and show it to her. After all, Sara had expressed an interest in it at the bar. It wasn't Jessie's fault Sara's curiosity was tempered by fear.

"Why did I say anything in the first place?" she said out loud. "Me and my big mouth. I need a motor scooter like I need another hole in my head."

Sara pedaled faster. A ribbon of sweat ran down her spine and into her spandex shorts. She stood on the pedals, forcing her legs up and down and up and down, burning against the uphill pace. She had been rude to Jessie. Plain and simple. Rude. And she needed to apologize. Today was Friday. And if past was prologue, it was the day Jessie bartended at Batch's. She'd swallow her pride and do it. She'd stop by the bar and with hat in hand, she'd apologize. Sara sat down on the seat and pedaled at a comfortable rate as she waited for her pulse to slow.

"I think it's time for a little visit to Batch's. What do you think, Gypsy?" She looked down at the mutt, wagging her tail insistently. Gypsy barked. "Yeah, my thought exactly."

Sara pulled a towel from the handlebars and wiped her face. Thirty minutes on the bike hadn't absolved all her guilt, but at least she had a plan. She climbed off the exercycle and went to take a shower. After work she'd muster up her courage, stop by Batch's Bar and Grill and nibble a little crow. With luck, Jessie wouldn't toss her out on the sidewalk.

It was six thirty when she walked through the door into Batch's and the smell of french fries.

"Excuse me, is Jessie Singer working this evening?" she asked the man behind the bar.

"Nope." He was preoccupied with the game on the television.

"When does she work next?"

"She doesn't. She quit." He finally looked over at Sara. In spite of his graying goatee and wrinkled brow, she recognized this man. Or at least his eyes and the square set to his jaw. It was as if she was looking at Jessie. Sara remembered she said her father worked at Batch's part time. This had to be him. The resemblance was too distinct to be anyone else.

"Jessie quit? When?"

"Couple days ago. Last week. I don't know." He shrugged indifferently.

"Did she say why?"

"All I know is she doesn't work here anymore. The old man better not take her back this time, the little shit." He rolled his lip in a deliberate sneer then gave Sara a long look up and down. "Are you one of her girlfriends?"

"No." Whatever went on here was none of Sara's business, but even if she was one of Jessie's friends she certainly wasn't going to confess it to this man. "Thank you anyway," she said, and turned to leave.

"If you find her, tell her we're doing just fine without her."

"Yes, I'll be sure and do that."

Sara drove away, frustrated she hadn't been able to appease her guilt, but more curious why Jessie quit her job. Other than her high-pressure scooter salesmanship, Sara liked Jessie. She didn't know why. She couldn't help but wonder if the BRCA test had come back positive. Maybe she was staring down the prospects of breast cancer. If the surly man behind the bar was her father, what kind of family history had them snapping and scratching at each other like feral cats in an alley. Or maybe Jessie just wanted something better.

"Well, I tried."

* * *

"Good Monday morning, all," Edie announced with a bounce in her step.

"What's good about it?" A young man in a lab coat and glasses sat at a computer entering data. He had a fresh-scrubbed collegiate look about him. An innocent naïveté.

Edie came up behind him and draped her arms around his shoulders.

"What's wrong, Trevor? Did your girlfriend have another headache?" she cooed in baby talk, then kissed his cheek, her bangs tickling his face.

"Quit." He swiped his palm over the spot.

"Did she? Huh-huh?"

"No. Now leave me alone." He leaned away and groaned.

"I know. She's on the rag."

"Edie, that sounds a little personal," Sara said, unable to ignore their foolishness.

"No, it isn't. I'm offering support and understanding for a co-worker." She gave him another quick kiss on the cheek then went to claim her lab coat from the hook. "We're here for you, Trevor. We want to help. Anything you want to share, we'll be glad to listen. Right, Sara?"

"Protect yourself, Trevor. Edie is in a mothering mood today." Sara carried a rack of test tubes to the refrigerator.

"No, I'm not. I'm a team player."

"But I don't want to be on your team," Trevor announced after checking to see if anyone was in Dr. Lesterbrook's office.

"Sure, you do." Edie grinned. "We offer great perks."

"PMS mood swings and shaved pits. Not exactly the kind of perks I'm looking for."

Sara chuckled to herself. Once again Edie, in her surreptitious way, was about to declare her sexuality. And it wouldn't be the first time she teased Trevor about being a sexually-frustrated straight man. Sexual harassment in the workplace, perhaps. But they seemed to enjoy the casual repartee, so long as Dr. Lesterbrook wasn't within earshot.

Edie collected a stack of printouts and headed out the door. A moment later she rushed back in the lab.

"Did you buy it?" she called in Sara's direction. "It's fun, isn't it?"

"Buy what?" Sara asked as she prepared a slide for the microscope.

"The scooter, of course. Did you talk her down on the price? You can always talk them down if they're desperate enough to post an ad on a hospital bulletin board."

"No. Why would I buy a motor scooter, and why would you think I did?"

"The ad is gone. It was there last week but it's gone now."

"Maybe someone took it down because they were interested. Or maybe she sold it."

"You're buying a motor scooter?" Trevor asked skeptically.

"No. I'm not buying a motor scooter."

"I thought you were interested in it," Edie said. "I saw you looking at the picture."

"Well, I didn't buy it, and have no intention of buying it. Maybe she changed her mind and decided to keep it."

"I never should have sold mine." Edie stared off in space dreamily. "It was the cutest thing. Pink and white with a basket in the back."

"Don't you have patients waiting for you?"

"Yeah." She slowly drifted back to reality. "You should have bought it, Sara."

"And you should go collect blood samples."

Sara tried to immerse herself in work. Between the whirling machines and banal chitchat, finding the concentration she needed to work was sometimes a challenge. Today was no different.

"Hello?" Margie said, tapping her knuckles on the lab table.

Sara looked up from the microscope.

"Hi." She blinked her vision back to normal.

"You didn't hear a word I said, did you?"

"What?" Sara hadn't heard Margie come in or anything out of her mouth.

"I said, hello. How's my personal blood glucose monitor doing?"

"No, I didn't hear you. I was counting. And if you mean Dr. Lesterbrook, he's in a meeting. How's the pump doing?"

"Okay, for now. I'm trying another brand of infusion set. So far, so good. And I didn't mean Dr. Lesterbrook. I meant you. I'm here to take you to lunch. Whatever you want from the cafeteria, lunch is on me. My way of saying thank you. I should have done it sooner."

"You don't have to do that, Margie. I'm just glad we got your blood sugar under control."

"Me too." She grinned. "Come on. Go to lunch with me. Join the pod."

"Pod?" Sara removed the slide from the microscope stage and went to enter the results in the computer. Margie followed along behind.

"Yeah. Pod. Group. You know. A bunch of people you work with and hang out with. People you can do stuff with."

"I've never heard it called a pod before."

"I had a pod when I worked in Phoenix. There were five of us. Six until Ronnie moved to Albuquerque." Margie rambled on, following Sara from table to table as she collected specimens for the fridge. "We rode the whitewater rafts down the Colorado

River one spring. Something I've always wanted to do. It was insane."

"In the Grand Canyon?"

"Yes. Did you know they take old ammo boxes, big ones, in the boats and set them up as potty chairs when they pitch camp. They say it saves the environment."

"You rode one of those big rubber rafts down the rapids?" Sara's eyes widened. "How did you do that with an insulin pump?"

"I didn't have it then, but it's no big deal. You ought to try it sometime. Be sure you go when the river is up. It's like riding a roller coaster. A really wet roller coaster. They have guided tours where you don't have to do anything but show up."

"And know how to swim."

"I don't think that's even mandatory. They strap this humongous life vest on you. Even if you fall overboard it's impossible to drown. You bob up like a cork. I ought to know. I did it. Twice. If I can do it, you can do it."

"I wonder what the lunch special is today." Sara retrieved her wallet from her purse and headed for the door.

"It's Mexican day. Enchilada plate with rice and refried beans."

"Hmm."

"Yeah. My thought exactly. I had my mouth all set for something that wouldn't make me gastronomically obnoxious the rest of the day."

"Think I'll check out the salads."

"Hey, if I get a fruit plate and you get a chef salad we could share." Margie nodded hopefully.

"Sure." Sara started down the hall.

"And remember, it's on me."

They entered the cafeteria and worked their way down the food line, maneuvering around the clog of traffic at the hot food station.

"Did you see that?" Margie nodded toward a blond woman at the coffee machine.

"See what?"

"The new x-ray tech." She gave a quiet moan of approval.

"Are you picking a fruit plate or one of these dishes of fruit?"

"I know what dish I'd like to pick." Margie heaved a throaty sigh as the woman disappeared out the door.

Sara selected a salad and took an extra plate for sharing as she processed Margie's not-so-subtle suggestion she was a lesbian. Like Jessie Singer, she suspected it, but until this revelation she didn't know for sure. And how did Margie know Sara was gay? Or, also like Jessie, did she not care she was outing herself to someone who may or may not harbor bias?

"Okay, yes. She's a little young," Margie added. "But she's so cute with her ponytail and perky little smile." Margie ate a grape from her plate then followed Sara to the drink dispenser. "She could have a husband and four kids for all I know. But maybe she just broke up with her girlfriend and she's in desperate need of comfort and compassion."

Margie paid for their lunch over Sara's objection and led the way to the employee's table. They sat down just as four others departed, leaving them temporarily alone at the table.

"Thank you again for lunch, Margie. But I wish you had let me pay for my own."

"You're welcome." She divided their plates, sharing everything right down to the blueberries. "Can I ask you a question? You can tell me to shut up if you want."

"Sure, what?" Sara dabbed a little salad dressing on the tomato and took a bite.

"I know you're the new girl in town, or at least new girl to the hospital, so to speak, but you make the rounds all over the building. So you might know people." She sprinkled salt on a piece of watermelon and took a bite. "You know, said hi, how ya' doing? That kind of thing."

"If you want to know if I've met Ms. Ponytail, no, I haven't."

"No, no. Not her. She's just a fantasy." Margie looked both ways then leaned in and said, "Someone asked me out and I want to know if I should accept. You know, is it safe? Have you heard anything I should know?"

"As far as I know there are no ax murderers or serial killers on staff but I'm new. I may not be the most informed person to ask. Who is it?"

"The one in navy blue scrubs at the coffee dispenser. Her name is Heidi." Margie touched Sara's sleeve. "If she's the devil incarnate, break it to me gently."

Sara discreetly wiped her napkin across her mouth as she took a look in that direction. She definitely recognized the woman.

"I think she works in pre-op."

"And?"

Sara went back to picking at her salad.

"Oh, God. You know something. I can tell. What is it? She's married? She's fresh out of prison? She's an escaped mental patient?" Margie placed her hand on Sara's arm, as if bracing herself. "Tell me. I can take it."

Sara chuckled.

"I know nothing about her past, Drama Queen. What I know wouldn't fill a test tube."

"You *do* know something. Tell me. *Please.* Is it bad?"

"No, it isn't bad per say. She's probably very nice." Sara stabbed a strawberry and popped it in her mouth.

"But?"

Sara chewed slowly as she formulated her response.

"Okay, here's the sum total of what I know about Heidi. And keep in mind, it isn't much. It was my second morning at Ocean Side and she showed up at the lab. She was dressed in scrubs and looked very professional and competent. She introduced herself and said she wanted to welcome me to the staff."

"And she asked you out."

"Yes, to dinner. But I told her no. Thank you, but no."

"Why? She's a hot-looking babe." Margie stole a glance in Heidi's direction. "Oh, wait. You aren't..." She laughed. "I'm sorry, Sara. I just assumed."

"Assumed what?"

"Nothing. Never mind." Margie buried herself in her salad, as if to hide her embarrassment.

"You meant you assumed I was gay?"

"Uh, huh."

"I am," Sara said quietly.

"You are?" Margie looked up with a broad grin. "Really?"

"Really. I don't advertise it, but yes." Sara pulled a friendly smile.

"Then it's true. You are dating a woman on a motor scooter. What's her name? Tell me all about her."

Sara nearly choked on a saltine.

"I'm not dating anyone on a motor scooter. Where did you hear that?"

"Around. The hospital has a very efficient grapevine. The word is she's a little younger, but taller and cute. We're talking capital q cute. And she wants to give you the scooter as a token of her love." Margie said it with dramatic overtones.

"*What*?" Sara laughed out loud.

"Carol in bookkeeping said she saw the two of you in the parking lot a few weeks ago. She said she had her hands all over you." Margie leaned in and added, "Between your legs. I told her that didn't sound like the Sara Patterson I know, but she insisted she saw what she saw. So, who is she? How long have you known her? She's the reason you didn't go out with Heidi, isn't she?"

"Okay, first of all, I didn't go out with Heidi because she was a little too pushy for my taste. And second, and let me squash these grapes once and for all, I am not now nor have I ever dated Jessie Singer. Yes, she has a motor scooter she is trying to sell. Yes, she brought it to the hospital for me to see because she thought I was interested in buying it. And yes, she touched my leg. But it was completely innocent. She was showing me how to sit on it. And just like Heidi, I told her no. And not surprisingly for the same reason. She was being too pushy." She went back to her salad.

"Not dating?"

"Not dating."

"So you would have bought the scooter if she hadn't been so pushy about it."

"What? No."

"But you just said you told her no because she was being too pushy. That sure sounds like you were interested if she had let you come to a decision in your own good time."

Sara had to admit it did sound that way.

"Now that you've had time to think about it, why don't you buy it?" Margie gave her a friendly nudge.

"Are you kidding? Me? I'd kill myself."

"From the way Carol described it, the scooter wasn't very big. What was it? One of those commuter scooters? The ones that sound like a juice blender going down the street?"

"Fifty cc, I think it was."

"Heck, most bicycles go faster than those things. And this might just be your chance." She raised a suspicious eyebrow.

"Chance for what? Date a bartender whose dream career is to be a professional pool player?"

"Okay, that too. But I was thinking a chance to do something outside your comfort zone. Something daring. It's just a motor scooter, but it's a start."

"Why does everyone think I need to be daring? What's wrong with practical and cautious?" Sara turned to Margie with a caustic scowl. "And don't you dare mention that cruise. I don't want to spend a week overeating and staring at gray water."

"Your choice." Finished with her lunch, Margie carried her tray to the conveyor, Sara right behind.

"Besides, I think she already sold it," Sara said as they headed back up the hall.

"See, you were interested."

"Thank you for lunch." Sara stopped at the doorway to the lab.

"You should buy it." Margie continued up the hall.

"You buy it."

"Heck no. I want a vehicle you can snuggle in."

CHAPTER SEVEN

It had been three months since Sara had come to work at Ocean Side and she was halfway through her probationary period. It had also been three months worth of Dr. Lesterbrook's hypercritical glances and judgmental overtones. She had expected to have to prove herself. She didn't expect his little surprise visits, watching over her shoulder as she was pipetting or preparing a slide. But it was his laboratory. If she wanted to work there, she had to follow his rules. She needed the job. And she liked the small regional hospital atmosphere. She certainly wasn't going to use her degree to apply at the local grocery store as a checker. Those days were all in the past.

Monday morning brought a flood of orders from the wards and two walk-in patients that kept Sara busy right through her coffee break.

"Have you cultured the swab from med surg?" Dr. Lesterbrook asked behind a stern expression.

Sara looked up from the microscope.

"Yes and we can rule out *E. coli*. It's not a gram negative rod."

"So, gram positive cocci?"

"Yes. I'm thinking strep or staph."

"I don't need a hunch. The ward nurse needs an answer. She's got patients with bedsores she can't treat with guesswork. Let me know when you isolate it." He started to walk away, but stopped and turned back, a curious frown on his face. "Is something bothering you? Have we got personnel issues in the lab I need to address?"

"No. Everything is fine." Sara wondered what she had done wrong. Nothing came to mind.

"You're sure everything is okay? No problems? Work environment? Co-workers?"

"No." Sara smiled pleasantly. "Why do you ask?"

"You didn't attend the employee picnic or the fund-raiser for the children's ward. I wouldn't attend those things if I didn't have to. Perfectly good waste of a Sunday afternoon. But I heard you and Edie talking about them so I just assumed you'd be there."

"I needed the extra time for work on my thesis."

"Oh, yes. Master's thesis. Immune deficiency or some such."

"Immune suppression secondary to long-term—"

"You'll make a good MLS, Sara," Dr. Lesterbrook interrupted before Sara could finish. "A master's in clinical laboratory science will serve you well."

"Thank you sir."

"You were smart not to stop at just being a lab tech. Too bad you didn't continue your education. Aimed for a doctorate." He headed across the lab. "I'll be waiting for the results on that culture." He went into his office and closed the door.

Sara glanced out the window, wondering if Dr. Lesterbrook was right. Was she acting differently? She knew better than to bring her personal problems to work. But she didn't have any problems. Nothing had happened to change her demeanor. Perhaps it was the pressure of completing her thesis. Was her topic relevant? Had she covered every point to the fullest? Would the long hours of research and rewriting earn her a master's degree? She made no apologies that it had taken her a few more years than some to finish. Graduate school was expensive. She had done it all on her own. The time she spent working odd jobs to earn her tuition made her all the more hungry to achieve it. It was almost hers. Almost within reach. If that made her more reserved, so be it. It certainly wasn't the residual guilt over how she handled Jessie Singer and that pesky motor scooter. Jessie Singer was just one of those people whose path had briefly crossed hers, then drifted away, never to be seen again. Her memory would fade. But it had been three months since that first meeting in the lab. Why had it lingered this long?

"I do not want a motor scooter," she said under her breath, and returned to her work. "I don't want a bartender either."

Sara finished her report on the culture for Dr. Lesterbrook and was in the middle of pipetting when Margie stuck her head around the corner. She held up a brochure and broadcast a wide grin.

Margie now made almost daily visits to the lab to visit and test her glucose level. She said it was cleaner and offered more privacy than the restrooms. "I refuse to sit on the toilet while I stick my finger," she had said. "It's not sanitary." Sara didn't mind. Margie stayed out of the way when things got busy, or when Dr. Lesterbrook wandered through with his challenging isn't-there-a-test-you-should-be-running look. Margie also provided pleasant, mature and intelligent conversation. Edie and Trevor frequently did not.

"Did you see this?" Margie said.

"See what?" Sara didn't look up.

"Cedar Ridge Trail Ride and Chuck Wagon Dinner."

"Is that one of those ATV things when you ride through mud holes and creek beds just to see how dirty you can get? I did that once in high school. I swear the girl steered for every water hole and mud pit she could find. I spit mud for a week."

"No. Horses. See? Women of Western Washington Annual Ride for Pride to benefit the women's center in Longview." She opened the brochure and spread it out on the lab table. "Doesn't a trail ride sound like fun? Look at these women. I'd let any one of them saddle my horse. Go with me, Sara. We'll have a blast."

"Go with you where?" Sara's mind was on the test she was running.

"On this trail ride. It's not a long one like the ride through the Grand Canyon and you should definitely do that someday. It was a hoot. S'mores by the campfire. Cowboy baked beans. Spectacular scenery. It was great."

"What are cowboy baked beans?" Sara was only half listening.

"Beans in a big pot with hamburger and onions. Not as good as mine, but edible. So, what do you say? Can I sign us up? It's not even that expensive. It's tax deductible since it's for charity plus we get a discount if we go as a couple."

Sara finally gave in and moved her attention to where Margie was pointing.

"I'm sure it's great, but I'm really not into camping in the woods and going potty behind a tree."

"This isn't a camping trip. It's just a one-day trail ride with a chuck wagon dinner in the evening, and it's all for charity. Actually, it's not even a whole day. It's only a one-afternoon trail ride and a dinner. Everything is supplied. Drinks. Tour guides. Meal. Even entertainment. See?"

"You want to go on a trail ride? I thought you already checked that off your bucket list when you did the Grand Canyon thing."

"I did. But I want to go again. Please, Sara. You know I won't do it without someone going with me. I'm a pod person."

"Ask that new woman from Astoria you're seeing. The dental assistant."

"Things aren't going very well with Arnie."

"Arnie?"

"Short for Arnelle and don't ask." Margie wrinkled her nose. "Come on, Sara. Go with me. Just this once." She whined childishly then smiled. "It's a short ride. How far can you go in one afternoon on circus horses?"

"Circus horses? Okay, I give up. What's a circus horse? Something with tassles?"

"The head wrangler on the Grand Canyon ride called them that. She said it's because they follow each other nose to tail. If you fall off the horse it just stands there until you climb back on."

"I don't want to fall off a horse, thank you very much."

"You won't fall off. These places only use really gentle horses. They have to or they'd have lawsuits up the hoo-haa. The only way you'd fall off is if you were either drunk or stupid."

Margie seemed to see the wheels turning in Sara's head as she contemplated the idea.

"What do you say, Sara? It's all for charity. One hundred percent of the money goes to the women's center. It's not nearly as dangerous as owning a motor scooter. Several of the gals from the hospital are going."

"When is this charity trail ride? And where is it?"

"It's the weekend after next. It's at some ranch off Highway Six on the way to Chehalis. Look at this gorgeous scenery. Pine trees. Mountain streams. Fresh air. And according to one of the girls who went last year, the food at the chuck wagon dinner is out of this world. Steak, ribs, chicken. They guarantee you won't go home hungry."

"And you're sure you don't have to be an experienced equestrian?"

"Heck no. That's the great thing about it. And hey, if I can do it schlepping an insulin pump, anyone can do it. Besides, you have to go. What if I need assistance?" Margie grinned innocently.

"That's not fair. That's medical blackmail. If you think you'll have problems with your pump we won't go."

"So, you'll go with me?" Margie was delighted.

"Okay, yes. I'll go. It's for charity," Sara agreed. It would be the weekend after she submitted her thesis. A change of pace might be the perfect way to recalibrate whatever was out of balance in her life.

"Great! I'll sign us up. You'll love it. By the way, have you ever ridden a horse before?"

"Does a pony ride at the state fair count? I was six."

"Sure. Works for me." She gave Sara a hug and hurried away, a chipper spring in her step.

Sara fought the urge to chase her down and cancel. If ER hadn't called needing a sample drawn stat she might have. It wasn't until that evening as she pulled into her driveway that she remembered she had agreed to go. Oh well. How bad could it be? Off in the beautiful Washington scenery, away from stress.

"Hello, baby," she said as Gypsy greeted her at the door, wagging ecstatically. "Yes, I'm home. I see Lucille brought you home too. Did you have fun at the children's center today?" She knelt on the floor as she cooed and patted the dog's head lovingly. "Guess what Momma did. She opened her big mouth and agreed to go on a trail ride. Yes, she did. Aren't you proud of her?" She gave Gypsy a pat then headed to the kitchen. Two yellow puddles and a small brown doggie-bomb were the first things she saw.

"Gypsy Patterson! What is this?" she said sternly. "Shame on you. It is not Christmas. I don't need presents."

Gypsy's wagging enthusiasm instantly changed to cowering humiliation. She sat in the corner and watched while Sara cleaned the mess and sprayed disinfectant. The dog seemed to know she had done a no-no.

"We had a talk about this, missy. You know how to use the doggie door. You have the entire fenced-in backyard for this."

It wasn't until Sara carried the trash bag out the back door that she noticed the doggie door was locked.

"Oh, no! Baby, it's not your fault. The door was locked again." She unlocked the swinging flap then knelt in front of Gypsy and loved on her, hoping to restore her trust. "Momma's sorry. Lucille forgot to unlock it. We'll have to remind her." She kissed Gypsy's head, gave her a pat then went to find something for dinner. Gypsy immediately disappeared through the doggie door. Sara stood at the sink eating a bowl of granola and a banana and wondering why she had agreed to the trail ride. Horseback riding wasn't one of her fantasies. Whatever it was that nudged her over the edge, she'd survive it. Tonight she had forty-six pages to edit.

* * *

The next morning Margie seemed to sense Sara had reservations about her decision to go along on the trail ride.

"You're not going to back out on me, are you?" Margie asked as they stacked their lunch trays on the cart.

"No. I said I was going and I am."

"But you're thinking about it, right?"

"Did I say anything? I'm going. I'm wearing jeans and my new sneakers and I'm going," Sara said proudly. She didn't need an excuse to back out. She had convinced herself to do this. She needed some social existence. She couldn't live like a hermit forever. Margie was right. It was time to be brazen. To throw caution out the window. Or at the very least, place caution on the windowsill.

"This month a trail ride. Next month skydiving," Margie said, waving her hand across the air as she sauntered down the hall.

"Not me. You'd have to shoot me and shove me out of the plane."

"We'll conquer an afternoon trail ride to start with and see how you do."

"I'm still not going on a cruise."

"We'll see," Margie said smugly.

"Sara, ER," Dr. Lesterbrook said and handed her a collection tray then returned to his office.

"Later, Margie," Sara said as she headed to ER.

"You're not backing out," she called after her. "You hear me? Not happening."

CHAPTER EIGHT

Margie climbed out of the car and took a deep breath.

"Smell the fresh air. Isn't it great?" she said, turning her face up to the late-morning sun.

"Yes. Absolutely." Sara gave a satisfied smile as she too took a long full breath. She was happy she had agreed to come on the trail ride. It was the perfect reward for having finished her thesis. It was done, the culmination of many months' worth of work, sweat and tedium. She had given up nearly a year of her social life to it. All she had left to do was wait for the university to schedule a defense of her work and she would have her master's degree in hand, a diploma to hang on the wall to declare for all to see that she had done this. She had accomplished something good. For a brief moment she wondered what her parents would think of it. After all, she was their only child. Neither of them had attended college. Surely they would respect those who have. Would they be proud of her accomplishment?

"Come on," Margie said, hooking her arm through Sara's and leading her toward the gathering women.

"Good morning, ladies. My name is Becky. Welcome to Bellsap River Ranch and the annual Cedar Ridge Trail Ride," a woman in a plaid western shirt and jeans announced from the back of a handsome palomino mare. The legs of Becky's jeans were tucked inside a pair of expensive-looking cowboy boots with soaring eagles tooled into the sides. A well-bent cowboy hat sat just above her eyebrows, unsuccessfully taming restless curls. She sat astride the horse, but had one leg hooked over the saddle horn, casually watching the twenty-six greenhorns mill around the registration table. The corral was full of horses, already saddled and waiting. Most were brown and indistinguishable from one another, their reins tied to the top rail of the fence. There was also one brown and white pinto, one white with gray spots and one jet-black horse with white feet.

"When you've finished signing in, if you'd gather around we'll see if we can get this party started." She smiled and raised the brim of her hat.

The women were an eclectic group including six senior citizens out to "try something new," a few women barely in their twenties sporting tattoos and athletic bodies, and five hospital employees. The rest were a group of middle-aged women from Portland who arrived in a van and sounded like they were out for a day of mischievous fun.

"What happens in the mountains, stays in the mountains," one woman joked. She mentioned a husband but her conversation suggested she was open to possibilities.

"Ladies, we've got three very capable wranglers here to help make this a memorable experience. In the blue shirt, we've got Allie. Best horse saddler this side of the Pendleton Roundup." She pointed to a middle-aged woman in a denim shirt. She had a dark tan and was adjusting a saddle. The woman gave a small wave then went back to what she was doing. "And over there we've got Laurie Ann. Three-time barrel racing champion. She also plays the guitar and after dinner if you all ask her pretty please, she just might sing us a song or two." A forty-something blond with a ponytail and long legs waved from the corral gate. She had trim hips and a big bust. Sara heard someone moan soulfully, presumably at the woman's full figure. "And last but not least, on the black horse, we've got JJ. She's made this trek more times than she can count." The woman tipped her cowboy hat to the crowd. She had gray hair, long, skinny legs and a leathered complexion. "The four of us have logged more saddle time than we'd like to admit. If you need anything, just ask. We want to thank you all for coming out today to help support the women's center. This is our eighth annual Ride for Pride. We've got the best scenery in southern Washington and the best food west of Chicago. Our cooks are preparing a feast for you and it'll be waiting at the other end of the trail. Before we pair you ladies up with one of our fine steeds, we've got a few do's and don'ts we'd like to share so you don't go home with gravel in your teeth."

The group listened to Becky's tutorial, some more intently than others. After a few questions about who had riding experience and who didn't, each woman was assigned a mount and helped up into the saddle. Margie was paired with a pot-bellied mare with a black saddle. Laurie Ann adjusted the stirrups to accommodate Margie's long legs, joking with her about entering a rodeo.

"Ouch," one of the women said with a chuckle as she swung her leg over and settled into the saddle. "Wait till I tell my girlfriend. She's going to be SO jealous. I haven't spread 'em this far in years."

Sara snickered quietly. It wasn't her kind of joke, but it was funny. She was the last to be assigned a horse.

"This is Brandy," Allie said as she led the pinto out of the corral. She gave a tug on the cinch strap to tighten it. "She's very gentle and loves to trail ride. She's got a nice easy gait. Just like sitting in a rocking chair." She positioned Sara next to the horse and showed her how to mount, then helped her slip her foot in the stirrup. "You might need to bounce a little to get yourself up but that's okay. She won't step out on you. She's used to that. Always mount and dismount from this side. And when you dismount, swing your leg over then take your left foot out of the stirrup before you lower yourself to the ground. You can just slide right down and you won't get your foot caught up in the stirrup."

The wranglers watched and offered assistance as the women practiced steering their horses around the paddock. The usual jokes about needing a crane or wanting a padded seat kept the mood jovial. It also masked the anxiety some of the women were doing their best to hide, including Sara.

"Where's the seat belt on this thing?" one of the seniors asked, her hands clutching the saddle horn. "It's a long way down to the ground, and I don't bounce like I used to."

It was just after noon when the instructions ended and Becky led the group out of the paddock and down the gravel road. Once they cleared the ranch house and fence line they headed across the valley, following a dirt trail that disappeared into a stand of tall evergreens. The first hour was slow, every horse plodding along at a steady pace. They stopped occasionally for pictures and adjustments to stirrups and saddles. And for bathroom breaks some of the women forgot to take before they left the ranch.

"Try to keep your horse's nose out of the tail of the horse ahead of you," Allie said loud enough for all to hear as she trotted up beside Sara. "If that horse ahead of you kicks, chances are she'll get you right in the knees. Give yourself some space, ladies." Sara eased back on the reins, leaving plenty of space between her horse and Margie's.

"Told ya," Margie said, looking over her shoulder. "Circus horses."

"You didn't tell me they'd kick."

"Surprise." She grinned.

Lunch wasn't part of the trek so everyone had brought snacks. Granola bars, jerky, candy bars and trail mix. A packhorse at the back of the line carried bottled water and juice that were distributed as needed. They were about to begin an uphill climb over a rolling hillside when Margie steered her horse out of line and stopped next to a tree.

"You have to go again?" Sara pulled up alongside.

"No. I need to test. I think I'm low. Can you hold my horse?" She handed her reins to Sara then dug in her pack for her test kit.

"How low do you think you are? Do you need help?"

"Heck, no. I just may need an extra snack or two." She stuck her finger and collected the blood droplet on the test strip then waited. "Yep. Peanut butter granola it shall be. You want one?"

"No, thank you. I had some trail mix. How low is it?" Sara asked, trying to see the meter screen.

"Don't worry. I've got it covered." Margie took a big bite of granola bar then repacked her test kit.

"Margie, how low?"

"You don't need to know. We're not at the hospital today, and I don't need you to get all in a snit fit. We're on a trail ride. Just pretend you're not a medical professional for one afternoon."

"And what happens if you fall off your horse from an insulin reaction? What am I supposed to tell the paramedics?" Sara handed back the reins and followed Margie onto the trail.

"Tell them to stuff a sugar cube in my mouth and go home." Margie looked back with a scowl. "If I fall off this horse you better not call the paramedics. I mean it, Sara. No overreacting."

"Fine. I won't overreact. I'll try not to let my horse stomp all over you as we mosey on up the trail."

"Thank you." Margie stuck her tongue out then threw her head back and laughed.

With switchbacks and winding trails, Sara had no idea which way they were headed. After nearly four hours on the trail they finally rode into a clearing where a fenced corral and three canvas shelters filled with picnic tables waited. Whiffs of smoke from a row of charcoal cookers filled the air with the delicious aroma of barbeque. Covered cast-iron pots simmered over open pit fires. Several large coolers and a buffet table staged for a meal welcomed the weary riders as they straggled into camp. Three women, all dressed in matching jeans and bright red western shirts, waited at the corral gate. Those who needed it were helped off their horses, moaning and groaning at their stiff muscles.

"I may never walk straight again," one of the women said, rubbing the insides of her legs.

"That's because you're not straight and you never will be, Josie. You be gay woomon," her friend said with an exaggerated Jamaican accent.

"A little longer on that horse and it would have jostled the gay right out of me. Where's the powder room? I need to re-apply," another joked.

"Never mind the powder room. Where's the damn bathroom."

Margie dismounted and rubbed her fanny as if the circulation had stopped to that part of her body. Sara was the last one to saunter into camp. Her horse headed directly toward the corral, picking up speed the closer it got.

"Whoa," she said, tugging on the reins as it trotted for the corner. "No, no, Brandy. Not back there. I need room to get off." She tried to turn the horse back toward the gate, rocking back and forth in the saddle and tapping her heels gently against the horse's belly. "Let's go. Come on, Brandy. Giddyap." But Brandy was content to stand in the corner, her nose touching the top rail of the fence. "Now look, horse. I need more than five inches to dismount. How do we plan to handle this?"

"Hold on there, Brandy. You need to cooperate with the nice lady," a voice called as a hand reached out and took control of the bridle.

It was Jessie.

She leaned her shoulder against the horse's rump and pushed, then led the horse back into the middle of the corral. She smiled up at Sara. "Hey there, laboratory lady. I saw an S. Patterson on the registration list. I wondered if it was you."

"Jessie? What are you doing here?" Sara hadn't noticed her as she rode in, but Jessie was dressed in one of the red western shirts.

"I'm the cook. I'm here to make your trail ride and starlight dinner a memorable and enjoyable experience," she said as if rehearsed. "I suppose you'd like to climb down from there." She stroked Brandy's neck then extended a hand up to Sara, who was still clutching the saddle horn.

A million questions flooded Sara's mind. Why did Jessie quit Batch's? Is this the job she considered better than working for her grandfather? When did she change career paths from professional pool player to chuck wagon cook at a horse ranch? Did she get the results of her tests back yet? But first things first. She needed to get off this horse and put her feet on solid ground. She had tried it once on her own but it wasn't a pretty sight.

"Can you hold the horse so she doesn't move while I do this?"

"I've got the horse. Drop on down here, slick."

Sara swung her right leg over. She remembered what the wrangler said and pulled her left foot out of the stirrup before lowering herself, but with both feet dangling and her butt extended she grabbed the saddle to keep from falling.

"That's it. You got it. Ease on down here." Jessie placed a hand on Sara's rear for support and guided her to the ground. "There ya go. Back on dry land."

"Thank you. There's no graceful way to do that, is there?" Sara was glad to be off the horse, but her legs felt like rubber.

"Looked graceful to me. But I'm just the cook." Jessie released Brandy into the corral and held the gate for Sara then closed it behind them. "What's it been? Three months? Four?"

"The last time we spoke was four months ago. But what are you doing cooking for a bunch of women in the middle of the woods?"

"It's sort of a long story. Let's just say I met the requirements for the job and it pays the bills."

In spite of the test results being Jessie's private medical information, Sara had to ask.

"I know it's none of my business, but did you get the results of your tests?" Sara expected Jessie to challenge her right to know.

"Those things aren't cheap, are they?"

"Unfortunately, no, they aren't. Genetic testing is new and costly. It won't do you any good now but it should come down in time." Sara followed Jessie down the line as she checked the cookers, waiting for her to offer the test results. But she didn't. "And?" she finally asked.

"And what? Back up. This one will spit at you." She opened the lid to the hissing sound of dripping meat juices.

"That looks delicious." Sara drew in a deep quenching breath, sampling the aroma.

"Brisket." Jessie stabbed a small piece with the fork, blew on it then tasted it. "Whoa, hot." She painted more sauce on the meat then closed the lid. "By the time we eat, this will be perfect."

"By the time we eat? How long will that be?"

"Not long. Why? Are you hungry?"

"A little, but I'm more worried about that long ride back after dark."

"It's not that long."

"It took us four hours to get here. Are we going to gallop all the way back?"

"Relax. It's right through there." She nodded toward the trail that led into the woods. "You made a big circle. It's less than a quarter of a mile to where you parked your car. She picked this spot on purpose. Some people are so stiff and sore once they make it this far they have to walk their horse back."

"Okay, so I won't worry about the ride back but how about answering my question."

"What question?" She made a test cut through a steak to reveal its pink middle. "How do you like your steak? Medium? Well done?"

"Medium. I like a little pink."

"You're going to be impressed. This beef is raised right here on this ranch. It's primo quality meat. You don't get that with frozen shipped-in stuff."

"You're not going to tell me, are you?"

"Tell you what?" Jessie made no attempt to hide a smug little grin.

"Oh, I get it. Payback. Okay, I'll ask nicely. Your test results, they came back okay, didn't they?"

"Yeah, they're fine." She chuckled, seemingly happy with herself for keeping Sara waiting. "No boob-ectomy for this girl."

"Good." Sara exhaled, relieved at Jessie's news. "It must be a great relief."

"To be honest, I remember very little of what you said that day. My brain was someplace else."

"I can understand that. Those tests can cause an anxiety attack by the mere fact of what they're looking for. I'm very pleased for you, Jessie."

"How are we doing over here, babe?" Becky hurried over and lifted the lid to a cooker. She fanned away the smoke and inspected the contents.

"We're ready. The one at the end needs another twenty minutes but we've got plenty to start."

"Good. Ten minutes." She wrapped an arm around Jessie's waist and gave her a squeeze. The twinkle in Becky's eye and her lingering smile told Sara there was more to their relationship than just boss and employee. It hadn't occurred to Sara that Jessie might have a girlfriend. Maybe it was her demonstrative personality, or her seemingly nomadic existence, but it just didn't occur to her. Becky, although attractive and amiable, seemed much older than Jessie. Come to think of it, Becky could easily be twenty years older. A mother figure. That's it, Sara thought. Becky was the maternal figure in Jessie's life, brought together through work, filling the void the death of Jessie's mother had created. Had to be. But her hand on Jessie's ass and the kiss she placed on her lips before she hurried away told something else.

Margie hurried up to Sara and grabbed her arm, saving her from asking Jessie what would have been an embarrassing question. Jessie's private life didn't belong in casual conversation over a barbeque grill.

"Did you see who's here?" Margie said through clenched teeth. She pulled Sara aside as if to divulge some sort of secret. Sara still wanted to ask Jessie about her change of job and offer an apology about the scooter misunderstanding but that would come later. Maybe.

"Who?" Sara asked.

"Gretchen whatshername. You know. The newscaster from Portland. The one who does the late news. She's gay and she is *so* hot." Margie panted like a dog then rolled her eyes. "I want to meet her. Come with me." She locked arms with Sara and pulled her along.

"Why do I have to go? We all rode in together. Just go over and say hi, I'm Margie. Don't be nervous."

"I'm not nervous about meeting her. I'm nervous that I'll say something stupid like, hey Gretchen, would you go out to dinner with me followed by a couple hours of heavy breathing."

"So, I'm supposed to be your muffle?"

"Yes, please."

As they crossed the camp to where women were congregating Sara looked back and noticed Becky once again standing at Jessie's side. Their eyes were locked in silent communication. Jessie was clearly in a relationship with that woman, Sara thought. They had the look. And Sara couldn't blame her. If it was a rustic outdoorsy type Jessie fancied, Becky filled the bill. If it was an attractive independent businesswoman she desired, Becky filled that bill as well, even if she was old enough to be her mother.

With Sara at her side, Margie walked up to a woman seated on a bench. She was dressed in designer jeans, sweater with the sleeves pushed up the elbows, white visor and sunglasses. She was fiddling with her phone and seemed unable to find a signal.

"Hi." Margie drew a deep nervous breath. "Aren't you the newscaster who did the report on using food stamps at fast-food restaurants? Gretchen, isn't it?" She sat down next to her and offered a handshake. "I'm Margie Snow. *Love* your newscasts."

The woman seemed startled, but accepted Margie's hand.

"Yes, that was us. Did you like that piece?"

"It had some good points. But you didn't mention there are many diabetics on assistance, and for them, access to fast food is critical sometimes. Brittle diabetics don't have time to go to the grocery store, buy something then take it home and cook it. They need carbs or quick sugar spikes in a hurry."

Way to pick a fight with the lady you're trying to impress, Margie, Sara thought. At least no one could say Margie wasn't direct.

"You know, you're right," Gretchen said. "But to be honest, I didn't write that piece. The news director got the idea from a national story. He cut it to fit the time slot we had. He's also a little right wing, so…"

"That explains the bias."

"You should see what we have to go through to cover Portland's Pride Parade. He expected us to show a five-second sound bite and call it good."

"You can't see all the lovely ladies walking up Burnside in five seconds. My God, what is he thinking?"

"No kidding." They both laughed.

Satisfied her help was no longer needed, Sara drifted away. She had worked up the courage to go visit with Jessie again, hoping this was the right time to apologize for the motor scooter misunderstanding. But before she got there Becky announced dinner was ready. The crowd of women immediately descended upon the buffet table like wolves ready to feast on a carcass. Jessie, Becky and the other ranch hands went to work at the buffet line, dishing up generous helpings of ranch beans, fried potatoes, corn muffins, salad and a selection of meats. The chuck wagon ambience was carried through from the red-checkered tablecloths and Mason jars used for drinks to the metal plates that looked like they could be used to pan for gold. The open air and trail ride had made the riders ravenous. Even Sara tried some of everything, piling her plate full.

"Aren't you eating?" Sara asked as she returned to the serving table for silverware. Jessie was slicing meat onto a platter.

"Later. You want some of this brisket? It's powerful good stuff," she said with a thick Texas drawl.

"No, thank you. I've got plenty." She looked up and down the table. "I hate to ask, but do you have ketchup?"

"Ketchup?" Jessie laughed then shouted, "We've got one, Becky. She wants ketchup. She's going to ruin a perfectly good steak with ketchup."

"Oh, my God. Tell me it isn't so. Where's my lasso?" Everyone hooted and cheered as Becky grabbed a lasso off the corral gate and began twirling it over her head, a wicked gleam in her eyes. "Where's that city slicker? Let me at her. I'll be darned if she's going to douse my steak with that crap. Where is she?"

The crowd became caught up in the fun as if it were part of the entertainment. They pointed at Sara, laughing and encouraging Becky's ire. Sara felt a flush of embarrassment warm her face, but stood silently as the drama built. She knew good and well if it hadn't been her, someone else would have been the brunt of this joke.

"Wait, wait, wait," Sara finally yelled above the laughter. "I'm not going to put it on my steak. I want it for my potatoes."

"Are you sure?" Becky scowled and kept twirling.

"I promise. Only on the potatoes." Sara held up a hand as a pledge.

Becky stopped twirling. The lasso settled to the ground around her feet.

"Okay, Jessie. Let her have some, but I'll be watching you, missy." She winked at Sara.

Jessie had already retrieved a bottle of Heinz from a cooler and set it on the serving table.

"Can I have A.1. for my, ah hum, potatoes?" someone shouted.

"Traitors. Infidels." Becky shook her head disgustedly and pointed to the condiment table. She and the other employees kept the mood light and fun. Laurie Ann circled the table with a pitcher of iced tea, refilling the Mason jars and making jokes. Becky encouraged everyone to return for seconds as Allie and JJ served apple cake for dessert.

"Try these. They're locally grown." Jessie reached in and set dishes of fresh berries along the table.

"Thank you, Jessie." Sara plucked a blackberry from the dish and ate it. "Oh, wow. Those are terrific."

"That's Jessie, the one with the scooter?" Margie whispered as she watched her move down the table.

"Yes."

"You should have bought it." She looked again at Jessie's nicely fitting jeans. "You should have kept your options open. I would have."

"First of all, why would I need to buy a motor scooter and second, Jessie Singer has a girlfriend."

"She does? Darn. Who?"

Sara nodded over her shoulder. Margie looked in that direction and gasped.

"Becky? The ranch owner?"

"Shh. Yes, I think so."

"Wow." She went back to eating. "I wonder if they do it in the saddle."

"Margie!"

"Hey, if you can do it on a barstool, why not on a horse?"

"You've done it on a barstool?"

"Yeah. Haven't you?" Margie shrugged.

"No."

"It wasn't in a bar, if that's what you're thinking. It was at home."

Sara had trouble getting the image of Jessie and Becky perched naked on a stool in Batch's dimly lit bar out of her mind.

"Do me a favor. Please don't ask them if they've *done it* on a barstool."

"Okay. But I know what you're thinking. And it really isn't that hard." Margie grinned.

Dinner and dessert gave way to a sing-a-long and conversation. As advertised, Laurie Ann had a lovely singing voice. She accompanied herself on a guitar and took requests for over an hour. Sara's rear had all the bench sitting it could take and she drifted across to where Jessie was scraping the dirty dishes into a trash bag. It was time to apologize.

"How did you like the steak? Good, huh?" Jessie asked.

"Yes, it was excellent. And no, I didn't put ketchup on it." Sara handed her the next plate in the stack. "Okay, I have to ask you something, but you have to promise you won't look at me like I'm an idiot."

"I promise." Jessie held up the rubber scraper solemnly. "But I know what it is. You want to change careers and become a waitress?"

"No."

"Bartender? Horse wrangler?"

"No. Now hush or I'll forget what I wanted to say. It's about the scooter."

"Yeah, I knew we'd get around to that sometime today. I'm sorry, Sara. I was a real ass and I feel bad about it. I should have never brought it over to the hospital without checking with you first. But you returned my backpack and helped me out when I was busy. I wanted to return the favor. You mentioned the scooter so I jumped to the assumption you were seriously interested in buying it. I'm sorry."

"You're apologizing to me? Wow. That's what I was going to do. Apologize for being rude."

"So, you accept my apology?"

"Sure," Sara handed her another plate and offered a smile, "if you accept mine."

"Accepted." Jessie nodded.

"What would you say if I said I know someone who might be interested in buying the scooter?"

"Who?"

"Well." Sara drew a preparatory breath. "Me. I think I want to buy it."

"You're kidding." Jessie dropped the plate she was scraping. She quickly retrieved it from the trash bag. "You?"

"Yes. Me."

"Really? You?" Jessie spat out a laugh, not the response Sara expected. "But you hated that idea. You didn't even want to sit on it."

"What I hated was being pressured into a decision when I wasn't ready. The way you were pushing me and insisting I try it out I was worried it was defective or something. But if you can guarantee there is nothing mechanically wrong with it, I'd like to reconsider."

"I'd never do that. I'd never try to cheat you. I'm not that kind of person. There's nothing wrong with the scooter. The engine is good. The tires and suspension are good. Everything works. I kept it garaged during the rainy season and changed the oil regularly. It's cherry. But I can't sell it to you."

"And why not?" Sara asked suspiciously. "Just because I didn't buy it four months ago I can't have a second look?"

"I'd be glad to give you a second look at it but I already have a buyer. He gave me fifty bucks earnest money to hold it until the end of the month. He's waiting for an insurance settlement. I wish I had known you were interested. I could have held onto it."

"I needed time to think about it. But that's okay." Sara felt a surprising stab of disappointment.

"Damn. Why didn't you say something?" Jessie demanded.

"Because you were being pushy and I'm not the impulsive type. I rarely buy anything without going home and sleeping on it."

"You do that for everything you buy?" She gave a wry smile. "It must make grocery shopping a huge ordeal."

"Not everything. But the big things, yes, I do. It drove my girlfriend crazy. She was just the opposite. She'd buy things on the spur of the moment then take it back the next day once she had a chance to think about it."

"You've got a girlfriend?"

"Had. The infatuation only lasted eleven months. Sweet girl, but not my style."

"So you don't like impulsive women."

"I don't like impractical women."

"It takes all kinds. That's what makes life exciting. But I wish you had said you were interested in the scooter. I would have waited."

"Maybe it's a sign. Maybe my guardian angel is telling me my first instinct was right. Motor scooters are way too dangerous and I shouldn't have one. They're far too impractical."

"Cripes. Don't you like having fun?"

"Of course I do. I came on this trail ride, didn't I?"

"I'm going to take a wild guess and say it wasn't your idea. Your friend over there talked you into it."

"But I came. And what about you? What brings you out here in the middle of nowhere? I thought you wanted to be a professional pool player."

"Who says I'm not?"

"Ladies," Becky announced as she climbed onto a bench. "I hope everyone had enough to eat. If you still have an empty spot, mosey on over there. Jessie will be glad to serve you up. Right, Jessie?" Jessie waved and pointed to a platter of meat, but the crowd moaned plaintively. "In case you haven't heard, it's only a short ride back to the barn. Yes, ladies, we rode you around in a big circle. We didn't want your city slicker butts to suffer any more than they already have." Laughter echoed through the trees. "When you're ready, we'll help you mount up and head back. You'll be back in your comfy cushioned car seats in thirty minutes. And if anyone doesn't think they can ride another inch, we've got transportation for you, too." Becky pointed at a pair of golf carts parked at the edge of the camp. "If you'd like to avail yourself to a motorized ride back, we'll be glad to take you. And the rest of us promise not to ridicule your sorry ass for being a wimp." More and louder laughter rose through the air.

One at a time the women mounted their horses and followed JJ along the trail back to the ranch just as the sun began to set. Margie and Gretchen were first to disappear through the trees, riding side-by-side and chatting incessantly. Even the older gray-haired women mounted spryly and headed down the trail. Jessie led Brandy out of the corral and helped Sara climb aboard.

"Thanks," Sara offered, settling herself in the saddle. "It was nice seeing you again, Jessie."

"You bet." Jessie gave a yank to tighten the cinch strap.

"You know, I went by Batch's to apologize, but you weren't there. I felt bad about the way that ended."

"Don't worry about it." She tucked the end of the strap through the loop.

"The bartender said you didn't work there anymore. He said you quit."

"I can just guess what he said."

"That middle-aged man with a goatee, was he your father?"

"Yeah." Jessie's jaw muscles rippled, as if stifling something else she wanted to add. She handed Sara the reins and turned the horse toward the trail. "Take care, Sara Patterson." She smiled and gave Brandy a swat on the rump, sending them on their way. Sara started up the trail then looked back. Becky's arms were around Jessie, sharing a passionate embrace.

CHAPTER NINE

It had been two months since the trail ride and the dog days of summer had settled over western Washington. Even the coastal region was unseasonably hot and muggy. Margie had established a fledgling relationship with Gretchen, one that included lunchtime phone calls from the privacy of her car. As the summer wore on, Sara was given more responsibility in the lab. She wasn't sure if it was Dr. Lesterbrook's growing acceptance of her ability or the additional obstacles he put in place, hoping to find her weaknesses. Some of her new duties included resolving employee disputes before they became troublesome. She was also given the task of breaking in a new phlebotomist fresh out of training, which should have been Dr. Lesterbrook's job. But she took the duties in stride, hoping to prove herself.

Sara shook her glass, coaxing a final swallow from the remnants of her iced tea. She wasn't a big iced tea drinker, but it was too hot to consider anything else. The on-shore winds mixed with brutal humidity and a week's worth of temperatures in the nineties had the hospital air conditioner struggling. Sara felt her slacks adhering to the backs of her legs. She discreetly wiped the perspiration from her upper lip and wished she could do the same for her underarms. She drank in an ice cube, wallowing it around in her mouth. She usually ate her lunch and immediately returned to the lab, but the cafeteria air conditioning was more tolerable than the window unit in the lab. Even Dr. Lesterbrook, who usually ate with other hospital administrators, lingered over a piece of apple pie at a nearby table.

"Hey there, groupies," Margie said as she placed her tray on the table and sat down. She had a wilted look about her, one that screamed phone conversation in a car.

"Hey yourself," Sara said, scooting over to make room for her. "How's the newscaster these days?"

"She has a new hobby." Margie mixed a glass of iced tea with some lemonade then took a long swallow.

"What hobby is that?"

"Yoga." She took another drink.

"I've done that," one of the nurses in scrubs offered. "It's very soothing after a stressful day."

"I've wanted to try it but my boyfriend thinks it's stupid," another one said.

"Take up yoga and dump the boyfriend, Holly," the one in scrubs replied. "Are you going to try it, Margie?"

"I don't know. It depends."

"It's not hard. Go slowly. Do whatever your body can handle."

"That's not the problem." Margie hesitated as if there was more she wanted to confess, but the other women at the table had commandeered the conversation, talking about yoga poses and classes for beginners.

"Why are you hesitant, Margie?" Sara asked quietly.

"I'm really not interested in it. I know, it's supposed to be healthy and something you can do even without instruction but, I don't know." She shrugged. "It's just not my thing. I'd rather do something like bike riding. I'm good at that. I can go for miles so long as it's flat. Gretchen gave me a Be*ginner's Guide to Yoga* DVD. I put it in the player and within two minutes I was ready to drop that disc through the shredder."

"So don't do it."

"Yeah well, I would, but it's a new relationship. You know how it is."

"Oh, you mean she wants you to do yoga together?"

Margie nodded and started on her ham sandwich.

"And you don't want to, but you don't want to say no, is that it?" Sara drank the last swallow from her glass.

"How do I get myself into these situations? I should have said no the first time she mentioned it, but noooooooooo. I hemmed and hawed and let her intimidate me. I always do that." Margie groaned disgustedly. "I want her to like me, Sara."

"Shouldn't you be honest with her?"

"I know." Margie looked to see who was listening. "To tell the truth, I get the feeling she's a flight risk so I'm trying to be cooperative."

"Try honesty, Margie. Maybe she'll surprise you." Sara felt Dr. Lesterbrook's eyes on her. She had already taken more than her allotted time for lunch and he seemed to be reminding her of that fact. She stood and pulled the back of her slacks away from her legs, ready to head back to the lab. "See you later," she said in Margie's direction.

"Hey, do you know how much yoga mats cost?"

"No." She gave Margie a puzzled look.

"I know. I know. Why buy a yoga mat when I don't like yoga?"

Sara had just stepped through the door into the lab when her cell phone chimed an incoming call. Normally she didn't acknowledge personal calls or texts during work hours, but it was her mechanic, hopefully reporting the oil change was finished and she didn't need a brake job after all.

"Ms. Patterson, did you know your alternator belt is frayed?"

"Alternator? I thought you were looking at my brakes."

"I haven't gotten to those yet. I saw the belt and figured I better give you a call."

"Is it bad?" Sara knew that sounded stupid. Of course a frayed belt was bad. "Does it need to be replaced now?"

"Yep. If that belt breaks the alternator won't charge your battery. The only way you'll know it happened is when your car won't start."

"It sounds like I have no choice. How much will that cost?"

"I'll have to check the parts store. Shouldn't be too bad. Couple hundred probably."

"That's your idea of not too bad?" Sara stared out the window, mentally calculating upcoming expenses and how long until payday. "Go ahead and replace the alternator belt since I certainly don't want a dead battery. But maybe I can get a few more months out of the brakes."

"I'll have to look at them."

Before she finished with her call Edie came into the lab, a small pizza box in one hand and waving a piece of paper in the other.

"Good news," she announced with giddy excitement.

Sara held up a finger, hoping she'd respect the phone in her hand and the conversation she was trying to have.

"Look at this," Edie whispered, as if her news trumped anything Sara was doing. She thrust the paper at Sara.

"It would really help if I could wait on the brakes." She accepted the paper but didn't look at it.

"Look!" Edie insisted.

Sara clutched the phone to her chest and glared at Edie.

"Wait one minute, please. I'm on the phone."

Edie nodded but stood nervously swaying from side to side as she waited. Sara finally ended the call and drew an exasperated breath.

"Now, what?"

"The ad. Look at it," Edie exclaimed jubilantly.

"I was on the phone, Edie," Sara said as she scanned the page then handed it back. But something caught her eye and she reclaimed it.

"I thought you'd recognize that."

It was Jessie Singer's red motor scooter. No doubt about it. Same photocopied picture. Same description. Even printed in the same font. The only thing different was the price, lowered by fifty dollars and a telephone number Sara didn't recognize.

"Where did you get this?"

"In the window at the dollar store. I thought you said she sold the scooter. That sure looks like the same ad that was on our bulletin board."

"I thought she did sell it." For a fleeting moment Sara wondered why Jessie didn't contact her. After all, she declared her interest in the scooter at the trail ride dinner. Even said she wanted to buy it. "Maybe this is an old ad, leftover from last spring."

"I don't think so. I go in there all the time and I would have noticed it. No, it's new. This-week new. Here's your chance. Buy it before she sells it for real."

"Don't start with me, Edie." Sara tossed the ad in a nearby wastebasket and went to turn up the air conditioner. "Why are you eating pizza in the lab and why are you eating it when it's sweltering outside?"

"The same reason I eat ice cream in January. Because I like it." She opened the box and picked an anchovy off the remaining slice.

Dr. Lesterbrook strode into the lab, a look of determination on his face.

"Sara, I need you to take care of this." He handed her a notice printed on bright pink paper. "Pass the word. Flu shots tomorrow. Everybody needs one now and again in December. No exceptions. Hospital rules."

Edie grimaced at his announcement. She opened her mouth, but he gave her a harsh stare before she could speak.

"That means you too, Edie. *No* exceptions." He looked back at Sara. "Take care of it. They're predicting a rough year for Influenza A."

"Yes sir. I'll make sure we all get one."

"What is that smell?" Dr. Lesterbrook scowled.

Sara pointed to Edie's pizza box.

"Get that thing out of here." He gestured toward the door. "You know the rules. No food in the lab."

"It wouldn't kill you to at least look at it, Sara," Edie said, heading for the hall.

"You are like a dog with a bone, aren't you?" Sara pressed the button on the computer and waited for it to print out patient orders. She wanted Jessie Singer's scooter and its recurring annoyance out of her mind. She wasn't going to let it consume her. Not this time. "She should have contacted me. I expressed an interest," she muttered as she looked down at the scooter ad in the wastebasket. "Sure, I take my time. It was a big decision. I'm not completely incompetent."

"What did you say?" Dr. Lesterbrook said from the doorway to his office.

"Nothing. Just me babbling about the incongruities of my existence."

"Incongruities aside, may I ask the status of your thesis? How's that going?" He raised an eyebrow suspiciously.

A grin came over Sara's face.

"Yes, you may ask." She pointed to the simple black-framed diploma on the wall. I just received it this week."

He crossed the lab, clasped his hands behind his back and leaned in to read it, slowly and deliberately, as if digesting every word.

"It's okay to display it in the lab, isn't it?" she asked, ready to defend its presence. After all it represented a major accomplishment in her field. Why not display it at work? She was proud of it.

He turned to her with a curious stare.

"Absolutely it's okay to display it but don't you think it needs a bigger frame? I do." He headed back to his office but stopped and gave Sara a pat on the back as he passed. "Nicely done, Sara. Very nicely done."

"Thank you, Dr. Lesterbrook." Sara hadn't expected that. A nod maybe. A dispassionate groan of acknowledgment. But his surprisingly simple and direct words, an almost fatherly compliment, touched her deeply.

* * *

It was after six when Sara walked the five blocks to the service station to collect her car. The repairs had ballooned to well over three hundred dollars, but it was too hot and she was too tired to complain about it. She stood in front of an oscillating fan in the corner of the shop while Mr. Harper finished under the hood. She turned slowly, holding her arms out in a feeble effort to dry her underarms. Each time the fan rotated toward the wall several flyers fluttered and rippled in the breeze. One immediately grabbed her attention. Even with the bottom portion of the ad ripped away, there was no doubt about it. It was Jessie's ad.

"Mr. Harper, how long has this ad been up here?" she asked, rereading it. "The one about the motor scooter for sale."

"I don't know, a week, maybe. People tape stuff up there all the time. When it falls down, I toss it." He closed the hood and wiped his hands on a rag. "All done. I test drove it and you're set to go. I guess you know you need tires."

"I know." She took a deep breath, afraid to ask what tires cost, but she needed to know before winter. "What's your best deal on tires? They don't have to be top of the line. Just decent tires with a good warranty."

"I've got a forty-five thousand mile tire for eighty bucks a tire, plus mounting, balancing, tire disposal and tax."

"Only forty-five thousand mile warranty? Anything else?"

"I've got a sixty-thousand mile Goodyear all-season, one fifty each. It's a good tire, but I've only got four left in your size. They're coming out with a new tread pattern and it'll be a little higher."

"I think I'll wait on the tires."

"Okay, but just so you know, tax on tires is going up in October. Don't wait too long to decide."

"I'll keep that in mind." She didn't have an extra six hundred dollars right now. And she didn't want to be pressured into buying tires anyway.

"You should at least get those back ones changed out. They're pretty bald."

"Thank you, Mr. Harper. I'll let you know." He must have gone to the Jessie Singer school of high-pressure salesmanship, she thought.

Sara sat waiting for a line of cars to pass so she could pull out into traffic and head home. The longer she waited the more her curiosity festered. Jessie was probably still serving barbeque to a bunch of saddle-weary buckaroos in Washington's backwoods, but that didn't keep her from wondering why she hadn't at least given Sara the right of refusal.

"Okay, possible reasons I should ignore the ad and go home," she said out loud, as she turned the car's air conditioning on high and pulled out into traffic. "I don't need a motor scooter. I can't afford one right now. Motor scooters are dangerous." She couldn't get past the idea that Jessie didn't contact her. She knew where Sara worked and how to reach her. With that she turned into the hospital parking lot and hurried inside. The telephone number had been ripped away from the ad at the repair shop but it was on the one Edie handed her, the one she had wadded up and threw away. She rushed down the hall, into the lab and headed straight for the wastebasket. But it was empty.

"When did they empty the trash?" she asked one of the technicians, but didn't wait for an answer. She roamed up and down the halls, looking for the janitorial cart, obsessed with finding the ad. "This is stupid," she finally told herself. "I'm going home. I need food. Not a motor scooter."

"Ms. Patterson, good. There you are," a nurse called as she strode toward her. "We've got an ambulance coming in with a possible stroke victim. We need CBC, lipids, pro time and a chem panel right away."

"I'm sorry, but I'm off duty. Check with the lab for who's covering."

"Dr. Lesterbrook said he saw you in the hall and that you were covering."

"Well, I'm not. I clocked out an hour and a half ago. Let him do it." Sara headed for the door. *Not this time, Doctor. Not this time.*

It was seven twenty and Sara was hungry. She could turn left out of the hospital parking lot, go home and heat leftovers. Or she could turn right and drive past Batch's Bar and Grill. As if her practicality needed an excuse to stop, a little voice reminded her Batch's burgers looked delicious and it was, after all, dinnertime. Why not stop? It had nothing to do with the ad. Nothing. She kept telling herself that.

* * *

Batch's was crowded. Every table was occupied, she assumed because of the cold blast of air-conditioning that greeted her as soon as she stepped through the door, cold enough to send a shiver down her spine. That and the two handwritten signs taped to the front window. One read Long Beach Nineball Tournament - Finals – Tonight. The other read Tournament Special – Hamburger & Fries - $5.95. Sara didn't want to sit at the bar especially since the only stools available were between burly men with pit stains and enough crack showing to spoil any appetite. She turned to leave, resigned to try Batch's food when it wasn't so crowded, but stopped when she heard a roar of laughter and a voice call, "Watch out. Jessie's going to run the table on you, Buck."

Sara worked her way through the tables to the end of the bar, bobbing her head back and forth to see through the crowd watching whatever was going on in the back of the room.

"Ha, you snookered yourself, Jessie." A man chuckled smugly. "You don't have a clear shot now."

Jessie stood at the corner of the mahogany pool table, rubbing a cube of blue chalk against the tip of her cue as she studied the ball placement. She was dressed all in black, black slacks and black shirt. Her hair was gelled and combed back in strict obedience. She seemed taller than Sara remembered. Older. Leaner. More refined. More self-assured. Like a panther stalking its prey, she said nothing but continued to study the table.

"Ten bucks says she scratches," the man said to a woman standing next to Sara. They each had a beer bottle in their hand.

He held up a ten-dollar bill between two fingers as if daring her to accept the bet.

"You're on," the woman said.

Jessie leaned down, her chin just millimeters above the cue stick as she slid it back and forth in practice. Her eyes were narrowed and focused as if she had walled out everyone and everything but the task at hand. She drew the cue back and struck the cue ball, dropping the blue number two ball into the corner pocket. The cue ball began to spin sideways, moving ever closer to the side pocket. She kept her hands on the table as she watched it, daring it, willing it to stop.

"Come on, baby. Come on," the man said, goading it closer. But the ball stopped short, partially hanging over the lip of the pocket.

"Thank you." The woman snatched the money from his fingers and grinned.

Jessie didn't seem to hear the cheers and hoots from the crowd or if she did, she ignored them. She began to circle the table again. She stopped at the corner and squatted, peering over the edge of the railing. Totally consumed with her next shot, she settled over it and stroked the ball softly. Another ball dropped into a pocket. She methodically moved around the table, sinking ball after ball until only the white cue ball was spinning in the middle of the table.

"That's five games, Buck," someone announced. "You're out. Jessie wins."

The man shook his head disgustedly as he unscrewed his cue stick and stuffed it into a case.

"Did Jessie win?" Sara asked the woman standing next to her.

"Yeah, five games to nothing."

"So she wins the tournament?" Sara was pleased for her, surprised to see her, but pleased.

"That was just semi finals. She has to play Marcus next. Nobody beats Marcus when he's on and he's been on all damn day." The woman took a drink from her beer bottle.

"Can I get you something, ma'am?" a waitress asked Sara.

"Thank you, but I don't have a table. You look a little crowded."

"Tournament," she said above the bustling conversation. "You don't need a table. I'll bring it to you here." She smacked her hand on the end of the bar.

"Well then, could I have a glass of iced tea with lemon and a hamburger with lettuce, tomato and mustard."

"Give me one without, Jimmy," the waitress shouted toward the pass-through window and went to get the iced tea.

Sara waited at the end of the bar hoping Jessie would see her or at least pass by so she could get her attention. But she never left the back of the room. She seemed focused on the tournament and only the tournament.

"Why aren't they putting all the balls in that triangular rack thing?" she asked the woman.

"They're playing nineball. They only use the one through nine."

"Oh. Could you explain what they're doing? I'm not familiar with this game." Sara wasn't familiar with any pool game other than she knew you hit the white cue ball into something else and hoped it goes in a pocket.

"They have to sink the colored balls in order, lowest number on the table first. Whoever sinks the nine wins the game. Then they have to call the pocket for the nine-ball. They'll alternate breaks."

"And the winner is the first one with five games, right?"

"Six. First one to six games in the finals." She took another sip then looked at Sara. "You don't play?"

"No."

"It's fun. You ought to try it sometime." She winked, then saluted with her bottle.

Sara wasn't sure but she thought she had just been propositioned in a bar. That was a first. Normally she'd be uncomfortable hanging out in a bar, but she had invested an evening working at Batch's. Except for the shoving match, it wasn't a bad place. And she took solace in knowing Jessie was just a few feet away. She arranged the lettuce and tomato and squirted the packet of mustard on her hamburger then took a bite while Jessie and a man in a white shirt she assumed was Marcus discussed the rules. Before they started, Jessie pulled a money clip from her pocket and peeled off several bills. The man in the white shirt did the same. They handed the money to a woman with a clipboard.

"Wonder what the bet is," the woman said to the man on the other side of her.

"I heard five."

"That's about right. Marcus won't even come to the table for less than three."

"They each bet five hundred dollars?" Sara's eyes widened. "I thought it was a tournament. Aren't they playing for that trophy?" She pointed to a small gold trophy on a nearby table.

"The tournament only pays one hundred to the winner. Marcus won't enter a tournament unless he can bet real money. Jessie too. This is what they came for. Not that dinky plastic trophy."

Jessie won the right to shoot first. They alternated, each running the table after sinking at least one ball on the break. It was as if each was waiting for the other to make a mistake and relinquish control of the table. Tied at three games apiece, Jessie stepped to the table, but didn't sink anything on the break. It was Marcus's table. His opportunity to forge a lead. He ran the table, giving himself a four-games-to-three lead and the break. Jessie stood against the wall, watching stone-faced, as he moved around the table, sinking ball after ball with cold efficiency. With only the nine-ball left and an easy shot to give him a two-game lead, Marcus smiled smugly. Even Sara could see it was an easy, straight-in shot and required little thought. But he took his time, chalking and rechalking his cue as he circled the table. He finally leaned over the shot, sinking the nine ball with a crisp click. Several of his supporters applauded and cheered as he slowly stood up, grinning pompously.

"Five games to three," the woman with the clipboard announced then went about racking the balls. "You're up, Jessie."

Sara didn't have to be an expert to know Jessie needed to win this game and two more or Marcus would win. Jessie stepped to the table without hesitation. She chalked her cue then drove a hard shot into the cluster of colored balls, sending them scattering. Only one ball dropped on the break, but it was enough to keep her at the table. She circled, a furrowed scowl growing across her face. She heaved an almost desperate sigh as if she didn't like what she saw.

"Double or nothing?" Marcus said with a devilish gloat.

The spectators fell silent as Jessie circled again, her eyes riveted on the yellow one-ball hidden behind the black eightball.

"She doesn't have a shot on the one," the woman whispered. "She can hit it but she can't sink it."

Jessie slowly slid her hand in her pocket, her eyes still on the table.

"I'll take that bet," she said, and pulled out her money clip. She handed several more bills to the lady with the clipboard. Marcus hesitated as if he didn't expect Jessie to take him up on his offer. But he counted out his money and handed it over.

"Nine in the side," Jessie said, pointing her cue toward the pocket.

"Ain't going to happen, Jessie," Marcus said with a chuckle, then took a swallow from a beer mug.

"Shit, she's going for the nine," the woman said, then downed the last of her beer.

"I thought she had to shoot the colored balls in order," Sara said quietly.

"You have to hit them in order, but if she sinks the nine with the one she's shooting at, she wins that game. But if she scratches, she loses the game."

Sara left her half-eaten hamburger at the bar and moved closer. Even though she didn't understand the strategy, she wanted to see Jessie's shot. After all, it was a two-thousand-dollar shot. Jessie leaned over the table, her eyes clued to her target. The crowd fell silent. Sara drew a breath and watched. With a sharp click, the white ball struck the yellow number one ball and sent it bouncing from rail to rail before rolling down the table. It finally struck the nine ball and neatly dropped it into the side pocket. Jessie slowly straightened to the sound of cheers, a small satisfied grin tugging at the corner of her mouth.

"Five games to four, Marcus. Your break," the clipboard lady announced.

He stepped to the end of the table. There was no doubt he was angry. His nostrils flared and his face flushed. He waited impatiently for the woman to rack the balls and step away. He hurriedly placed the cue ball and took a shot. It was a hard shot, bouncing several of the balls across the table. But nothing dropped. It was Jessie's table. Her game to win or lose. She circled once, chalking deliberately as she eyed her first shot. Methodically she began sinking shots, moving around the table, always leaving the cue ball just where she wanted it for the next shot. She neither showed emotion nor looked up until the nineball dropped into a pocket.

"Five games all. Jessie's break for the last game."

Jessie leaned back against a tall stool, her cue standing between her legs while she waited for the balls to be racked. Her quiet confidence was in direct contrast to Marcus. Perspiration dripped from his sideburns. His shirt was stained with sweat. Sara was surprised Jessie didn't seem the least bit nervous or intimidated. She sat expressionless, as if two thousand dollars was no big deal. Jessie was right. She was a professional pool player. At least she was tonight.

Jessie stepped to the table and drove the cue ball deep into the cluster, scattering them across the table. Nothing dropped at first, drawing murmurs from the crowd. It took a few moments, but the red three-ball finally made its way to the corner pocket and fell in with a plop. Sara exhaled and drew another breath as she nervously watched Jessie take the next shot, sinking two balls. Marcus stared at Jessie then at the table, his forehead furrowed.

"You're not going to have a shot at the eight, kid. It's frozen against the side," he said with a nervous chuckle.

Jessie didn't reply. With her next shot the cue ball sank the six then bounced into the eight, spinning it across the table.

"Not anymore," she whispered as she leaned over the shot and drove it into the corner. "Side pocket." She tapped the tip of her cue on the pocket.

All that was left was the nine. Sara wouldn't blame Jessie if she took her time over this last shot. Gloat a little. Revel in it. Marcus did. Why shouldn't she? She came from behind with cold, calculated precision and now was one yellow-striped ball away from victory and two thousand dollars. But she took the shot without fanfare, sinking the nineball and winning the tournament. The woman with the clipboard handed Jessie the trophy and an envelope containing the money. Marcus congratulated her, though briefly, before leaving. Sara stood at the end of the bar while Jessie received a few handshakes. It didn't take long for Jessie's eyes to move around the room and find her.

"Well, hello there," she said with a warm smile. "I didn't know you were a billiard fan."

"To tell the truth, I'm not. I had to ask what was going on."

"Nineball tournament. We have one every summer. How long have you been here?"

"Long enough to know you're pretty good. I had no idea."

Jessie shrugged and reached for her cue case.

"Once in a while things work out. Sometimes Lady Luck steps in and lends a hand."

"It looked to me like you took matters into your own hands. You didn't need Lady Luck. But how do you stay so calm? I'd be a nervous wreck playing for that much money."

"Oh, you saw that bet?" She chuckled softly. "It's like facing a bear in the woods. You can't let your opponent see fear. You have to act like it doesn't matter one way or the other. Win or lose, you don't care."

"But what if you did lose?"

"I didn't play to lose."

Sara glanced over at the man behind the bar.

"Your dad?"

"Yes," Jessie replied without looking.

"Does your being here at the tournament mean you're back working at the bar instead of cooking barbecue?"

"No, not really."

"So you're a full-time pool player now?"

"Not exactly. It's hard to be a full-time pro unless you're ranked high enough to receive endorsements. A handful of players do, but it's rare. There's good money in some of the tournaments, like the one coming up next month in Las Vegas. But most of them don't pay enough to cover travel expenses."

"Are you entering that one?"

"Yes. I've sent in my registration fee. Five grand for first place in the women's division."

"Wow. Then this tournament was sort of a warm-up for that?"

"That and it pays the bills. And I'll bet everything in this envelope you didn't come here by coincidence." She waved the envelope.

"Wow, that's a bold bet when you consider I didn't even know you were in the tournament. How do you know I'm not just here for a hamburger?" She pointed at the remnants left on her plate. "It is dinnertime, you know. They're very good, by the way."

"But that's not why you're here, is it?" Jessie picked the pickle off the edge of Sara's plate and ate it.

"Um, no. Okay, I'll admit I had ulterior motives."

"You saw the ad I posted, didn't you?"

"Yes."

"And you want to know why I didn't let you know the scooter was still available?"

"Yes."

"I was tempted to tell you the guy didn't buy it. He bought a dirt bike instead, the idiot."

"So, why didn't you?"

"Jessie," a woman called through the crowd. Sara assumed it was another well-wisher, come to offer congratulations. But the woman threw her arms around Jessie's neck and hugged her. "Way to go, baby. Way to go." She placed a quick kiss on Jessie's cheek then looked over at Sara. This was not the same woman kissing Jessie at the trail ride. Becky was older, more outdoorsy and more matronly. This woman was none of those. She was Hispanic, with dark expressive eyes and a radiant complexion artfully detailed with lipstick and eye shadow. Somewhere in her twenties, this beauty had a sultry come-hither look about her.

"Stephie, this is Sara."

"Hi." She clung to Jessie's side, gleaming proudly. "Isn't she great? My little pool shark."

"Hello, yes." But Sara wasn't satisfied. She wanted an answer. "Why didn't you?" she repeated.

"Because I didn't want you to have it." Jessie wrapped an arm around Stephie's waist.

"And why not? My money is as good as anyone's." Sara straightened all of her five feet six inches, refusing to be intimidated.

"I'm sure it is and but that's not the reason."

"Jessie, can we go soon? I've got to work in the morning," Stephie said, smoothing her hand over Jessie's shoulder.

"Sure." Jessie gave her a squeeze.

"No, you can't go," Sara bristled. "You're not leaving until you tell me why I can't have the scooter."

"Oh, my God. *She* wants to buy your scooter?" Stephie declared.

"No, she doesn't." Jessie shook her head adamantly.

"Yes, I do. I told you at the trail ride dinner I did."

"No, you don't. A motor scooter is something you buy impulsively. You don't think about it for weeks and weeks. You just go out and buy one. I did. That's why I have one for sale. There is nothing practical about a motor scooter, especially for someone your age who has never ridden one before. You'd always regret it. I took that burden off the table. It's not for sale. At least, not to you."

Sara didn't know what to say. Jessie was right. A motor scooter was the most impractical thing she ever considered buying. And why was she arguing with her. She didn't have the money for it anyway.

"Shouldn't I be given the opportunity to say no?" Sara demanded.

"You already did. Months ago in the parking lot of the hospital." Jessie stuffed the envelope of money into her back pocket and tucked her cue case under her arm. "It was great seeing you again, but this subject is closed." She took Stephie by the hand and started for the door.

CHAPTER TEN

"Hey, what's with all the looks?" Stephie said with a sneer.

Jessie opened the passenger door, slid the cue case behind the seat and waited for her to climb in.

"What looks?"

"There. You did it again. You keep looking back up the sidewalk. You're looking for that woman to come out the door, aren't you?"

"I have no idea what you're talking about." Just the suggestion of it drew Jessie's eyes back toward Batch's front door.

"Stop that."

"I'm not doing anything. Get in. It's hot out here."

Stephie hesitated but finally climbed in, a disgusted look on her face. It was still there when Jessie circled the pickup and slid in the driver's seat.

"What?" Jesse asked as she slipped the key in the ignition.

"I don't want to talk about it." Stephie checked her looks in the visor mirror then declared happily, "Drive up to Ocean Park. It's low tide."

"You want to walk on the beach now? I thought you had to work tomorrow."

"Yeah, I do. But I'm hot. It'll be cooler on the beach. Come on. I'll make it worth your while," she said temptingly, and placed a hand on Jessie's thigh.

It took a half hour to navigate the narrow highway north along Long Beach and out onto the deserted beach. The roar of the surf filled the darkness. Jessie pointed the headlights toward the water and turned off the engine. She was tired. It had been a long day. A long, tense day. She had argued with her father over refusing to cover for him at the bar instead of playing in the tournament. He knew she was in it and that she stood a good chance of winning. Even though she didn't show it, the nineball tournament had been stressful. Her insides were still a mangled mass of nerves. And now Stephie wanted to wander the beach in the middle of the night so she could dangle her toes in the ocean.

There was that other thing gnawing at her. Sara Patterson. Stephie was very perceptive. Jessie had looked back up the sidewalk, hoping to see Sara come out of the bar. Their meeting had been all too quick and didn't end the way Jessie had intended. She didn't handle it well. She should have explained it was Sara's safety that concerned her the most. A nervous rider wasn't a safe rider. She'd never forgive herself if Sara did a pavement slide on her pretty little nose first crack out of the box.

"Are you still thinking about her?" Stephie gave a sideways glance.

"Who?"

"You know who. The blonde with the curly hair. The one who wanted to buy your scooter. I think you should sell it to her."

"Why?"

"So I can stop hearing you bitch about it. First you're going to sell it. Then you aren't. Then you are. Sell the damn thing and be done with it. Let the dumb blonde buy it."

"She's not a dumb blonde. She works at the hospital. And I'm not selling it to someone who will just end up hurting themselves on it."

"That's not your responsibility. She's an adult. Let her worry about that. Come on." Stephie kicked off her sandals and climbed out. "I'll race you."

"You don't race on the beach after dark. You stroll." She peeled off her shoes and socks, rolled up her pant legs and followed at a leisurely pace, her hands in her pockets. Stephie ran ahead, turning a cartwheel in the moonlight.

"I was a cheerleader. What do you think? Still pretty good, huh?" She turned another one then added a handspring.

"Not bad." Jessie had to admire her athleticism.

Stephie stood in an incoming tide as the water surrounded her ankles.

"Come down here and get wet. This is great."

"You go ahead." Jessie moved the envelope of money to her front pocket, then sat down on the sand, almost immediately feeling the cool wetness soak through the back of her pants.

Stephie turned a cartwheel in the shallow surf, giggling as she splashed, then sat down next to Jessie.

"What's wrong?" Stephie leaned over and wrapped an arm around her.

"Nothing. I'm just wondering why we drove all the way out here in the middle of the night."

"Don't be a spoilsport. It's romantic." She blew in Jessie's ear then tried to give her a hickey.

"Hey, stop that." Jessie leaned away. She didn't need a hickey on her neck for everyone to gawk at while she leaned over a two-rail bank shot.

"Then kiss me."

Jessie obliged with a quick kiss on the lips, but Stephie had something else in mind. She pushed Jessie down onto the sand and stuck her tongue deep into her mouth. Stephie wiggled out of her clothes and crawled on top of Jessie. She was turned on. No doubt about it. Jessie wasn't sure she needed to do anything for Stephie to reach an orgasm. All she had to do was lie there and enjoy the woman's body writhing against her own. Stephie's orgasm happened with lightning speed and intensity. She let out a squeal then a sigh. But that wasn't unusual.

Their three-week courtship had mostly been about Stephie's orgasms and how easily she achieved them. She didn't hide it. She couldn't. What the three weeks had not been about was Jessie's satisfaction. Stephie's sexy body and lack of modesty stirred an animal instinct in Jessie but she had yet to have an orgasm herself. That usually happened later when Jessie stood in the shower. She blamed it on insomnia or fatigue or the fact it just took her longer than some to reach climax. Perhaps it was that she and Stephie had nothing in common. Arm candy, yes. But there was no future with Stephie. Just another disappointing check mark in Jessie's little black book.

"Let's go home," Jessie said, while Stephie brushed off the sand and pulled on her clothes.

"Aw, what's the matter? Not in the mood?" She grinned coyly.

"No, I'm not. And I have sand in my pants."

"Take them off, baby." Stephie began pawing at Jessie's zipper. "Go naked."

"I'm not going naked."

Jessie brushed the sand from the back of her slacks then pulled off her shirt, gave it a shake and put it back on. She thought about taking off her wet sports bra, but that would just provoke another roll in the sand while Stephie got off on herself.

They headed back to town. Jessie was busy constructing an excuse why she couldn't spend the night when she pulled up in front of Stephie's apartment and kept the engine running. She wanted to go home and take a shower. They both smelled like sea foam and dead fish.

"I'd ask you in but my roommate has her boyfriend spending the night. He's a real jerk." Stephie said, and gave her a kiss.

"That's okay. Another time." Jessie leaned over and released the passenger door handle. "Good night."

She waited for Stephie to go inside before she pulled away, a sense of relief at not being invited inside. The downtown streets were nearly deserted as she turned onto Spruce and drove past Batch's. She pulled to the curb and stared across the street. The bar was still open, the neon beer signs flashing brightly.

The remaining customers would probably be the regulars, the drinkers, the lonely and a few ball-banging pool players. The kitchen was closed, but there would be the residual smell of grease and fried onions. She wondered how well they had done. Had the tournament brought in extra customers? Had her father kept his hand out of the till? She had only worked sparingly throughout the summer. The bartending shifts she had been offered barely paid the bills. She could have accepted the job as waitress while her father worked the prime shifts but that was an argument waiting to happen. She made more playing in local billiard tournaments and side bets with arrogant men who underestimated her skill. When things got tight there were always the odd jobs that attracted her attention. Being a cook for Becky's chuck wagon dinners only lasted a few weeks, but it was fun. It was something to add to her résumé. She knew it was time to move on when Becky wanted her to move into the ranch house and fill the role of wife, forsaking all others. That was not happening. Becky wasn't the one she'd do that for.

Jessie was about to pull away from the curb when her cell phone chimed. It was Batch.

"Hey," she said happily. "How's it going?"

"Is that you sitting out there?" He chuckled.

"Yeah."

"You coming in?"

"No. Heading home. I need a shower."

"I wondered where you went. I thought you'd stick around after the tourney. Nice job, by the way." He sounded proud. "You want to work tomorrow? Bartending. Five to close."

"I thought he was working all this week."

"Nope." Something in Batch's voice told Jessie there was a problem. He hesitated a moment then added, "Ron has some business he needs to take care of in Denver."

"You only need me tomorrow? Just the one day?" She knew the answer to that question even before Batch could reply.

"Might be a week or so."

"When will he be back?"

"It won't be long. You want the job?"

"He doesn't know when he'll be back, does he?"

"You want it or not?" Batch demanded.

"Sure. Why not?"

Jessie had no reason to say no. With her father gone there would be no arguments. It would be like it used to be, at least until he came strolling through the door again, wanting his job back.

"Thanks, Kid. See you tomorrow." In spite of his gruff nature, Batch sounded relieved.

"I'll be there. Don't worry."

"I know you will."

"I love you, Granddad," she said softly, and ended the call. She leaned back against the headrest and closed her eyes, also relieved. She had her job back. At least for now. Sure, it didn't allow her to hopscotch across the country and try her hand at the big tournaments, but it gave her roots and permanence, and she found comfort in that.

* * *

Jessie arrived early the next morning and let herself in the back door. Just as she suspected, Ron had left the night before without doing the cleanup expected of the bartender at closing. She washed several tubs of glassware, restocked shelves behind the bar and emptied trash, all before Batch arrived.

"How's it going there, Kid?" he said as if there was nothing new.

"Hey, there." She smiled. She didn't need to question why Ron had left so suddenly or what lame excuse he gave. It was none of her business. Batch looked tired. That was answer enough. "We need to add a case of paper towels and a case of t.p. to the order. And we're going to need a new dispenser head for the soda. It's got a crack in it."

"There's a new one in the storeroom on the shelf behind the door. No one's gotten around to installing it."

"I'll take a look. It shouldn't be that tough," she offered.

Batch gave a satisfied nod as he headed to his office, seemingly pleased with her offer to fix it. Jessie filled her morning with odd jobs around the bar, small jobs that should have been done but weren't.

"Hey, Kid." Batch backed his desk chair into the doorway. "I forgot. Someone left a phone number on a napkin for you to call. She made it sound important."

"Oh, yeah? What about?" Jessie rested a case of beer against the doorjamb.

"She said it was about a motor scooter. Are you finally selling that damn thing?" He tossed a cocktail napkin on top of the beer case. "Good-looking woman. Nice too." He smiled.

Jessie didn't recognize the number, but she sure recognized the name. Sara Patterson, with a note that read *In case you reconsider.*

"You know her?" He looked up at her with a cocky grin.

"Oh, yeah. I know her. And I'm *not* reconsidering." Jessie headed to the bar to stock the beer cooler. "Not in a million years," she announced.

"But you're going to call her, right?"

"Not in a *hundred* million years," she shouted even louder.

CHAPTER ELEVEN

The humid summer finally gave way to autumn with shorter days and cooler weather. Sara passed her probation period. She now had two weeks' paid vacation and full medical coverage. Dr. Lesterbrook also awarded her the job of scheduling for the lab. It didn't take long to know why that wasn't his favorite duty. It was hard to make everyone happy. More often than not she ended up with the unpopular shifts on holidays or working overtime.

"Hello again," a soft voice said.

Sara was busy with a differential count at the microscope and didn't look up until she was finished. A professionally dressed woman in a beige pantsuit, pulling a sample case, stood in the doorway. Naomi Upland was a sales rep for one of the laboratory supply companies. This was her fourth visit since Sara had started work at Ocean Side, visits Sara found more than coincidental. After all, Dr. Lesterbrook didn't need Naomi to be there to place an order. It could be done online. But she was a pleasant enough woman, so on her last visit Sara had accepted her invitation to lunch in the cafeteria.

"Hello. If you need to see Dr. Lesterbrook he isn't here right now. Some kind of monthly administration meeting."

"That's okay. I just wanted to drop off our new catalog. Nothing earth-shattering. Nothing you can't find on our website but we are going to carry a new line of Vacutainers." She pulled a booklet from the front pocket of the case and handed it to Sara. "It seemed like a good enough excuse to drop by and say hi." She opened the catalog and leaned against Sara's arm as she flipped through the pages.

Naomi smelled like Chanel and coffee. And she was definitely flirting. Sara felt her eyes studying her, as if touching her cheek. This wasn't the first time either. Sara had to admit it was nice to have someone show her attention. It had been a long time since anyone leaned into her just for the sake of being close. Naomi was an intelligent professional. A pleasant conversationalist. A charismatic forty-something woman whose breast pressed against Sara's arm sparked a curious response Sara hadn't felt in a long time.

"I really came by to see you anyway. You can pass the message on to Dr. Lesterbrook that we're using a new invoice code for our preferred customers. It should cut shipping time by fifty percent. Of course, I could come back another day and tell him myself. That might not be a bad idea." She raised an inviting eyebrow. "What do you think?"

"I'll be glad to tell him, but I don't think we need anything right now." Sara went to the computer to enter the test results as they were needed urgently. And to put space between her and Naomi's persistence, persistence that had Sara wondering.

"Say, would you like to have dinner with me?"

"It's only ten thirty," Sara said, checking her watch. "I won't take my lunch break until noon, at least."

"Not lunch. Dinner. This evening. I've got a meeting in Astoria at two but I should be back by six. I hate to eat dinner alone. When I'm on the road, eating dinner by myself is boring. I end up eating delivery pizza at the hotel. You'd be doing me a huge favor if you suggest someplace local with good home cooking. My treat. Or rather, my expense account's treat. Please." Naomi whined dramatically. "Pretty please."

"I'd hate to think I'm the reason you ate delivery pizza for dinner," Sara replied with a laugh. It sounded like an innocent enough offer. "Okay. I accept. It's perfect timing. My dog is spending the evening at the VFW. The vets love it when Lucille brings her to bingo. Besides, I forgot to set anything out to defrost."

"Where's a good place around here for dinner? Steak, seafood, burgers? Something other than pizza."

"It depends. Seafood would be Griffith's out by the wharf. Steak would be Big R's. Hamburgers, hmmm." Sara thought a moment then said, "Batch's Bar and Grill. I know it doesn't sound like the kind of place you'd go for good food, but I had a hamburger there a few weeks ago and it was wonderful. I was genuinely impressed."

"I've heard about that place. And you're right. Not the kind of place I frequent for food, but if you say so, Batch's it is." Naomi looked at her watch and gasped. "Oh, God. I've got to get out of here. I'm going to be so late." She gave Sara a hug and added, "You've saved me from a fate worse than death. I've already had pizza twice this week. Thank you. See you later." She hurried to the door, rolling her sample case along behind.

"And who was that?" Edie said from the doorway to the storeroom, drying her hands on a towel.

"Sales rep from Foley Lab Supply." Sara turned on her heels and went back to work, hoping Edie would do the same.

"I didn't know sales reps hug their clients and invite them to dinner. Do I sense something bubbling up here? Does Sara have an admirer?" Edie giggled wickedly.

"No, you sense Sara being polite to a sales rep. Nothing else." Sara looked down at the computer screen, but did have to wonder about Naomi. "Did you run the glucose tolerance on Mr. Willis, room three-sixteen?"

"Not yet. I have to go draw the last sample."

"Good. Go do that." Sara handed her a phlebotomy tray and gave her an expectant glance.

"Sara, are you busy?" Dr. Lesterbrook asked as he came striding through the lab, a determined look on his face.

"You caught me between tests. What do you need me to do?" Sara slid a rack of tubes into the refrigerator.

"I need you to draw a red top and lavender top."

"Sure. On who?" Sara looked toward the waiting room door.

"On me." He headed for the drawing cubical as he rolled up his sleeve.

"Okay?" Sara knew better than to ask why. He was her boss. If he wanted a test run, she would run it. She couldn't help wonder if someone had complained about her technique. Or had he seen something to question her competence. Whatever the reason, as she went about gathering what she'd need, she felt his eyes on her, watching every move she made. Like she did with every patient, she pulled on latex gloves and then secured the band around his bicep. "Is there a problem, Dr. Lesterbrook?"

"No, no problem. I just want to check my H and H. While I'm at it I'll go ahead and check my cholesterol." He reached up and released the tourniquet as she slid the needle in his vein, all without a flinch.

"You want me to run a hemoglobin and hematocrit or go ahead and run a complete CBC?" she asked as she changed tubes.

"I'll take care of it." He watched the blood fill the second tube. "I've been a little tired. I'm probably anemic. Comes with age. I told my doctor I'd have it checked."

As soon as she pulled the needle out of his vein and attached a Band-Aid he took the two tubes from her hand and headed into the lab. He hesitated in the doorway and looked back.

"You did a good job. Thank you, Sara." Not overly vociferous but a compliment, nonetheless. Something he didn't offer very often.

Sara returned to work, curious why Dr. Lesterbrook didn't want her to do the grunt work of running his routine blood tests. She hoped it wasn't because he didn't trust her ability to do it correctly. He trusted her enough to run every other test in the lab. Why not his? And why so secretive?

Sara also wondered why she had suggested Batch's Bar and Grill for dinner with Naomi. There were other places within an easy drive that served a decent hamburger. Whatever the reason, Batch's seemed to have an almost mystical attraction. And she wasn't into mystics.

"Oh, crud," she gasped, grabbing for the bottle. But it was too late. She had already knocked it over and a stream of purple stain ran across the lab table and dripped onto her slacks. She capped the bottle and hurried into the restroom to wash it out but she knew it was useless. It would take several washings and even then the stain would probably be permanent. She suspected her thigh had a lovely purple blotch as well. She returned to the lab, blotting a large wet spot that was still bright purple.

"Nice," Edie said as she closed the lid to the centrifuge and turned it on. "What happened? Did Barney attack you?"

"Very funny."

"That's going to look really nice at dinner tonight. That sales rep is going to think you're wearing purple camo."

"I'll have to go home and change. And I'm going to be late." She gave a last swipe of the towel across the stain then sat down at the microscope, resolved to wearing damp pants the rest of the day. She thought about asking Edie if she could stay and cover for her, but it wasn't worth it. Edie hadn't worked fifteen minutes of overtime since Sara started at the hospital. Why did she think that would change? Edie was only a tech. Sara had to stay.

She was right. She was going to be late. A last-minute walk-in and an emergency room patient kept her busy until just before six. She hurried home, checked Gypsy's food and water dishes, even leaving a doggie treat where she would find it if Lucille brought her home before Sara returned. She left a note on the table for Lucille then changed into her new jeans with bling on the flaps of the back pockets and topped it off with her favorite cinnamon-colored sweater. She quickly raked her fingers through her hair and headed downtown.

"I hate to be late. I hate it. I hate it," she muttered as she scurried along the sidewalk, her dress boots tapping a quick pace.

Naomi smiled at her as soon as she came through the door, having staked out the table in the window.

"There you are. I was afraid I was eating alone after all." She stood and gave Sara a hug.

"I'm sorry. I had every intention of being here on time. That is until I knocked over a bottle of crystal violet and stained my tan slacks purple."

"Ew, that would be a mess. Does this mean you need me to drop by and fill out an order for more CV?" She had a wicked grin.

"It wasn't our only bottle and I didn't dump it all." Sara hitched her chair in to the table. "Although Edie said it looked like purple camouflage." They both laughed, unaware of the woman waiting to take their order.

"What can I get you ladies this evening?"

Sara glanced up to see Jessie, dressed in jeans, an apron and the bar's green polo shirt. Her hair, though short, hung in rambunctious squiggles over her forehead. It was a different look than the last time Sara saw her at the tournament. This was softer, more approachable, Sara thought. Mellow. One that looked good on her.

"Hey there, slick." Jessie looked over at Naomi then back at Sara and smiled. "What brings you back to Batch's?"

"Jessie! What are you doing back here in an apron?"

"Batch needed a bartender."

"But I thought you said you had other plans."

"Nope. I'm still here and kickin'. So, what can I get you? Slow gin fizz? Glass of wine?"

"I'll have a Cuba Libre. With 10 Cane Rum, please," Naomi said.

"Very nice choice, ma'am. And you, Sara? What would you like?"

"Eek. I have no idea. I was all set to order a hamburger. I hadn't given much thought to what I want to drink." Sara glanced around at nearby tables, hoping something looked good. "Something light. Something simple."

"How about a strawberry margarita?"

"That sounds good."

"Crushed ice or cubes? Salt or no salt?"

"Let's see. Crushed ice and no salt."

"Perfect." Jessie gave them both a hospitable smile and returned to the bar.

"Do you know her?" Naomi asked as she looked down the menu card.

"Yes. It's a long story, but let's just say our paths have crossed a few times."

"You know, I've never dated a bartender. Sounds kind of kinky."

"I've never dated one either. My only association with her was purely business, one way or the other." Sara glanced over at the bar. Jessie was staring back, expressionless.

"What's good here? Hamburger, right?"

"Yes, very," Sara said, unable to take her eyes off Jessie's slowly growing smile.

"I don't know if I'm really in the mood for a hamburger."

A red-haired waitress returned with their drinks and took their food order. Just as Sara remembered, the waitress handed it through the window to Jimmy, who was now sporting an extremely short haircut, almost nonexistently short. Sara ordered a cheeseburger. Naomi took several minutes to decide, contemplating every item on the card. She even considered a pizza but settled on a hamburger. Jessie was busy behind the bar, filling beer glasses and mixing cocktails, but somehow found the time to deliver their food orders.

"Cheeseburger?" she said, balancing a tray on one hand.

"Here," Sara said, raising her hand. "She has the hamburger."

"Who gets the onion rings?"

"We're sharing," Naomi said, clearing a spot for the basket.

"And you'll want these." Jessie pulled bottles of ketchup and mustard from her apron pocket. "Can I get you anything else? Refills, ladies?"

Sara had barely touched her drink. Naomi's glass was still half full but she tapped the rim.

"Yes. I'll have another Cuba Libre."

"Absolutely. With 10 Cane, right?" Jessie added.

Naomi nodded as she picked an onion ring from the pile.

Sara and Naomi ate their dinner and chatted about work, travels, life experiences and even old girlfriends. Sara's list was shorter than Naomi's. Although Naomi seemed to be a vigorously energetic woman, Sara wondered why she talked so dispassionately about her past relationships. Sara's failed relationships were all heartbreaking to her. She worried she had been too critical or too reserved or too cautious. Whatever the reason, her breakups had always been devastating. That didn't seem to be the case with Naomi. She seemed strong enough to bounce back unscathed and unbruised, ready for the next great love of her life.

"Did you see they have pool tables in the back?" Naomi said with a gleam in her eye. "I think pool is so much fun. Talk about a great icebreaker. Do you play?"

"Me? No. I think I've held a cue stick exactly one time in my life and that was at college. They put a pool table in the rec hall. I never got the hang of it. The balls never went where I wanted them to go."

"We ought to come play sometime. It'll be fun. And if you wear a low-cut blouse, we won't have to pay for our drinks." She winked. "What do you say?"

"I really don't know anything about pool."

"It doesn't matter. Come on, what do you say? Maybe we can reserve a table for an hour or so." Before Sara could stop her Naomi waved Jessie over.

"What can I get you? Another Cuba Libre?" Jessie wiped her hands on her apron.

"Who do we see about reserving a pool table?"

"Well, other than the Wednesday night ten-ball league, we really don't reserve them. It's pretty much first come, first served. When did you want one?"

"Tomorrow evening. Say eight o'clock." She looked over at Sara and grinned. "I should be back from Portland by then. We can meet here, okay?"

"I'll tell you what. I'll hold the first table over there by the cue rack." Jessie nodded over her shoulder. "Eight o'clock."

"Do you play?" Naomi asked.

"A little bit." Jessie gave Naomi a quick up and down look. It wasn't a lewd glance. More curious than anything else.

"You're sure we won't be taking the table from someone else?" Sara asked, looking in that direction.

"If you mean would someone be using it if you weren't, sure. Some beer-belcher who can't shoot straight anyway." Jessie laughed. "I'd rather hold one of the tables for a couple of lovely ladies any day." She placed a hand on each of their shoulders and smiled an inviting smile. "It will be my pleasure."

Sara felt Jessie's fingers curl around her shoulder, holding her softly. She wondered if Naomi felt the reassurance. Or was her touch and the look in Jessie's eyes meant just for her?

"Now, if you'll excuse me, I better get back to work. As Sara knows, the bartender's work is never done."

As soon as Jessie left, Naomi grinned.

"And you've never dated a bartender?"

"No." Sara sipped at her margarita, hoping she didn't have to explain. And hoped the blush she felt rising over her face was from the alcohol, not Jessie's lingering touch.

"Are you all right?"

"Yes, I'm fine. Why?"

"You look a little flushed."

"I'm not a big drinker. It's probably just alcohol blush."

"Oh, yeah. I get that sometimes, but it usually takes three or four. You've only had one."

"Like I said, I'm not a big drinker."

"Cheap date." Naomi laughed as she tossed her credit card on the check. "Before I head back to the hotel, I need to find the ladies' room."

"Back corner to the left," Sara offered. "Don't be surprised if there's a line."

"Restrooms at bars always have lines. So long as it's clean, I don't care." Naomi headed in that direction.

"Can I get you another margarita or maybe an apéritif?" Jessie asked.

She startled Sara who hadn't seen her coming.

"Oh, no, thank you. This is fine." She took the last sip. "It was very good though."

"Fresh strawberries give it more flavor. How was your dinner?" Jessie collected the empty plates and glasses, balancing them in an artistic pyramid.

"Very good. I enjoyed it."

"And your friend?" Jessie looked back as Naomi disappeared through the ladies' room door.

"Naomi?" Sara looked that way as well. "She liked hers too. I have to ask, what's special about 10 Cane, or whatever it is?"

"A Cuba Libre is really just a rum and Coke. 10 Cane is high-grade rum made with fermented cane sugar while most darker rums are just fermented molasses. It's not top shelf but it's up there."

"Wouldn't eating onion rings mask the taste and defeat the purpose?"

"You bet. But the customer's always right. If that's what she wants, I'm certainly going to make it."

Sara glanced back to make sure Naomi wasn't coming. "Before you go, I want to say thank you."

"For?"

"For not saying anything about the you-know-what in front of Naomi. It would just raise a bunch of questions, and then I'd have to explain everything and I just didn't want to. You know what I mean?"

Jessie scowled curiously.

"What you-know-what?"

"The scooter and the ad and me saying I wanted to buy it and you saying no. The whole convoluted situation."

"Oh." Jessie chuckled. "That subject is closed."

"I know. But I wanted to thank you for not bringing it up."

"It wasn't even on my mind."

"Actually, you did me a huge favor. I know I said I wanted to buy it, but I didn't have the money for a scooter. I didn't need another debt."

"Closed subject. Don't worry about it. I yanked down the signs and threw a tarp over it. It's not worth the hassle right now." Jessie turned to leave, but stopped and looked back as if there was something else she wanted to add, but Naomi came striding back to the table before she could say it.

"Shall we go?" Naomi said, drinking the last of her cocktail as she stood at the table.

Sara knew she was going home and Naomi was headed to her hotel. The date was over. Nothing would happen and that's the way she wanted it. Sara didn't sleep with women on the first date. Would there be more? Was Naomi worth considering? Possibly. But Sara wondered what Jessie was thinking as they walked out together. And she was definitely watching.

CHAPTER TWELVE

Sara stood at her kitchen window, watching the rain puddle in the yard, and waiting for someone to answer the phone. It was the fifth ring before someone picked up.

"Batch's," a man finally said.

"Hello. Is Jessie Singer there?"

"Just a minute." The receiver rattled, presumably dropped on the bar. A long minute later it rattled again.

"Hello," Jessie said breathlessly. "Is anyone still there?"

"Yes, I am."

"Sara? He said it was a woman, but he didn't say who it was. Sorry it took so long."

"That's okay. Was that your grandfather?"

"Yes. Let me guess. He dropped the phone. He always drops it or rather tosses it on the counter. What can I do for you? And by the way, I did put a reserved sign on table one. It's all yours, whenever you and your friend get here."

"That's why I called. I tried to call her, but she doesn't answer and her voice mail won't pick up. I don't think I'll be able to make it this evening. It's raining pretty heavily and it's supposed to get worse throughout the evening."

"That's not news in the Pacific Northwest."

"My dog isn't happy about it. When she's home by herself in a thunderstorm she pants and shakes and almost has a panic attack." Sara smiled down at Gypsy and said, "It's okay, baby. Momma's here."

"You have a dog?"

"Yes, a beagle. Gypsy is a therapy dog, but she gets nervous when it thunders. When Naomi gets there could you tell her I'm really sorry, but we'll have to do this pool thing another time? Let her know I tried to call."

"Bring her."

"Bring Gypsy? No, no. That's okay. I'll just stay home with her."

"She's housebroken, right?"

"Yes, of course."

"Then bring her with you. She can sit in Batch's office. He won't mind. He likes dogs. Cats, not so much. He thinks they're insolent. But she'll probably get something to eat out of the deal."

"Are you sure? We don't have to do this, Jessie. Naomi and I can play pool another time when it isn't pouring."

"Bring her. I like dogs too."

"Thank you. This is very sweet of you."

* * *

The sun had already set by the time Sara and Gypsy entered Batch's Bar and Grill. Like everywhere else in Ilwaco, it smelled slightly musty from the week's worth of rain. Sara shook out her umbrella and stood it in the holder by the door. She unbuckled Gypsy's yellow vinyl raincoat and slipped it off, allowing her to shake.

"So, this is Gypsy," Jessie greeted them with a wide grin. "Can I pet her?"

"Sure. She loves attention."

Jessie squatted in front of the dog and stroked her coat. Gypsy wagged and wiggled enthusiastically.

"Hello, little dog. Your mommy is smart. She dressed you in a raincoat."

"This is very nice of you to let her come with me. I really appreciate it. I could have left her home, but then I'd feel guilty and worry all night."

"She'll be fine."

"I guess Naomi isn't here yet." Sara scanned the room.

"Not that I've seen." Jessie led the way to the office and flipped on the light. "I put a blanket down for Gypsy to sit on. The cement floor might be a little cold."

"Look, Gypsy. A blanket all for you." Sara patted the blanket, encouraging the dog to try it out. Gypsy sniffed it then turned a few circles, tamping a spot for herself.

"Gypsy, sit. Stay," she said firmly and held up a hand. Gypsy lowered herself onto her haunches and cocked her head, as if waiting for further instructions.

"Wow, she is well behaved. Better than some people I know."

"If I keep it simple, we have no problem."

"Does she know any tricks?"

"Hold out your hand."

Jessie leaned down and held out her hand. Gypsy placed her paw in it.

"Good girl," Jessie said, patting her head.

"Now point your finger at her, but don't say anything." Sara watched proudly as Gypsy performed. As soon as Jessie pointed her finger Gypsy lowered herself and placed her snout on her front paws. "Gypsy, speak." The dog sat up and gave a quick, happy bark. "That's as far as we've gotten. We're working on a couple more, but they're still works in progress."

Sara's cell phone rang in her pocket.

"There's Naomi. I better take this and let her know I'm here." She stepped out of the office as she accepted the call. "Hello. I'll have you know I won't be late tonight. I'm already here. Are you on your way?"

"You're at the bar already?" Naomi seemed distracted.

"Yes. I was determined not to make you wait this time. And they've got a table reserved for us."

"That's great, but I'm afraid I'll be late. You know how it is. The sales rep is always the last on the priority list. I'm sorry. Hopefully it won't be too long. Have one of those luscious-looking strawberry margaritas and I'll be there as soon as I can. By the way, did you wear one?"

"One what?"

"A low-cut top, of course." She giggled.

"Actually, no." Sara hadn't thought about it. She wasn't the type to dress provocatively to get free drinks. She hoped Naomi wasn't either, and that she was only joking. Sara had chosen a long-sleeved blouse with a metallic sheen to it, mostly because it was clean and comfy. It was open at the neck with a wide collar but didn't afford a direct view through to her belly button. At least she hoped it didn't.

"I have to go. I think the department manager is ready to see me."

Sara heard voices in the background then the call ended. When she returned to the office Jessie was filling a stainless steel bowl with bottled water. Gypsy sat on the blanket, watching intently.

"You thought of everything."

"This *is* a bar. We serve drinks. That is unless we think our customers have had enough. Gypsy, you haven't over-indulged, have you?" The pup tilted her head and perked her ears. "I didn't think so."

"You may want to reconsider holding a pool table for us. Naomi will be late."

"How late?"

"I don't know. She just said she'd be here as soon as she could."

"That's okay." Jessie shrugged. "There's no big rush. Mid-week is usually slow and the rain has kept people away." She headed back to the bar.

Sara gave Gypsy a last look and command to stay, and then followed Jessie out. There were only a handful of customers scattered around the room and two playing pool.

"What can I get you?" Jessie asked.

"Nothing for me. Thank you. I'll wait for Naomi."

"Are you sure? It might be a while."

"Well, maybe a small glass of water." She settled onto a barstool.

"That's not very imaginative." Jessie filled a stemmed glass with ice. She opened a small bottle of Perrier, raising the bottle as she poured. She added a stemmed cherry and set it in front of Sara. "Your water, ma'am." She rested her hands on the bar as if waiting for Sara to try it.

"I would have held a glass under the faucet and called it good."

"We aim to please." She waited for Sara to take a sip then dropped another cherry in the glass.

"This is good." Sara took another drink and then plucked a cherry from the glass and ate it.

"You're kidding. You've never had Perrier or Pellegrino before?"

"Not like this, no. I've never been served sparkling water dressed up in an elegant glass with a cherry."

"So, I'm the first person to introduce you to the wonderful world of fizzy water?" Jessie propped her foot up on the shelf.

"Yes, you are. Motor scooters and fizzy water." Sara fished out the other cherry.

"Okay, I have to explain something about that. The real reason I wouldn't sell you the scooter is because I didn't want you to get hurt. I know scooters like mine aren't very powerful but they go fast enough and I didn't want that on my conscience."

"Thank you, but I thought that subject was closed."

"You brought it up."

"No, I didn't."

"You said motor scooters and fizzy water." Jessie poured the rest of the bottle into her glass.

"That's different."

"I think maybe you've had enough fizzy water. I'm cutting you off."

"Another Corona, Jessie," the man in a rain-dampened suit called from his stool at the end of the bar. "If my wife asks, I was here alone."

"Don't get me involved with your domestic problems, Ernie." Jessie pulled a bottle from the tank, popped the top then stuck a lime wedge in the top.

"Every damn time I go out the door she thinks I'm screwing around."

"Don't give her cause." Jessie set the bottle on his cocktail napkin and took away the empty.

"Too bad I can't use fizzy water as an excuse for why I can't play pool." Sara glanced over at the row of pool tables.

"So this Naomi person knows how to play?"

"She says she does. I don't know why she thought this was a good idea. I told her I don't know how."

"You shouldn't worry about it. Most of the people slugging quarters into our tables don't know how either. Trust me. You'll fit right in. No one would even notice."

"Knowing how well you play, doesn't it drive you crazy watching that? You should give lessons. Teach people like me how to hold the stick."

"It's called a cue and I do."

"You have pool classes?"

"Private lessons."

"Oh, private lessons." Sara raised an eyebrow.

"Just billiard lessons for people who can afford one-on-one instruction and don't want to do it in a bar," Jessie stammered.

"Women who want private lessons?"

"Uh-huh."

"Like Becky? I'm sorry, Jessie. That's none of my business."

"That's okay." She didn't seem bothered by Sara's curiosity.

"I couldn't help but notice that Becky wasn't with you during the tournament. Should I offer sympathy that it didn't work out between you and her?"

"Nope. That relationship reached its sell-by date pretty quick. Actually, both of them did."

"I'm sorry. That can be rough."

"It was fun while it lasted, if you know what I mean." Jessie flashed a wicked grin.

"Margie said dating someone with a horse ranch begs to wonder certain things."

"Such as?"

"This is embarrassing. How did we get onto this topic of conversation?"

"Blame the fizzy water." Jessie added more Perrier to her glass. "I'm guessing Margie wants to know if cowgirls are good in the hay, right?"

"In the saddle I believe was her quandary." Sara laughed. "I can't believe I'm repeating that."

"You tell her yes. On two occasions." She dropped two more cherries in Sara's glass.

"What about the tournament you were going to enter? Las Vegas, wasn't it? Did you win?"

"Yes, it was in Vegas but no, I decided not to go. Something came up."

"But I thought you were all registered, ready to go."

"Nope. Maybe next time." Jessie's jaw muscles clenched as if she were holding something back, something she didn't want to admit.

"I'm sorry it didn't work out for you. I bet you would have done well."

"No big deal. So, how long have you been dating this Naomi person?"

"I don't know that I'd call it dating. She's a sales rep for a laboratory supply company. She's in southwest Washington every few weeks or so. We're just friends."

"She travels a lot then."

"Yes. She's on the road for days at a time."

"Sounds exciting."

"Did you know she's ridden in a hot air balloon, taken flying lessons and bungee jumped off a bridge in California? And before you ask, I admire her courage, but I have no interest in doing any of those."

"Me either. I prefer my feet on the ground." Jessie picked three limes from a bowl and juggled them before lining them up on a cutting board to be wedged.

"She's got a good job. She's very successful. But being on the road so much makes me wonder how anyone can establish roots or permanence."

"Maybe she's got a girlfriend from hell back home."

"She does not have a girlfriend back home, from hell or otherwise. She said after her last breakup a year ago she rented an apartment, but hasn't been home long enough to finish unpacking the boxes."

"You're right. No permanence there. But hey, if the sex is good," Jessie said with a wicked grin.

"I beg your pardon." Sara swallowed the sip and frowned up at her. "I'm not discussing my sex life."

"We discussed mine."

"Well, I'm *not* discussing mine." She stirred the straw around in her glass. Before she could stop herself, she added. "But, no, we haven't."

"So you're worried you'll look bad because you can't shoot pool, right?"

"Something like that."

"Here's your chance." Jessie nodded toward the pool table closest to the bar. "Grab a cue and have at it."

"Really? You think it'll help?"

"Sure. A little practice never hurt anybody." Jessie unlocked the coin slot compartment and flipped a lever. The balls released and rolled into the tray. "There you go. You won't need any quarters."

Jessie filled the triangular rack then positioned it for the break.

"How do I know which one of these to pick?" Sara stared at the cues on the rack, lifting several to compare the weight. Jessie picked one, rolled it on the table as if checking for warping then slid it up and down between her fingers.

"Try this one."

"Any final words of advice?" Sara stood at the end of the table, feeling awkward. Put a test tube or syringe in her hand, she would feel right at home. But a long wooden stick, a cluster of colored balls and a woman watching who could clear the table as if it were child's play, not so much.

"Yes. Try not to rip the felt."

"That's not much help." Sara set the cue ball in the middle and leaned down to take a shot.

"Wait." Jessie pulled the ball back and positioned Sara behind it. "Try it now. You have to break from behind the head string. It's an imaginary line across the table."

"Head string, huh?" She leaned slightly forward, preparing to break. "And what if I miss the group of balls altogether?"

"It's a pretty big target. You should be able to hit something."

"Seems like there should be more tidbits you could share." Sara closed one eye as she lined up the shot. "Pearls of wisdom. Some tenets all pool players live by."

"Never eat beans before a match." Jessie perched her hands on her hips as she watched.

Sara snickered and made the shot. The cue ball struck the cluster, but only hard enough to scatter a few of the balls. "That wasn't very good, was it? Most of them are still all grouped together."

"That's okay."

"Now I shoot them in numerical order?"

"Yep. In the game of eightball one person shoots the solids and the other person shoots the stripes. Seven of each. The first person to sink all theirs gets to shoot the black eightball to win."

"How do you decide who shoots what?"

"Whatever you sink first. Usually something drops on the break. I don't think you need to worry about shooting in order right now." Jessie looked over the table then headed back to the bar. "Shoot the blue one."

"Okeydokey. The blue one," Sara muttered as she circled the table. She lined it up and gave a healthy whack, sending the blue ball bouncing around the table from rail to rail but the only thing that dropped in a pocket was the cue ball. "Oops."

"What happened? You scratch?" Jessie stood at the beer tap, filling a tall glass.

"If that means the white ball went in instead of the blue ball, yes. I scratched."

"It'll come out on the other side." Jessie seemed to show great restraint in not laughing out loud. "First piece of advice. Keep both eyes open."

While Jessie tended to a few new customers, Sara moved around the table, whacking at one ball then another. She tried several grips and stances, all with frustrating results. Jessie made it look so easy. Lean down, line up the shot and stroke the cue ball. Sara made a dozen shots. She sank only four and scratched five times.

"How's it going over there, slick?" Jessie called.

"I'm not sure this is helping my self-confidence. Could you do me a favor when you have a minute?"

"Sure. What?" Jessie came out from behind the bar, drying her hands on a towel.

"Shoot one. I want to see how you do it."

"You're doing fine. It just takes time."

"I don't have that kind of time. Shoot one." She handed the cue to Jessie.

Jessie chalked it then stood her stance, the same one she used during the tournament. She placed her hand on the table, bridging the cue between her fingers. She leaned down, her chin nearly touching the cue as she slid it back and forth in practice. Her eyes became riveted on the target, her jaw muscles clenched. With one smooth stroke she tapped the cue ball and dropped the red three one into the side pocket with a firm plop. The cue ball stopped immediately.

"Do it again," Sara said, watching her stance and the way she gripped the cue.

Jessie rechalked the cue and lined up another shot. With almost robotic consistency, she sank another ball. Then another, each time leaving the cue ball in perfect alignment for the next shot.

"Okay, that's it. I'm going home. There is no way I can do that." Sara shook her head.

Jessie laughed and grabbed for her arm.

"Yes, you can. Come over here." She put the cue in Sara's hands and positioned her at the table. "You're right-handed so put your left foot forward enough to feel balanced. Bend at your hips, not your waist. Keep your head, arm and cue all lined up along your aim line." Jessie wrapped her arms around Sara, one hand on the cue and one on the table next to Sara's to form the bridge. "Nice smooth stroke."

Sara felt Jessie's hips snug against hers, her breasts against her back. She looked down at the table where Jessie's long fingers curled around hers, cradling and protecting Sara's hand. Sara didn't have to look to know Jessie's cheek was just millimeters from hers. The sound of her breathing in her ear.

"Just easy does it. Nice and parallel," Jessie said softly as she helped guide the cue back and forth. "You don't have to over-power it. Everything good comes from an easy stroke."

Jessie took her hand off the cue and rested it on Sara's hip, allowing her to shoot. In that split second before the cue struck the ball Sara swore Jessie's hips bumped her bottom and a million things raced through her mind. Was she sending some kind of subliminal message? Was she making a pass? What if she was? What would it be like to have Jessie's naked body pressed against her own? And where in the world did those thoughts come from? With Jessie's help, the cue ball rolled down the table and deposited two colored balls into the corner pockets.

"Wow. Two." Sara remained bent over the table, Jessie still at her back.

"See what I mean? Easy does it and you'll be satisfied with the results." Jessie gave Sara's hip a pat then stood up. "It's all about consistency and practice."

"Thank you." Sara circled the table, needing a few deep breaths to clear her thoughts.

Her timing impeccable, Naomi came through the door, flapping and shaking her umbrella. Her slacks were rain-splattered from the knees down and her jacket was soaked but her hair was perfectly coiffed. She had a don't-start-without-me energy about her.

"Oh, my God. I made it," she announced and scanned the room. "There you are. Am I terribly late?" She rushed up to Sara and hugged her more warmly than she had ever done before. "I'm sorry I made you wait. Was it terribly boring?"

"No, you're fine. Jessie was just showing me how to hold a cue so I don't look like a complete imbecile. Unfortunately, I don't think it will make any difference at all. Are you sure you want to do this?"

"Absolutely, I do. And it's okay if you don't know how. I can teach you. But first I need something tall and cold and refreshing." She looked over at Jessie and thought a moment. "Vodka sunrise. Something mid-shelf."

"Absolut?" Jessie offered.

"Yes. That'll be fine. And fix Sara another of whatever she's having." She patted a barstool for Sara to come join her.

"Sara?" Jessie said with a reserved smile, pointing to her glass.

"Yes, I think I will have another. Two cherries this time." Sara took a seat at the bar. "How was your meeting?"

"Canceled. The department head left at noon. His secretary forgot to tell me so I met with his assistant, but he doesn't know anything about anything. He spent the entire meeting staring at my crotch." Naomi threw her head back in disgust. "I should have just ordered in a couple sandwich trays and called it good." She turned to Sara with a sparkle in her eyes. "You look good. How was your day? Is Dr. Lesterbrook running you ragged?"

"No. Not at all." Sara wasn't going to trash the boss over a drink at a bar. It wasn't good practice now or ever. "Where are you off to after Long Beach?" Sara wanted a different subject.

"Seattle next week then up to Vancouver. I'm trying to schedule a long weekend in Whistler mid-November. Skiing will be fabulous. They've already had six inches at the summit. Do you ski?"

"No. I tried it once, but skiing and I don't get along."

"You're kidding? You lived your whole life in Washington and you don't ski?"

"I was raised in the middle of the state. Apple country. Skiing is a sport performed in the mountains in frigid conditions and I don't like snow in my pants." Sara gave a deliberate shiver. It seemed easier to sound wimpy than explain skiing was an expensive sport her family hadn't been able to afford. As the only child of deeply religious blue-collar parents such frivolity was considered wasteful. Reading a good book in front of a fireplace or while snuggled in bed was another matter. That she loved to do, and had since she was a child, experiencing adventure vicariously through characters on a page.

"I love skiing." Naomi gave a dramatic moan. "St. Moritz at Christmas is to die for."

"St. Moritz, as in Switzerland?" Sara felt like the small-town girl she knew she was.

"Yes. I've only been once, but it was fantastic." Naomi took a long slow sip then headed to the pool table. "Is it time for me to teach you how to shoot pool?"

"If you're tired we don't have to do this tonight." Sara followed, hoping she'd change her mind. But she didn't.

Naomi racked the balls as if she knew what she was doing. She returned Sara's cue to the rack and selected two different ones, seemingly because they had identical handle decoration.

"Do you want me to go ahead and break so you can see how it's done?"

"Sure." Sara looked over at Jessie. She looked back, a curious arch to her brow.

Naomi crouched over the shot but everything about it was different from Jessie's instruction, from her stance to the way she held the cue. She gave a hefty whack, scattering the balls but nothing dropped. She circled the table as if it was still her turn. Sara didn't care. She wasn't ready to show off her lack of skill.

"It's all in the wrist," Naomi said as she took her next shot. She finally sank one.

"That was a good one."

"Your turn."

Sara stepped to the table. She tried to remember everything Jessie had showed her. Left foot forward. Cue parallel. Aim line.

Easy stroke. It was all too much. The only thing she was certain of was chalking the tip of the cue with the little blue cube.

"Doing that really doesn't make any difference," Naomi said.

Sara heard a disapproving groan coming from where Jessie stood behind the bar. She leaned forward at the hips but everything else was a blur. She whacked the cue ball into a cluster of three, scattering them in all directions. She sank nothing.

"That's okay. It takes time to learn." Naomi barely waited for the cue ball to stop spinning before she leaned over her shot. She didn't sink anything either, but lined up for another anyway. "Didn't the bartender say she plays?"

"Yes, she does. Jessie's pretty good."

"Maybe she'd play me a game," Naomi said, looking in that direction. "You don't mind, do you, Sara? She's not very busy."

Before Sara could suggest she not, Naomi invited Jessie to play. She half expected Jessie to decline, but surprisingly accepted.

"What do you want to play?" Jessie asked, keeping an eye on the bar and her customers as she racked the balls. "Eightball?" Naomi didn't seem to know what that meant. "Stripes and solids?" Jessie added.

"Yes. You can be stripes. I'll be solids." Naomi waited at the end of the table to break.

Sara started to say something about the rules of the game, but Jessie shook her head as if it didn't matter. She offered her cue to Jessie and was a little surprised she accepted it. She expected her to choose one from the rack or perhaps take out the case where she carried her own. Jessie chalked the tip while Naomi broke. Nothing dropped and she scratched, which gave Jessie the cue ball in hand to shoot at whatever she wanted but she abided by Naomi's rules.

"I'm stripes, right?" Jessie studied the table intently.

"Yes."

"Do you have to shoot them in order?" Sara asked, although she already knew the answer.

"I think so," Jessie said, and leaned over her first shot. The nineball rolled into the corner pocket, the cue ball left just inches from the ten.

Sara knew this was going to be a very lopsided victory. Naomi would probably never get another chance to shoot. She had chosen the wrong woman to challenge. Within two shots Naomi seemed to realize her fate and stood silently watching, all expression drained from her face. Jessie circled the table. Her concentration was unwavering. But her next shot seemed deliberately off-line. She didn't sink anything and the cue ball stopped in perfect position next to one of the solid color balls.

"Oops," Jessie said. "Your turn."

Naomi sank that one, but didn't leave herself another shot. When she missed Jessie came back to the table and made another off-line shot, again leaving the cue ball next to one of Naomi's.

"Damn." Jessie stamped the butt of the cue on the floor angrily, her eyes rolled to meet Sara's.

Naomi grinned and quickly sank it. She took a drink from her cocktail then excused herself to the ladies' room.

"No cheating while I'm gone," she teased. "I know exactly where every one of those little balls are."

"I promise." Jessie returned to the bar and filled a beer pitcher for a group of bikers. Sara sat on the stool, sipping her fizzy water.

"I know what you're doing." She chased a cherry around the bottom of the glass with a straw.

"What's that?" Jessie mixed a shot of vodka into a tall glass of orange juice and set it on a tray.

"You don't have to do that, you know."

"Do what?" She popped the top of two bottles of Corona and added them to the tray then signaled the waitress.

"You're letting her win."

"No, I'm not." Jessie chuckled innocently.

"Yes, you are. You could beat her blindfolded. You know it. I know it. Everyone in this bar knows it." Sara leaned in so only Jessie could hear. "You don't have to do that."

Jessie just smiled. She held the bottle of Perrier over Sara's glass, ready to pour the rest of it.

"No, thanks." She covered the glass with her hand. "I'm fizzied out."

Instead of capping the bottle Jessie slowly brought it to her lips and drank, her eyes locked on Sara's.

"I'm ready," Naomi said, returning to the bar for another sip before stepping to the table. "My turn, right?"

"Yep. Have at it," Jessie said, mixing another drink.

Back and forth they went, each of Jessie's errant shots leaving Naomi in perfect position to sink something. Naomi didn't seem to realize what was happening, but Sara did. Naomi finally sank the eightball, proudly raising the cue over her head in victory.

"Sorry, Jessie. I guess it just wasn't your night."

"I guess not. Good game, Naomi." Jessie shook her hand and returned to her customers without a word to Sara.

"I'm glad we did this. It was fun." Naomi tossed the cue on the table. "But you're right. I'm tired. I've got an early meeting and lunch with a bunch of clinic administrators. I've got to get some sleep. Do you mind?" She smiled sweetly at Sara, her arm around her waist.

"No, absolutely not. I need to head home myself. I've got an early day tomorrow too."

Sara didn't see it coming, but Naomi pulled her close and kissed her, the tip of her tongue exploring Sara's mouth. It wasn't a long kiss. But long enough for Sara to feel embarrassed. She wasn't in a kissing relationship with Naomi, at least not yet. They were barely at the hugging stage. But there it was. The kiss that said this woman is spoken for. Sara wasn't ready for that and it made her uncomfortable.

"I'll call you tomorrow," Naomi said with a wink. She tossed a twenty-dollar bill on the bar and headed out the door.

Jessie waited until the door closed then turned to Sara.

"I think you're going to have to change your résumé. You'll be adding something real soon. And I don't mean bungee jumping," Jessie teased.

"I need to collect my dog and go home." Sara headed for the office, ignoring Jessie's remark and the sinister grin on her face.

"How'd you like the taste of Absolut? Smooth, huh?"

"I'm not discussing this with you," Sara called without looking back.

"But you'll keep me updated, right?" Jessie chuckled, juggling lemons as Sara claimed her umbrella from the holder.

"No. It was a kiss. One kiss. Now drop it or I'm taking my fizzy water business elsewhere." Sara opened her umbrella and stepped out into the rain, Gypsy at her side.

"Good night, Sara," Jessie called.

CHAPTER THIRTEEN

Sara and Naomi had only been gone a few minutes. Jessie carried a tub of dirty dishes into the kitchen and returned with a rack of clean glasses as Batch came through the front door. The hood of his rain slicker was doing little to keep his face, beard and hair dry.

"Hey, Kid?" He dripped a wet path as he crossed the room to her. "Was there a dog in here? I saw one leaving."

"Yep." She heaved the rack onto the counter and began stacking the glasses in rows.

"How come?"

"Because I told Sara she could bring it. The dog doesn't like thunder." Jessie held a wineglass up to the light, examined the spots then set it aside to be rewashed.

"Was it that motor scooter blonde?"

"Her name is Sara Patterson and yes, she's the one on the napkin. She was meeting someone here so I let her bring her dog. And before you ask, no, she isn't buying my scooter."

"Not in a million years, my ass," he said with a hearty laugh, and headed for the office.

"I didn't call her. She called me."

"But you will. You will." He closed the door. It opened again, a frown on his face. "Was that dog in here?" he shouted.

"Yes."

"I stepped in the damn water bowl." He mumbled something Jessie presumed was a long string of profanity and slammed the door. A moment later the door reopened. "Where's the damn mop?"

"Storeroom."

He retrieved the mop, still mumbling and grumbling. Once he cleaned the mess and made the rounds, greeting and joking with the customers, he stepped behind the bar. He dropped a couple ice cubes in a glass and filled it with iced tea. He added three spoonfuls of sugar but didn't stir it.

"Any mail?" he asked.

Jessie handed him the stack from where she always kept it next to the cash register.

"You got something official looking."

"Probably the tax bill." He tucked the mail under his arm, grabbed a handful of popcorn from the machine and headed to the office.

Jessie knew it wasn't a tax bill. It didn't come from the tax collector's office. It was from the health department. But she'd let him discover that for himself. If it was important, he'd let her know.

"Hi." A woman in a tank top and blazer propped her arms on the bar and leaned forward, pushing her ample bosom together.

"Hey there." Jessie looked up and smiled, then went back to muddling mint leaves for a mojito. Audrey was a regular. She was a beauty school instructor who loved to tinker with new products and styles. This week it was pink highlights and a row of piercings up the edge of one ear. She and Jessie had a short history together. A few dates. Nothing serious. An escape from boring solitude. She represented no demands. No jealousy. Dinner. A movie. Sex. All the banal characteristics of a noncommittal relationship. For both of them. A booty call, nothing more.

"I've been waiting all evening to visit with you. First it was that blonde, then the one with the big laugh."

"What can I get you, Audrey?"

"Guinness, I guess." She watched as Jessie drew the glass of dark ale from the tap, providing just the right amount of head. "Who was the blonde, by the way?"

"What blonde?" Jessie sat the glass on a napkin and slid over a basket of popcorn.

"The one in the shiny shirt. The one who didn't know which end of the cue to hold."

"Just a friend. And she knew how to hold it."

"Her eyes were all over you." Audrey cocked an eyebrow.

"She asked for a few tips on shooting pool. That's all. Like I did for you."

"So, you're not dating her?"

"No."

"Are you closing tonight?"

Jessie recognized the question as Audrey's invitation for a date. An uncomplicated invitation. There was no reason Jessie couldn't accept. She was between girlfriends and owed allegiance to no one. But somehow she wasn't interested. A quick sweaty trip down lover's lane with Audrey didn't appeal to her. And Sara Patterson seemed to have everything to do with it.

"Not tonight, Audrey."

"You sure?"

"Yeah, I'm sure."

Audrey shrugged and returned to her friends at a nearby table. Jessie glanced over at Sara's glass still sitting on the bar, the cocktail napkin artfully folded and ruffled around the base. A single cherry sat in the bottom among the remnants of her fizzy water. Jessie hadn't cleared it away and didn't plan on it. She clinked the top of the Perrier bottle against the rim of the glass then downed the last swig, holding it in her mouth a moment before swallowing.

"This ain't no damn tax bill," Batch said as he came striding up to the bar. He held out a letter for Jessie to read. "The health department says we got to have CPR certification."

Jessie scanned the letter.

"It says this is your second notice. Where's the first one? Why didn't you do something about this before?" Jessie went to the opening to the kitchen. "Hey, Jimmy. Do you know CPR? Batch needs an employee who's certified."

"Nope." She was scraping the grill and didn't look up.

"How about you, Charlene?" she asked the waitress as she returned to the bar with an order. "Do you know CPR?"

"Is that where you squeeze someone when they choke?"

"No, that's the Heimlich Maneuver. I know how to do that."

"Then, nope. I don't."

"Sorry." Jessie handed the letter back. "Wish I knew how, but I don't."

"I wonder if Ron knows how. Maybe he's certified."

Jessie scowled suspiciously, hoping he would come to his own realization about that. Nothing in Ron Singer's makeup suggested he knew CPR or any other lifesaving, socially redeeming skills.

"Damn," Batch said disgustedly, and headed back to the office.

* * *

"Sara, you've got a visitor. She says she knows you," the hospital security guard said quietly, resting his hand on her shoulder. He nodded toward the side door of the cafeteria where Jessie was waiting. Sara looked professional in her business attire. Fresh and crisply efficient as always, she showed no trace of the late hours she and Naomi spent at the bar the night before.

Jessie combed her fingers through the sides of her damp hair, wondering if she looked like a creature from the swamp. Sara looked up from her sandwich, smiled and waved her over.

"Sorry if I'm interrupting your lunch."

"Sit down. Would you like something? The food here isn't bad." Sara scooted her chair over to make room at the crowded table.

"No. I've already had lunch." Jessie's eyes drifted around the table. "Are you sure I'm not bothering you? You're not in a meeting or something?"

"We try not to do anything constructive during lunch," Margie said, raising a chuckle from the others. "Sit down and take a load off."

"What can I do for you?" Sara asked, eating the last bite of a sandwich. "By the way, thanks again for letting me bring Gypsy last night."

"You're welcome."

"Is there something I can help you with?"

"Can you teach me CPR?"

"I beg your pardon."

"I need to learn CPR. Someone at the bar needs to know how. Safety regulations."

"I'm not a licensed instructor. You need someone trained as an instructor who can certify you. I think the Red Cross has classes."

"So, you don't know how to do it either?"

"I know how. All hospital employees are taught how to administer CPR. It's part of our employee training."

"So you know how but you're not an instructor. Is it that difficult to learn?"

"It really isn't hard. It's basically circulating oxygenated blood to keep the person, and specifically their brain, alive. It's a pretty straightforward technique."

"It sounds complicated. I wouldn't want to kill someone."

"First of all, you don't do CPR unless the person needs it, which means they aren't breathing. If they aren't breathing eventually their heart will stop, if it hasn't already. So if you do nothing, they are going to die anyway."

"That's a happy thought." Jessie grimaced. "A person has a heart attack and I kill them because I do CPR wrong."

"There are lots of reasons to need CPR. Drowning, choking, electrocution, diabetic coma, gunshot."

"Falling down drunk."

"If they've stopped breathing, yes."

"So you'll show me?"

"You'll have to take a certified class." Sara stuffed the sandwich wrapper in her sack.

"Can you find me one before ten o'clock tomorrow morning?"

"Why ten o'clock?"

"Because that's when the inspector is coming. The health department is sending someone to inspect and certify that we are compliant. They'll shut us down if we aren't."

"Seems like they should have given you more notice."

"Actually, they did. My grandfather got a letter months ago, but he forgot about it. He's a good restaurateur but he's not that great at paperwork. The old man drives me crazy sometimes but I can't let them close him down. I need to make this happen, Sara. Can you help me?"

"Is anyone here a certified CPR instructor?" Sara asked, scanning the others at the table.

"I know how, but I'm not certified," one of the nurses said. The others agreed.

"I know someone who is," said one of the hospital volunteers, as she picked at her salad.

"Who?" Sara and Jessie said in unison.

"Your boss."

"Dr. Lesterbrook?" Sara seemed surprised.

"Yes. He used to teach the CPR and first aid classes. He hasn't done it in several years but he used to. They tried to talk him into doing it again, but he said no. He was very adamant about it too."

"Anyone else?" Sara asked hopefully but no one volunteered. "I wish I could help you, Jessie. But a certified instructor is the only one who can sign the paper."

"Thanks anyway. I'll let you get back to your lunch." Jessie stood and pushed her chair in, ready to leave. But Sara reached over and took her arm.

"Wait a minute. I owe you one. Come with me." She strode out of the cafeteria and down the hall toward the lab with a determined impatience in her step. Jessie followed. They entered through the waiting room and stopped at an office door where a man in a white lab coat sat working on a computer. Sara took a preparatory breath then knocked.

"Dr. Lesterbrook, can I speak with you a minute?"

"Sure," he said after a reluctant sigh. He hit the save key then closed the computer and looked up. "What can I help you with, Sara?"

"Dr. Lesterbrook, this is Jessie Singer. She needs to learn CPR and she needs to do it in a hurry." She pulled Jessie into the office and closed the door.

"Singer. Jessica Singer," he said with a reflective scowl. "Should I know that name?"

"It's Jessie Singer," Sara corrected. "And yes, she was a walk-in months ago."

"Ah, yes, Singer." He looked Jessie up and down. She couldn't tell if his steeled expression was good or bad.

"She needs CPR certification before ten o'clock tomorrow morning. I understand you are an instructor. You would be doing her, and me, a huge favor if you could teach her. She's a very quick study. It shouldn't take very long at all."

"I don't know who told you I was an instructor but I haven't done that in years. The Red Cross handles all instructional classes for the hospital now. You'll have to contact them."

"I have sir," Jessie inserted. "But their next class isn't for two months. I don't have that kind of time."

"Sara, you should know how to perform CPR, especially working in a medical facility like this. You should be able to teach her how to do it."

"Dr. Lesterbrook, I do know how to do it and I could show her. That isn't the problem. She needs certification and that's something I can't provide."

"I don't teach anymore," he replied succinctly, and turned back to his desk. "You'll have to find someone else. You shouldn't have waited until the last minute."

"Yes sir. You're right. My grandfather should have taken care of it when he got the first notice. But he didn't. Now he's screwed. He has until tomorrow morning to come up with at least one employee certified in CPR or they'll shut him down. I'm trying to avoid that happening. I'm sorry to have bothered you, sir. This isn't your problem. It's mine." Jessie opened the door and headed out into the hall. She somehow expected Sara to follow, perhaps offer words of sympathy or encouragement for her plight. But her own footsteps were the only ones echoing down the long hallway. She wasn't sure where she was going next but she wasn't giving up. She had just opened the door to the parking lot when she heard running footsteps and a breathless voice.

"Jessie, wait. Wait!" Sara called. "Wait a minute. Where are you going?"

"Going to find an instructor who gives a damn," she said, and let the door close behind her.

Sara pushed the door open with a frantic look on her face.

"Wait. I've found you one."

"Who?"

"Me." She stood in the doorway as rain dampened her hair and wind whipped her white coat. "I'm going to teach you."

"Thank you, Sara. I appreciate your offer to show me how, but I need to spend what little time I have finding someone who can certify me."

"If I said you will be certified when I'm finished with you, would you come back inside?"

Jessie stood in the middle of the parking lot as rain dribbled down her neck, wondering if she could believe her.

"I promise," Sara added with a smile. "And could you hurry up and decide because I'm getting soaked out here."

Jessie followed Sara back into the lab, their shoes squishing as they walked. Jessie noticed Dr. Lesterbrook wasn't in his office. Or anywhere else in the lab, for that matter.

"Can I ask how this is going to get me certified?"

Sara handed her a towel and took one for herself, blotting the rain from her face.

"This way, please," she said as if she didn't hear Jessie's question. She opened the door to the storeroom and flipped on the light. She pulled a large plastic case from the top shelf, struggling to get it to the floor. It was covered with dust and padlocked shut. She took a key from her pocket, unlocked it and peeked inside before removing the lid. Beneath a layer of cardboard and bubble wrap she uncovered the torso of a manikin dressed in a blue and red jogging suit jacket, its eyes closed and mouth open.

"Jessie Singer, meet Resusci Anne." Sara lifted the manikin from the tub and placed it on the floor of the storeroom. "She's going to help you become certified in cardiopulmonary resuscitation. And if you do everything you're told and pass the class, you'll get one of these," she said as she pulled a folded paper from her pocket. Jessie's name was written on the top. Dr. Lesterbrook's name was signed on the line marked instructor.

"But I thought he wouldn't do it." Jessie looked toward the door, waiting for him to appear.

"He isn't. I am. He said if I instruct you and verify you can perform CPR, he will certify you. The only stipulation, this goes no further than that door." She gave Jessie a stern look. "Consider this as privileged information."

"So you're putting your rear on the line for me?"

"No, I'm putting his rear on the line for you. Please, don't chop it off."

"What made him change his mind? What did you say to him?"

"I didn't say anything. I was ready to run after you when he stopped me. He said sometimes people deserve a little help. He pulled a certificate from his drawer, signed it and handed it to me."

"And he trusts you to know how to do this?"

"I had to promise one tiny little thing."

"Which is?" Jessie was almost afraid to know.

"I have to take the class at the Red Cross to become an instructor."

"I'm sorry I got you into this mess," Jessie said.

"Actually, I'm glad you did. I think being a CPR instructor is something I should do. I work at a hospital. The more knowledge I have, the better."

"I really appreciate this, Sara." Jessie placed her hand on Sara's arm. "Really."

"We're friends, aren't we?" Sara smiled softly.

"Yes, I guess we are."

"I wanted to do this for you, and for your grandfather. It's what friends do for one another. And you're lucky. It's a slow day in the lab."

"Anytime you and Naomi want to come by and play pool, let me know. I'll make sure there's a table available. Even if it's tournament night, I can usually set one aside."

"Thank you. I'll let her know." Sara knelt beside the manikin and unzipped the jacket.

"Or if she's not in town and you want to practice, that's okay too."

"There's a thought. Maybe I can get good enough so I don't scratch every time I shoot." Sara grinned sheepishly. "So, shall we begin?"

Jessie watched and listened while Sara went over the basics of why and when CPR was appropriate. Sara seemed well-educated on the subject and a good communicator. She also seemed to sense when Jessie understood a concept and when she needed more information. They knelt side-by-side as Sara showed her how to check for breathing and a pulse, clear the airway, where to place her hands and how to compress the chest.

"Compressions need to be two inches at a rate of about one hundred per minute." Sara sang the song "Staying Alive" as she pumped the chest. "Forgive my singing. That's not one of my skills. But that song fits the compression rate perfectly."

"Sounds good to me." They sang a few bars together as Sara demonstrated again.

Sara's hands cupped over the manikin's chest were meant to be instructional but Jessie felt a tingle of excitement with each thrust. She tried to concentrate on the lesson, but it was as if Sara's fingertips extended over the nipples were trying to massage and coax them to full erection. Jessie perched her hands on her knees and pulled her elbows in tight to relieve the sensation in her own breasts.

"Okay, now you try it," Sara said.

Jessie's hands trembled as she placed them on the manikin's chest for the first time. She locked her fingers together as she had seen Sara do, ready to administer the first compression.

"Put the heel of your lower hand on the sternum, like this." Sara cradled her hands around Jessie's, repositioned them. "This reminds me of you showing me how to shoot pool. It's all in the hand placement."

"This is a little more intense than that," Jessie chuckled nervously.

"You're doing very well. Now, lean over the victim and press straight down. Not at an angle. You can't sit back on your heels like that and do the compressions successfully."

Jessie began compressions, doing her best to mimic Sara's technique.

"A little quicker," Sara encouraged.

"It's harder than it looks, the amount of pressure, I mean."

"And once you start, you can't quit until you are relieved by an EMT or someone else who knows how to do it. It's a commitment you are making to save someone's life. That's why they say call nine-one-one first, before you start. You can stop every few minutes to check for breathing and a pulse, but then you start again. The American Heart Association says conventional CPR consists of chest compressions and rescue breathing. But not everyone will consent to putting their mouth on that of a stranger. So they acknowledge hands-only CPR is better than nothing. Let me show you how to add rescue breathing if you should choose to do that."

Sara explained the rate and technique for incorporating breathing into the mouth of the victim as well as chest compressions. It was all mechanical and scientific until the moment she tilted the manikin's chin upward and covered its mouth and lips with her own. Oh, shit, Jessie thought, as a full-fledged bolt of electricity shot down her body and out her crotch. Was that what it was like when Naomi kissed her? Was that the thrill awaiting whoever was lucky enough to press their lips to Sara Patterson's? Jessie envied that manikin. With every fiber of her body, she envied that doll.

"Now your turn." Sara leaned back so Jessie could try.

Jessie took a deep breath and leaned down, placing her mouth where Sara's had been. It was the closest thing to kissing her she could imagine. But there was no way she could tell her that. This was just one of those fleeting fantasies, not the first she'd had about Sara Patterson since she first smiled at her in the lab waiting room nearly a year ago.

CHAPTER FOURTEEN

"Hey there, woman." Sara caught up with Margie in the hall and locked arms with her. "Where have you been hiding?"

"Hi." Margie's usual jovial spirit seemed dampened. Her furrowed brow and thin-lipped nod suggested she wasn't in the mood for chitchat.

"Are you okay? How's your blood sugar since you came off the pump? Are you having better luck keeping it under control now that you're back to injecting?"

Margie turned to Sara, her eyes glistening and red.

"What's wrong?" Sara pulled her to a stop.

"It didn't work out," she said with a shaky voice.

"You're going back on the pump? I thought the doctor said your tissue wasn't absorbing well enough for an insulin pump."

"It's not the pump. Not the insulin." She lowered her eyes as a tear ran down her cheek. "Gretchen said she tried, but she can't deal with it."

"Can't deal with what?"

"The needles. The blood. The injections. The whole thing. She doesn't want to be with someone who's diabetic." She looked up with a pained expression. "I never asked her to do anything. I tried to be discreet so she didn't see anything, but sometimes I have to test five or six times a day. She said it didn't matter where I did it. She still knew what I had in my tote."

Sara wiped the tear from Margie's cheek. "I am so sorry, honey."

"We were going to move in together." Margie closed her eyes and drew a deep breath then straightened her shoulders. "I shouldn't blame her."

"But you do. And that's okay."

"I loved her, Sara. I truly did."

"I know, Margie. I know. Come talk with me." Sara motioned toward the lab.

"I can't. I wish I could, but our computers are down. I've got to get back to the office." She forced a smile. "I'll be okay. It'll just take some time."

"You know where I am. Anytime you need to talk, you come find me. I'm a good listener." She hugged Margie, and sent her on her way. She wished she could diminish the pain for her. But Margie was a strong woman. She'd get through this. She had her friends for support. Sara wanted to visit with Margie about something else that had been preying on her. But this wasn't the right time. Margie had enough stress. Sara didn't need to compound it. She'd figure out her feelings about Naomi and the kiss for herself. If her texts and phone calls were to be believed, Naomi wasn't due back in Ilwaco for a couple weeks. There was time.

* * *

Margie showed amazing resilience. Within a week she was back to her witty, happy self. At least she was on the outside. It was her occasional vacant stare across the cafeteria that told Sara her friend was still suffering.

"Live it up, girls," Margie said, dumping a plastic bag of candy on the lunch table. "Halloween has come to Ocean Side, even if the administration won't decorate for it."

"They did." Sara reached for a Hershey's Kiss wrapped in autumn-colored foil. "There's a cardboard pumpkin taped to the front door."

"One anthropomorphized squash does not a decoration make." She popped a bite-size Snickers in her mouth. "I like the holidays, especially ones in the winter with snow."

"So, Christmas?" a nurse said, raking two candy bars into her pocket.

"Yes. And Christmas shopping in the snow. Love it, love it, love it."

"But we don't get snow along the coast. We get ice. Windy, rainy, nasty ice."

"I know, and it should be illegal. I like snow," Margie declared.

Sara checked her watch. Lunchtime was over, or nearly so. She carried her tray to the dirty dish cart and headed back to the lab, knowing she had work waiting.

"Sara," Margie called, trotting after her. "Are you doing anything Saturday? I need to go shopping and I thought maybe we could go together. Grab lunch somewhere and generally hang out."

"Saturday? Nope, I don't have anything on my calendar. I'm not on call. Sounds like fun. What are we shopping for? Anything in particular?"

"Yes, a new food processor and gym shoes."

"Gym shoes. You mean sneakers?"

"White, canvas, tie. Simple attributes to simple shoes. Nothing fancy. And certainly not yoga shoes." She gave a stern look.

"Ah, demoting the yoga shoes to the back of the closet, are we?"

"I'd do more than demote them if I hadn't paid sixty bucks for Primo Zen Walkers. They hurt my toes. Besides, I need to get out in the world. I need to reconnect with my life. I can't continue to sit in my house and feel sorry for myself. What better way to find balance than a shopping trip, right?" She grinned.

"Absolutely. Shoes. Lunch. Girl talk. What a great way to spend a Saturday."

"You're sure I'm not crowding your Sara-time?"

"Nope. I'm looking forward to it. We haven't been shopping together in months."

"I know. Not since…" Margie smirked. "I swore I wouldn't do that. Why is it our worlds revolve around who we're dating? Everything is either before Gretchen or during Gretchen or after Gretchen. Why is that?" She closed her eyes and held up her hand. "No. Don't answer that. It doesn't deserve an answer. It was rhetorical."

"Good. Because I'm not sure I had an answer." She patted Margie's arm. "You'll get through this. I know you will. But I need to get back to work. Every doctor in town is ordering CBCs and sed rates."

"Which means?"

"Looking for secondary infection. Elevated white counts." Margie continued to stare at her curiously. "The flu, Margie."

"It's a little early for that, isn't it?"

"Not for the elderly and those with compromised immune systems. Which means, you take care of yourself, you hear me?" She wagged a finger at her.

"Yes, Mother," Margie said and curtsyed. "How about Bay Shores for lunch?"

"Oh, fish and chips. Yum." Sara was going to suggest burgers at Batch's but this was Margie's shopping trip. Her choice.

"But shoes first."

"Of course. Shoes first."

Sara held her breath that Naomi wouldn't call or show up for the rest of the week. The bouquet of flowers and the *Thinking of You* card were a reminder Naomi was pursuing their friendship to a deeper level even though she was on the road and hundreds of miles away. Sara enjoyed the roses and the attention they represented but did they come from the person of her dreams? Was Naomi's kiss the one she longed to taste? Sara still didn't know how she felt about her, and where she thought their relationship was going.

Maybe a shopping outing with Margie would help. Stewing over it wasn't providing any clarity. There had been a few fleeting moments when she considered dropping by Batch's and visiting with Jessie, but somehow that seemed counterproductive. Every time Sara tried to decide what to do, it was Jessie's face that came into focus. Not Naomi's. And that wasn't making this decision any easier. She didn't want to hurt Naomi's feelings. That was the last thing she wanted to do. Shopping, shoes and lunch. Maybe there was clarity mixed up in that somewhere.

* * *

"You're here early." Batch looked up from his newspaper as Jessie came into the bar. He looked like he had been there awhile. Several empty creamer cups lay on the table along with his coffee mug and a half-eaten bagel.

"Couldn't sleep." Jessie pulled a picture frame from a sack and sat down at the table next to him.

"What's that?" He had a curiosity for everything Jessie. And always had.

"The health department said you're legal now but this frame hanging on your wall let's everyone know you are." She opened the back of the frame and inserted a letter behind the glass. She checked to see if it was straight then turned it for him to see. "It's your CPR certification." She headed to the office to hang it, Batch following along behind. "Where do you want this?"

"Take down that picture of the bowling team. I ain't bowled in years and don't plan to."

She hung the certificate then stepped back for his approval.

"I know it's not fancy-looking but it's signed and it means you're certified."

He nodded and touched a corner as if it needed adjustment.

"Thanks, Kid."

"No problem." She didn't make eye contact with him. She knew better. Batch Singer didn't like to show emotion. He was pleased with her efforts and that was enough. His shoulder bump was his way of offering a hug of thanks.

"Did you hear Ron had a car accident? Son of a bitch on a motorcycle ran him off the road then took off."

"Is he okay?" Jessie's daughtering instinct engaged in spite of herself.

"He was in the hospital overnight. Broken nose. Some cuts. No concussion though."

"Good."

"Totaled his car."

"Insurance should cover it."

"They're giving him some crap about coverage and deductible."

"He has insurance, doesn't he?"

"Yep. He and I are on the same policy. It's cheaper to cover two cars under one premium. It's like a family plan."

"So, you pay his premium?" Jessie knew that sounded judgmental.

Batch smirked and headed back into the bar.

"We pay it," he grumbled. "I called my agent. He'll take care of it as soon as we bring him the paperwork."

Jessie stopped short of asking why Ron didn't take care of it himself. He was an adult. But the word *bring* suggested something else. Not *send*, but *bring*. Jessie hoped it didn't mean what she suspected.

"When is he coming?"

Batch looked back at her with surprise.

"In a couple days."

Jessie said nothing. There was nothing to say. Her father was returning to Ilwaco. She took a deep breath as she felt her blood pressure rise, a flutter of anxiety washing over her.

"He wrecked his car and the insurance ain't enough," Batch added. "He lost his job because he couldn't get to work."

"Did he lose his job first or after the accident?"

"I don't want to hear it. He's coming home. That's all there is to it."

Jessie rolled her eyes to the ceiling, unable to stop a tear from pooling in each one.

"Work with me here, Kid. He needs a damn job."

Jessie was too mad to discuss it further. She knew if she stayed she'd argue with him and that would benefit no one. Batch's mind was made up. She'd have to live with it, like she always did. She headed to the storeroom. There was always work to do in there that would hopefully take her mind off this thorn once again jabbing into her side. She spent two hours lifting and sorting boxes of liquor and restaurant supplies and mulling over this development. She could hiss and spit about it. Or she could just accept it as an opportunity. She might never get a better one. She walked back into Batch's office where he was revamping the work schedule. Her blood pressure was back to normal. Her anxiety and frustration diminished to an acceptable level.

"Take a look at this and see what you think," he said, penciling in another name. "I tried my best to balance the hours for you and Ron. It might be a little off but we can work it out."

"Take me off the schedule."

"I've got you working the evening shifts through Wednesday. He'll start on Thursday and work through next weekend. You'll make good money tonight. The game's on at seven." Batch didn't seem to hear her.

"I'll work through Wednesday, but that's it. I'm turning in my notice."

"Don't get your nose out of joint. I've got you down for four days that next week. I told him you two would have to share the hours."

"He can have them all. Every day, every shift. It's all his, with my blessing. I've got another offer."

He looked up at her with a worried scowl.

"What offer?"

"Las Vegas."

"What the hell does that mean?"

"It means I'm leaving Batch's and Ilwaco and trying my luck in Las Vegas."

He laughed out loud.

"You can't win at those damn crap tables and slot machines. Take my word for it, Kid. The only one who ever wins at those is the house. You'll blow through your money in twenty-four hours."

"I'm not going for the crap tables or slot machines. I'm going for the billiard tables."

"We've got billiard tables," he grumbled, motioning his thumb over his shoulder.

"I'm going for the tournaments. And the leagues. Nineball. Ten-ball. Snooker."

"Hey, we've got leagues and tournaments. You won the last one."

"That's chump change compared to the tournaments in Vegas. Remember last year that guy offered me two grand to promote Ballard Cues. All I had to do was win three tournaments in a year. He didn't care where. Professional players make almost as much from their sponsors as they do winning the big tournaments. And sooner or later, they all come through Vegas."

"Tell you what. You hang around and we'll up the prize money on our next tournament. How about two grand, winner take all? You're a damn good player. You'd win that."

Jessie pulled a chair up and sat down, staring into her grandfather's worried eyes.

"Batch, I want to do this. I *need* to do this. I'm good enough to win here in Ilwaco, sure. But I need to know if I'm good enough to be a pro. What if I am? This could be my chance to find out." She rested her hand on his arm. "I have to know."

"You're a hometown girl. You're not ready to do something like this."

"This isn't some hairbrained impulsive notion. I've been thinking about this for two years. I'm not asking for your help. All I want is your blessing. Please. Offer me your blessing."

"What about that woman? Sara? You like her. I know you do. For once you've found someone smart and mature."

"What makes you think there's anything between us. She's just a friend. That's all. Besides Sara deserves more than I can give her. She wants someone with roots and stability." Jessie chuckled. "And that's not me. We both know it's not. Anyway, she isn't available."

"Maybe you should think it over, Kid." He sounded desperate.

"I have. I'm a dues paying member of the Women's Professional Billiard Association. I know where there's an apartment within walking distance of the strip and I can bartend to keep food on the table while I get started. I've already made some contacts. Ballard Cues. Crest and Eagle Tables. There's even a company talking about instructional DVDs."

They sat staring at each other for a long moment.

"Your grandmother would try to talk you out of this. She'd say its foolishness. You know that."

"Yes, I know she would."

"She'd say you need to stay here. Save your money and build for a future."

"Probably."

He took an exasperated breath then stood, pushing himself up straight.

"But she's not here anymore. She's gone and this is up to me. I wish you weren't going, but I won't stand in your way." He extended his hand to Jessie. "You won't need it but I'll offer you my blessing anyway."

Jessie placed her hand in her grandfather's, his large hand callused and rough but warm around hers.

"Thank you." She couldn't resist and pulled him into a hug.

"You'll be back." He held her for a moment then pushed her away. "It's Saturday. We've got work to do. Meat truck ought to be here any time now. And there's a box of new menu cards on the bar. Let's get busy here." He shooed her out the door then closed it.

Jessie went about preparing for the bar to open, a broad grin on her face and a spring in her step as she thought about her plans. Fear didn't enter into it. Even her father's impending return wasn't enough to discourage her enthusiasm. She was going to Vegas. Sink or swim, she was going to Vegas.

* * *

Sara sat in her car, listening to an instructional CD on the integration of laboratory results while waiting for Margie. It was dry and boring and she found herself daydreaming as she listened to it. Margie was late. It wasn't like her to be late. Sara was beginning to think she misunderstood where they were to meet. It was a beautiful Saturday morning. Perfect shopping weather. No rain. No threatening clouds. No chilly autumn wind. Sara didn't need anything. She could have easily stayed home and done laundry or taken Gypsy for a walk on the beach. But like Margie, she needed an outing, to think, to reflect, and to just be. She tapped the power button and leaned her head back.

"Come on, Margie. Shoe shopping is waiting."

Her cell phone jingled in her pocket and she scrambled to retrieve it. She expected it to be Margie explaining her delay. But it wasn't. It was the hospital lab.

"Hello." She wasn't on-call, but she answered it anyway.

"Sara, this is Terry. The controls for the chemistry analyzer are not in range. Any suggestions?" The lab tech on the other end of the line sounded frantic.

"We just got a new shipment of control sera. They're in the back fridge. Use those," Sara said, catching a glimpse of Margie coming up the sidewalk. "Call me back if that doesn't work." She ended the call and climbed out of the car. It was a casual jeans and sweater kind of day and just what Margie was wearing. Sara too. Usually Sara was dressed in slacks and a long white lab coat that covered everything from her neck down. Today she felt liberated. Daring, even.

"I'm late, I know. I'm sorry. My test meter is giving me fits. It said I was six eighty-two." Margie greeted Sara with a hug.

"I hope that was wrong."

"Yes. I changed the batteries and it decided to cooperate. One seventy."

"Good. So, shoes or food processor first?"

"Shoes."

They started up the sidewalk, arm in arm, Margie plotting their stops. It was four blocks to the shoe store, plenty of time to catch up on hospital gossip. Sara could live without it, but Margie was a people person. She treated all her co-workers as friends and instantly became engaged in any problem they cared to share with her. Sara listened. She added appropriately placed sighs and nods as if she too was interested in John's mother's cancer treatment or Helen's son's DUI.

"Eight medium," Margie said to the clerk and pointed to the shoe on the shelf. "What do you want to try on?" She looked in Sara's direction. "How about those sparkly pumps with the six-inch stiletto heels?" She laughed.

"No, thanks." Sara didn't need shoes but why not try something on, just for fun. "Do you have the blue rain boots in seven wide?"

"Rain boots are boring. Necessary in Washington, but boring. Try on something else. Something weird."

"Weird? Why do I want to try on something weird? That sounds like something Edie would do. I'm not the glitter high-top sneaker type. But I do like the looks of these," she said, wandering down the row of dress boots.

"Try them on. Pretend you're related to Imelda Marcos."

They tried on shoes, boots, sneakers and even a pair of slippers. The clerk was very patient with them. She seemed to realize they were out for a day of fun. Margie bought her simple white gym shoes and an extra pair of laces. Sara bought two pairs of dress socks and a paisley scarf. But no shoes.

Leopold's department store was next. The annual fall appliance sale was in full swing. It meant Margie could afford a Cuisinart food processor for the price of a store brand.

"Don't you just love the word Cuisinart?" Margie said as they waited in line at the register. "It just sounds artistic. Like my chocolate cream-cheese brownies belong in the Louvre."

Sara had been staring absently across the store. Her mind was on Naomi. And on Jessie, although not intentionally.

"Hey, are you okay?" Margie asked.

"Sure. Why?" Sara brought her attention back from wherever it had wandered.

"Something's on your mind. I can tell." She squinted at her. "Some deep dark secret you're trying to hide."

"I have no deep dark secrets, other than I'm hungry. Is lunch next?"

"Yes, me too. And yes, lunch is definitely next." She handed the cashier her credit card. "Fish and chips at Bay Shores, or do you have someplace else in mind?"

"This is your choice, Margie. Wherever you want to go is fine with me."

"My first thought was Bay Shores. I love their fish, but we'd have to drive. I think I'd rather find someplace downtown within walking distance. Any suggestions? What's within two blocks?"

"Two blocks?" They stepped out onto the sidewalk with their bundles and looked both ways. Sara knew exactly what was in the next block but she hesitated to mention it. She didn't want to start another rumor.

"Hey, how about Batch's?" Margie nodded in that direction. "Isn't that where Jessie works? I heard they have pretty decent food for a bar. And it's just right there."

"Works for me," Sara said, taking one of Margie's packages. "And yes, they have great burgers."

"Then why didn't you suggest it?"

"This is Margie Snow's Saturday to reconnect and find balance. Not mine."

"I beg to differ. I still think there's something on your mind, Sara. I don't know what, but something. And I plan to worm it out of you before this day is over."

"You're going to be disappointed." Sara smiled and opened the door, then followed Margie inside. Batch's lunch crowd was noisy and the lights seemed brighter than they usual were. Sara assumed it had something to do with Saturday and a lunchtime atmosphere. Three waitresses shuffled between the tables, delivering food, soft drinks and pitchers of beer. A college football game aired silently on the three televisions above the bar. Jessie was busy filling drink orders but looked up and offered a smile of recognition. She pointed to the only available table and said something to a waitress.

"This way, ladies," the waitress said. "What can I get you to drink? It's on the house."

"Really? Just because it's football Saturday?" Margie asked over the roar of applause as a player scored a touchdown.

"Because Jessie said so." The waitress gave the table a quick wipe and set the menu cards in front of them.

Sara looked over at the bar. Jessie held up a green bottle of Perrier water and grinned. Sara nodded in agreement.

"I'll have half unsweetened iced tea and half lemonade," Margie said as she scanned down the menu.

"One Arnold Palmer. Do you know what you want to eat?"

"I'll have a hot dog with mustard and onions. No, wait. A Kosher dog with mustard, sauerkraut and grilled onions." Margie pointed to the card. "And a side of potato salad."

"And you, ma'am?" She turned to Sara.

"That sounds good, but I'll have a cheeseburger with mustard and pickles, no onions."

"Rabbit food?"

"Yes, please."

"And to drink?" The waitress scribbled on the pad, something Jimmy would understand, she assumed.

"I think Jessie knows."

As soon as the waitress left Margie leaned in and smiled.

"Jessie knows? And how does Jessie know what you like to drink? Huh, huh, huh?"

"When I was in here with Naomi I had sparkling water with cherries in it. It's good. You should try it."

"It is true then. You had a date with Naomi Upland, the sales rep."

"I don't know if I'd really call it a date. We met here for dinner. She was tired of hotel takeout. Did you know she has ridden in a hot air balloon?"

"And?"

"And she skis."

"I didn't mean what else does Naomi do. I meant how did the date go."

"Fine." Sara offered a noncommittal shrug. She wasn't ready to mention the second meeting or the kiss.

"Okay, what is it? You keep drifting off into la-la land with a little squinty look on your face. Is there some big decision you need to make and can't figure out what to do? Is it work? Is Dr. Lesterbrook pinching lab hours again? Is it Gypsy? Is she okay?"

"Work is fine. Busy but fine. Dr. Lesterbrook isn't doing anything strange. He's just being Dr. Lesterbrook. And Gypsy is great. She's busier than I am. They have her working alongside a new dog they're training. Lucille said the patients in the nursing home love it when Gypsy sits up on her hind legs during morning sing-along. Evidentially she loves "'You Are My Sunshine.'"

"Okay, it's not work and it's not the dog. What else?"

The waitress delivered their drinks, a tall glass with a lemon wedge on the rim for Margie and a stemmed goblet of fizzy water and three cherries for Sara. Sara took a sip. It was just as she remembered it. Jessie's smile was just as she remembered it too. In fact, Jessie seemed happier today. She laughed out loud at someone's joke, and chatted with the customers seated at the stools. She juggled a jigger, a lemon and a lime before filling the shot glass with tequila. She even seemed to be doing a cha-cha step as she waited for a pitcher to fill under the beer tap.

Margie fumbled something out of the small tote bag on her lap. After a minute she rezipped the bag and hung it on the back of her chair.

"Do you need to test?" Sara asked.

"Nope. All done. No need to test."

"You injected already?"

"Yeah." She took a sip from her glass then placed a napkin in her lap. "I can usually do it so no one sees anything. I've had lots of practice."

"If you didn't test how do you know how much you need?"

"I had five units ready. I'll test later and add a little more if I need it."

Laughter and applause erupted from several people at the bar. Jessie was juggling cocktail shakers, occasionally flipping one behind her back. She finished and took a bow.

"Jessie looks like she's having fun." Margie squeezed the lemon into the drink. "Is she still dating that rancher woman?"

"Becky? I don't think so."

"Probably just a summer fling. I wonder who she's seeing now." Margie leaned in and added, "I bet she never has to worry about being single. She's cute and self-confident and has a dynamite smile. She probably has charisma that glows in the dark."

"Glows in the dark? What the heck does that mean?"

"All I'm saying is Jessie, the bartender, is way better than Naomi, the sales rep."

Margie flashed a suggestive grin then blew bubbles in her drink. "I'm just saying."

Sara's mind was playing tricks on her again. The image of Jessie leaning her back against the bar and demonstrating how Naomi's kiss should have been performed was hard to ignore. It also had her repositioning herself in the chair.

"Wait." Margie gasped, almost choking on her drink. "That's it, isn't it? That thing that has you so preoccupied has something to do with Naomi. Am I right?" Margie offered a mischievous grin. "Have you slept with her yet? Was it great?"

"Margie!"

"Well, have you? How about Jessie? Have you slept with her? I hear you had her in the storeroom teaching her CPR," she teased.

"No, I have not slept with either one of them."

"What are you waiting for?" She giggled and took another sip. "I'm sorry. I'm just joking with you. But seriously, is something going on with you and Naomi?"

Sara ruffled the edge of her napkin around the base of her glass.

"She kissed me," she said finally.

"Did you kiss her back?"

"No. It came as a complete surprise. But it was pretty much a self-explanatory kiss. She covered all possibilities." Sara raised an eyebrow.

"Oh, *that* kind of kiss. Tongue and all. Do you think she meant it?"

"Oh, she meant it. That's the only thing I'm sure of. Her phone calls and texts suggest she really meant it. She's looking forward to seeing me again. I think she expects more than just a kiss, and soon. She said she'll be in town next week sometime."

"And you're not sure if you're ready yet?"

"I don't know if that's a scenario I'll ever be ready for with her."

"Naomi Upland is a catch, Sara. At least that's the word around the hospital. Her family has money. She loves to travel. And she's good looking. She even has a tattoo of a swan on her right hip. It's as big as your hand."

"My God, the hospital grapevine is more invasive than the FBI."

"All I'm saying is you could do worse."

"But maybe I could do better." Sara released a sigh. "Margie, when she kissed me I didn't feel anything. I take that back. If anything, I felt embarrassed."

"Why embarrassed? Where did this kiss take place? In the lab? In the car?"

"Here. We were standing right over there by the bar. She pulled me into this open-mouthed French with customers watching."

"Don't worry about it. That kind of thing happens in bars all the time."

"Not with me, it doesn't."

Margie looked over at the spot. Her eyes drifted over to where Jessie was filling a tray with drinks.

"Did Jessie see it?"

"I'm sure she did. It was hard to miss."

"Would it have been different if the kiss took place in private? Would you have enjoyed it then?"

"I don't know." Sara lowered her eyes. "I doubt it."

"Is there someone else, Sara?" Margie asked gently.

"No. Well, maybe. No, there's no one else." Sara couldn't keep herself from a quick glance toward the bar. "This is just about Naomi."

Somehow she knew it wasn't. She wanted to admit she had feelings for Jessie. Feelings she didn't understand. But before she could say anything Margie's cell phone chimed. She pulled it from her pocket and watched as it continued to ring.

"Aren't you answering it?" Sara asked.

Margie rolled her eyes up to Sara's and turned the phone so she could see Gretchen's name and picture on the screen.

"Why is she calling you?"

"She's upset about the way we ended things." The call went to voice mail.

"This isn't the first time she's contacted you then?"

"No. She sent two texts this morning. That's why I'm late. The meter wasn't the only reason." She watched the phone, as if expecting something more. Sure enough, within a minute an incoming text flashed on the screen. Sara could tell by the quiver in her chin that Margie still had feelings for Gretchen. "Here. You read it," she said, thrusting the phone at Sara.

"No, you read it. Answer it. Delete it. Reply to it. Whatever feels right for you." Sara squeezed her hand. "Or call her back." She stood and crossed to the bar, leaving Margie staring at her cell phone.

Jessie was busy loading beer bottles into the tank. Sara could wait for her to finish, but she was afraid she'd lose her nerve. She stood on the foot railing and leaned over the bar.

"Jessie?"

"Hi. You need another fizzy water?" she said with a quirky smile. "By the way, Batch says thanks for the CPR class."

"You're welcome but no, thank you. I don't need another drink. But I need to talk to you."

"Sure. What about?"

"Not now." Sara moved down the bar, making room for the waitress. "Can we talk sometime when there aren't so many people around?"

"Sure. Let me know when."

"Three Cokes. Seven and seven. JW rocks," the waitress said.

Sara turned back for the table, but Jessie reached across the bar and took her hand.

"Are you okay, Sara? Is everything all right?" She gazed into Sara's eyes with gentleness and concern.

"Yes. At least I think it will be."

"We don't open tomorrow until eleven. How early can you be here?"

"Is eight o'clock too early?"

"That works."

By the time Sara returned to the table Margie was reading the tiny screen on her test meter.

"Well, was I gone long enough?" she said, hitching her chair in to the table.

"Long enough for me to write four texts." Margie heaved an exasperated sigh.

"And?"

"And I didn't send any of them. Where's our food?"

CHAPTER FIFTEEN

Sunday morning was chilly with drizzly fog hanging over the coast. Sara scurried up the sidewalk and tapped on Batch's locked front door. She could see Jessie in the back, shooting pool. She waved and trotted to open up.

"Where's your umbrella?" she said, pulling her inside.

"In my front closet." Sara pushed some shape into her damp hair. "I thought it was just foggy."

Jessie was dressed in her normal bartending attire. Black jeans and a forest green polo shirt. She looked freshly washed and combed. She smelled good too. Not the greasy fried food and alcohol smell that permeated everything and everyone who spent the day in Batch's. Sara had opted for slacks and a sweater over a collared shirt. She left several outfits tossed on her bed, tried on and discounted. It wasn't like her to leave them in a heap but she didn't want to be late, not this morning. Jessie's welcoming smile made her glad she wasn't.

"Come on back." Jessie took her hand and led her to one of the high tables. "I've got a fresh pot of coffee and some apple fritters." The coffee and pastry were already set up, as if awaiting her arrival.

"Something smells good."

"I've got a pan of cinnamon rolls in the oven. You can have one of those, too, but it'll be a while." Jessie poured coffee in the cups as Sara took a seat.

"I didn't know you made cinnamon rolls."

"It's my grandmother's recipe. Simple enough even I can make them. It's sort of a Sunday tradition. I make a pan or two and sell them until they're gone."

"The domestic side of Jessie Singer."

"Yeah, well." Jessie shrugged. "But I don't sew or do flower arrangements," she said with a chuckle.

"Did I interrupt your practice?"

"Nope. I'm always practicing. Did you want another lesson?" She nodded toward the table.

"No, not today."

"Oh, yeah. That's Naomi's job, right?" Jessie took a big bite of the fritter.

"Probably not."

"I didn't want to show her up in front of you. There was no victory in that."

"That was very kind of you to allow her to win. I don't think she suspected what you were doing. Could you have sunk every one of those balls without missing any?"

Jessie cocked an eyebrow and took another bite.

"By the way," Sara started, pulling apart her fritter into a manageable bite. "Right before Naomi left, after the pool game—"

"Yeah, when she kissed you," Jessie inserted.

"Yes. So, it was that obvious?"

"Obvious? People in Oregon saw that kiss. People in China saw it," Jessie teased as Sara covered her face with her hands. "Every bathroom wall on the West Coast has graffiti that reads, 'For a great kiss, call Sara Patterson."

"Stop. It wasn't that bad."

"No, she didn't throw you down on the pool table and take you right there."

"You're having way too much fun at my expense, Jessica," Sara shot back.

"Okay, okay. I'm sorry. It was a good kiss, though. Right? It looked like it was. Hey, I was jealous."

"Jealous of what?"

"The woman can't shot pool worth crap, but she has great technique when it comes to kissing. She even picked an excellent partner." They each took a bite of fritter then a sip of coffee, neither of them offering to fill an awkward silence. "All kidding aside, she seems nice, Sara. I'm happy for you. I'm sorry I'll miss your next billiard lesson, if Naomi decides to give you another crack at it."

"What do you mean miss? Are you working a different shift?"

"Nope. I'm going to Las Vegas." She looked at Sara for a reaction.

"Las Vegas? Why there?" Sara gasped.

"I told you. I plan to become a professional pool player. And Vegas has more casinos and tournaments than any other place in the country. I won't have to motel-hop from town to town, following a regional tour."

"You had a tournament here."

"You sound like Batch. He thinks Ilwaco is enough too."

"But Las Vegas. That's a thousand miles away. Where will you live?"

"I've got an apartment lined up. It's small but it's furnished and just a few blocks from the strip. I think I've got a bartending job lined up too." The more Jessie explained her plans the more excited she seemed to become. "And I'm working on an endorsement deal. It's a small company. They make really high-end cues and cases. I met the CEO last year at a tournament in Seattle. If I can prove myself at the table, they might be interested in signing me to be their spokesperson."

"It sounds like you have this all planned out." Sara found it hard to sound enthusiastic. Jessie was moving several states away and seemed to have no regrets. "You're going to just leave your home and move?"

"I'll keep my garage apartment here in Ilwaco. I own it. My grandmother deeded it to me as a graduation present right before she passed. She and my grandfather bought the property years ago. They were going to remodel the old house and live in it, but it burned down before they got it finished. The detached garage survived so they gave it to me. I'll never sell it. Besides, I'd need a place to stay when I'm in town. You know, holidays, birthdays. I haven't missed one yet."

"I'm not thrilled you're going so far away, but I'm very proud of you, Jessie. You know what you want and you're going after it. I wish you every success. You deserve it."

"I bet your parents are proud of you too. College degree hanging on the wall. Working in a hospital. How could they not?"

"I'm not sure they know where I'm working." Sara forced a smile.

"Why? Don't you tell them what you're doing? Heck, Batch knows every move I make, sometimes before I even make it."

"I don't have that kind of relationship with my parents. You're very lucky."

"Where do they live? Way across the country?"

"They live in a little town in central Washington. Rock Island. I doubt you've heard of it. My dad works at the Rock Island Dam. It's the first hydroelectric dam to span the Columbia River."

"That's where you were raised? Rock Island, Washington?"

"Yes. Tiny little place. Rock Island's population is about eight hundred, give or take. Wenatchee is just seven miles down the road. It's about thirty-five thousand. That's where I went to high school. Go Panthers." She gave a cat-claw sign.

"It sounds like you were a big sports fan. Did your team win lots of Friday night football games?"

"A few. I know we won the Central Washington High School Knowledge Bowl my senior year."

"And you were on the team I bet."

"Yes. David Lebrowski was responsible for English and geography. Susan Jones was math and history. I covered the sciences. Chemistry, biology, physical science. I was a bookworm. And Jillian Berry was on the team because she looked good in a sweater and her dad was on the school board."

"You look good in a sweater yourself." Jessie grinned. "You were one of those really smart kids, weren't you? Your folks were probably very sorry when you left home and went off to college."

"Actually, they were relieved."

"Why? Because their little girl was going off to make something of herself?"

"Because their little girl was moving out of town so they didn't have to deal with her shameful behavior."

"I can't believe you ever did anything shameful. What did you do? Have sex under the bleachers on prom night?" Jessie joked as she refilled Sara's coffee cup.

"Nothing that tame. At least in their eyes, it wasn't. They probably would have preferred that. I was an only child. I lived a very sheltered life. A very conservative life. My parents never missed a Sunday church service. Even when you were sick you were expected to go. It was right after Christmas my senior year. I told my parents I was gay. I had been wrestling with my need to tell them for months." Sara swallowed hard, forcing back the lump in her throat. "They didn't approve. They said they'd never approve. And they would never support me as long as I chose that path. The day after my high school graduation I took my college scholarships and moved out. They assumed I was going off to live a life of sin and would go directly to hell." Sara lowered her eyes. "I sent them an invitation to my college graduation. They didn't reply."

"How can they do that? Families are supposed to love unconditionally. You're their daughter. You're a wonderful person. You're smart and dedicated and you're good with people. I've seen you. I've been one of those people. You helped me through a very tough time. For all I knew I had cancer. You don't deserve to be treated like that, Sara."

"Maybe not." Sara shrugged. "I think these past seventeen years have made me strong. I'm not sure that would have happened if I hadn't gone out on my own."

"Could you share a little of that strength with me? Sometimes I wish I was more settled. More practical, like you."

"Are you having second thoughts about moving to Las Vegas?"

"No. That's what worries me. I can't wait. I want to do this so bad I can taste it. Does that sound stupid?"

"It sounds like you've given this a lot of thought. And I say go for it."

"You're sure? Wow." Jessie heaved a sigh. "Thanks. I wanted to hear somebody tell me that. Batch offered his blessing but I don't think he meant it. He thinks I'm making a mistake. He doesn't understand."

"It's called a dream and we all have them. You'll never know if this is the right one for you unless you follow it, right?"

"Exactly."

"And whatshername, Stephie? She's okay with this?"

"Stephie is last summer's fruit," Jessie said, staring into her coffee cup.

"I'm so sorry, Jessie."

"I'm not. Being single is great. I don't need anyone's permission to do this. Sex only complicates things."

"You made love to her, but don't feel a connection?"

"I didn't say I made love to her. I said I had sex with her. There's a difference. She wasn't the one anyway."

"The one?"

"Yeah." She looked up at Sara cautiously. "You know, the forever after one. The one you can't get out of your thoughts. The one who takes your breath away."

"Oh, that one."

"I'll know her when I meet her." Jessie took a sip, her eyes on Sara over the rim of the cup.

Jessie's glance was like a gentle embrace, one that Sara could feel clear down to her soul.

"I'm sorry, Sara. I railroaded the conversation. What did you want to talk about?"

"We already did it." Sara pushed her coffee and pastry aside. Jessie was moving away. Disappointment would take her place and Sara could say nothing to stop her. "When are you leaving?"

"Thursday morning, early. I want to make it at least to Reno."

"Promise you'll drive carefully." Sara placed her hand on Jessie's.

"I promise."

"And you'll keep in touch."

"Of course. I'm not going to the moon. But you'll be busy. You won't have time to think about the bartender with the motor scooter."

"I'm sure I will. Has Batch found a replacement for you?"

"Yes. Or rather a replacement has found him. My father will be bartending. He'll be back in town in a couple days."

"That's perfect timing."

"You'd think so." Jessie carried their cups into the kitchen. Sara followed and watched as she pulled the huge pan of cinnamon rolls from the oven. "Make yourself useful, slick." Jessie handed Sara the pastry tube of icing and pointed for her to decorate the tops.

"Those smell *so* good." Sara took a deep delicious breath then began drizzling the frosting across the rolls. "Who's going to make the cinnamon rolls while you're in Las Vegas?"

"No one. I'm the only one who does it. Batch thinks I'm nuts for doing it but he always has a couple."

Sara finished then squeezed the last glob of frosting onto her finger and ate it.

"Wow, that is incredible."

Jessie cut one from the pan and divided it onto two napkins.

"This is the way they should be eaten. But be careful. They're very hot." She handed one of the napkins to Sara.

They each took a bite, moaning in unison.

"Oh, wow. This is better than that kiss, believe me." She bumped Jessie and snickered. "Probably better than sex too."

"Take that, Naomi," Jessie teased, giving a fist pump. "You know, I'm going to miss you, Sara."

"I'll miss you too," she said lightheartedly. She couldn't tell Jessie how much she would miss her or how much her feelings for her were growing. Jessie was ready to spread her wings and take flight. As painful as it was, Sara would say nothing to interrupt her pursuit of happiness. She knew what it was like to have a dream. And for all Sara knew, what she saw in Jessie's eyes and in her touch were just those of a friend. Nothing more.

CHAPTER SIXTEEN

Sara jogged the beach with an easy stride as foam-crested waves rolled ashore. Her sneakers patted a measured beat against the hard wet sand. It was a chilly day with a low-hanging fog bank just offshore. Perfect jogging weather. Pins and needles stung at her cheeks. Her hands were cold even inside her gloves. She could feel the cold water soaking through the back of her stretch pants, picked up by her shoes and flipped up onto her rear. But it was all part of the charm of running along the beach. That and driving home smelling like fish and seaweed.

"Come on, Gypsy," she called without missing a stride. "Quit chasing the seagulls. You know you can't catch them."

The dog jumped and pranced in and out of the surf, barking her territorial demands at the low-flying birds, and then ran to catch up with Sara.

It had been two months since Jessie had moved to Las Vegas. Christmas was just around the corner. Ilwaco's business district was decorated for the holidays with giant plastic wreaths and candy canes hung from light posts. Even the hospital had a tree in the lobby and tinsel hanging from the ceiling. Each day brought expectations Sara might hear from Jessie. A letter. A phone call. A text. Something to let her know how things were going. Would she be back for Christmas? Was the move everything she hoped it would be? The two texts Sara had sent came back as undeliverable.

She continued up the beach as she imagined all the possibilities of Jessie's reply. She was homesick and would return within the week. She was working on a dude ranch in the Nevada desert. She was a bartender where women and men alike stuffed twenty-dollar bills down her shirt. The scenario that seemed the hardest to reconcile was the one where Jessie was a successful professional pool player. It meant she was doing exactly what she dreamed of and would stay. Sara considered stopping by Batch's for a burger and to catch up on Jessie's whereabouts but she couldn't bring herself to go inside knowing Jessie wasn't there.

Naomi's invitations to dinner had become less frequent once Sara confessed they could be friends, but not lovers. Naomi still occasionally stopped by the lab with updates on her company's new products but she didn't linger. Sara was just as happy she didn't. It only made an awkward situation worse when Naomi's eyes drifted down Sara's lab coat and hesitated at her breasts.

Sara finished her run and returned home. She showered and gave Gypsy a bath before settling into her chair with a cup of hot tea and a novel she had swapped on the hospital's Trade-n-Share table. A love story set in the mountains. At least that's what the synopsis on the back cover led her to believe. She expected to be whisked away on a romantic adventure, but halfway through the first chapter she knew that wasn't happening.

"No wonder someone left this on the table." She tossed the book aside and went to start a load of whites. She didn't usually fight with anxiety, but she felt the need to go somewhere and do something. Where? She had no idea. But she dressed and drove into town. The store windows were full of decorations and gift ideas. Bows, garlands, twinkle lights and Christmas trees were everywhere.

Sara had already done her Christmas shopping. Gifts for Margie, Edie and Trevor—even a little something for Dr. Lesterbrook and Naomi had been wrapped and were under her small tabletop tree. Gypsy had the most presents. A new collar and leash, a doggie sweater, two bags of rawhide bones and a bright red ball, one Sara hoped Gypsy would learn to fetch. The presents were small but heartfelt. She sent her parents a Christmas card and, in spite of her inner voice telling her why bother, she included a fifty-dollar gift certificate to their favorite restaurant in Wenatchee. She wouldn't get a reply or a thank-you but that wasn't why she did it. She sent it because they were her parents. No other reason.

She drove into town and pulled into a parking spot near Mulberry's Bakery. She didn't need anything but went inside anyway. It smelled like gingerbread and almonds. Sara studied the choices, almost too many to decide. Gingerbread cookies, cannoli, cheesecake, pies, holiday decorated cupcakes, scones, muffins. Everything looked decadently scrumptious. She wasn't sure what she wanted or even why she'd stopped in until a little voice in her head took command.

"Can I help you, miss?"

"Yes, I'd like one of those." Sara pointed to the tray on the top shelf.

"A cinnamon roll?"

"Yes, please."

She headed up the sidewalk with her pastry sack in hand, happy she had bought it, but wondering why. She didn't normally indulge herself like that. The anticipation of the holidays was in the air. She strolled for several blocks, stopping to window shop as she hummed "Jingle Bells." Before she realized it she was staring in Batch's window at the evening dinner crowd.

"Why not?" she muttered and stepped inside. She stood waiting for her eyes to adjust to the dim lighting, dimmer than she remembered. It didn't smell like french fries. It smelled like holiday-scented potpourri and lots of it. Pine and clove and vanilla, all fighting for her senses. Jessie's father was behind the bar. He was wearing a Santa hat with a sprig of mistletoe pinned to the band over his forehead. He was laughing with two female customers as they sipped their drinks. The waitresses hustled back and forth between the tables and the bar. The pool tables in the back were all occupied. Sara knew Jessie wasn't there but she scanned the room anyway, just in case.

"Just one?" the waitress asked Sara after delivering drinks to a nearby table.

"Yes. A table please. How about that one?" She pointed to the table against the wall, furthest from the bar and the man who had taken Jessie's place.

"What can I get you?"

"Fizzy, I mean, a Perrier with two cherries and…" Sara scanned the menu card, looking for something different. "How about chips with spinach artichoke dip?"

She had had a big lunch and wasn't all that hungry but she wanted a reason to stay. The waitress brought her drink, served in a regular glass with a few ice cubes. It was sparkling water, but it wasn't the same. Jessie served it in a stemmed goblet. A small detail but it had made it special. She sipped her drink, but left the cherries in the bottom of the glass. Picking them out seemed unnecessarily crude. And Jessie wasn't there to drop another in the glass for good measure and tease her about drinking fizzy water.

"You need a refill, miss?" A gray-haired man stopped at the table with a pitcher of ice water in his hand, poised to fill her glass.

"No, thank you." She covered the glass with her hand. "This is fizzy water. I mean sparkling water."

"Fizzy water?" He laughed out loud. "My granddaughter calls it that. Perrier, right?"

"Granddaughter? Jessie Singer?"

"Yep. You know her?"

"Then you must be Batch Singer."

"I am." He grinned and extended his hand to her. "And you are?"

"I'm Sara Patterson. Yes, I know your granddaughter."

"Sara Patterson. I remember you. You're the napkin girl." He chuckled.

"What napkin girl? Oh, the message about the scooter. Yes, I'm the napkin girl."

Batch looked down at the table as if checking for another person.

"You here alone?" he asked, cocking an eyebrow.

"Yes. I was doing some shopping." She held up the pastry sack. "Have you heard from Jessie?" That sounded stupid. Of course he had. She was his granddaughter. "I mean how is she doing? Any tournament wins?"

"So, you know the story?" He grinned.

"I know she planned to move to Las Vegas, but that's as much as I know. I haven't heard from her."

"She's working at Caesar's Palace. I don't know where. They've got a butt-load of bars in that place. At least she's putting her bartending skills to use."

"She's happy then?" Sara felt the words catch in her throat. She had no claim on Jessie. Their connection was completely platonic, but the passing of time hadn't made it any easier. "Maybe I can catch up with her during the holidays. She'll be back in town for Christmas, won't she?"

"I doubt it. She's playing in a Vegas Mistletoe Nineball Tournament."

"But it's Christmas."

He shrugged and walked away, as if disgusted by the direction the conversation took.

Sara finished her drink and a few of the chips then left. She was disappointed at the news Jessie wouldn't be home for Christmas. Somehow she'd envisioned her return in time for eggnog and caroling. She hadn't thought past it.

* * *

Dr. Lesterbrook was in his office with the door closed when Sara arrived for work Monday morning. He usually exchanged greetings, however brief, before discussing plans for the day. But today he seemed preoccupied and didn't look up, or perhaps didn't see her. He sat hunched over his desk, unwrapping an alcohol prep. She knew he was a neat-freak but he seemed obsessed with cleaning the end of his middle finger. Before she could knock on the glass she noticed him open a lancet and stab his finger. She watched as he collected several drops of blood into a fingerstick vial. He marked the tube then spun in his chair and stood up. His eyes met Sara's and instantly narrowed, as if she had intruded on something very private. He opened the door, his stare still locked on her.

"Good morning, Dr. Lesterbrook," she said, swallowing her embarrassment at being caught watching.

"Good morning, Sara. They need you down in pediatrics." He clutched the tiny tube in his fist and rotated it back and forth as he headed across the lab toward the Coulter counter.

"Can I run that for you, Dr. Lesterbrook?"

"Nope, I've got it. You're needed elsewhere." He continued to rotate the tube and watched as she collected the paperwork and a phlebotomy tray from the shelf and walked out into the hall.

Sara entered the pediatric ward and stopped at the nurses station. The patient she needed to stick was a toddler. In her hurry to leave the lab and escape Dr. Lesterbrook's suspicious glare she hadn't checked the tray. She needed the small twenty-two gauge butterfly needles to draw from a toddler and she didn't have any. She returned to the lab, formulating the excuses and apologies he would undoubtedly demand. When she entered the lab Dr. Lesterbrook was dropping the fingerstick vial into the biohazard bucket and ripped the test results off the printer.

"Done already?" he asked, wadding the paper.

"No. I forgot to check the tray. I don't have any twenty-twos." She expected a scowl and a reprimand for wasting time. She got neither. He just nodded and went into his office. She collected what she needed and returned to the ward, ready to get her morning underway. Whatever tests Dr. Lesterbrook had run were none of her business. He was the same as any other patient. His medical records and test results were protected by law and were private. She was beginning to wonder if he was not only a neat-freak but a hypochondriac as well.

Edie and Trevor conducted their usual banter throughout the day, teasing each other about dating, clothes and who had the best electronic gadgets. Only once did Sara have to remind them of waiting samples. A courier delivered a cooler of samples, most marked as urgent, from local doctors' offices and clinics, which only added to the lab's congestion.

"Hey, hey, hey," Edie complained as the tractor-fed paper began twisting through the printer. "It's all chewed up. How am I supposed to read this?"

"Wait. Don't pull it," Sara said and hurried over to help. She released the crumpled paper and rethreaded it through the printer. "We'll have to reprint some of these pages." Before resetting the printer, she pulled several pages of the duplicate printout from the back capture tray, looking for the spot where the printer began creasing the paper. She noticed a computer time stamp that read eight fifty-three a.m. with an ID code of one-two-three. Normally the ID code for test results was a patient's initials. As Sara remembered, eight fifty-three was about the time she was on her way to pediatrics. And about the time Dr. Lesterbrook was in the lab with the fingerstick vial in his hand. The printout showed the test run was a white cell count, nothing unusual. A normal range for the white count was five to ten thousand. Usually elevated when a patient has an infection, this one was four thousand. Slightly low, but not significant. Many things could account for that reading. If this was Dr. Lesterbrook, perhaps he was one of those people who normally ran a slightly low white count. The test result that caught her eye was the lymphocyte percentage. Normal range was twenty-five to thirty-five. This was twenty percent. Again, not significant but it represented a slight decrease of what should be expected. Coupled with the low white cell count, this could be meaningful. Her scientific curiosity couldn't help wonder what he was looking for. She repaired the printer feed and went back to work, hoping to put it out of her mind. She promised herself not to ask him. She didn't want to raise his critical attitude toward her any higher than it already was.

"Merry Christmas, Sara." Margie leaned around the doorjam, grinning like one of Santa's elves. She was wearing a holiday vest and wreath pendant with flashing twinkle lights.

"Merry Christmas, Margie," Sara called from the drawing station where she was collecting a blood sample from an elderly woman.

"It's only Christmas Eve," the woman said. She kept her eyes on the wall poster as Sara slipped the needle in her arm.

"We make allowances for Margie. She's been saying that all week. She loves Christmas. How are you doing, Mrs. Vogel?"

"I'm doing okay." She took a deep breath then coughed.

"You've got the best med tech in western Washington, Mrs. Vogel," Margie said as she watched the procedure.

"There. All finished." Sara attached a Band-Aid then gave the woman's hand a reassuring pat. "Your doctor will have the test results this afternoon." She walked her out then returned to process the samples.

"I didn't see you at lunch. Did you change your lunch break?" Margie followed her across the lab.

"Is it lunchtime already?"

"Not now, it isn't. It was lunchtime an hour and a half ago."

"We've been swamped with walk-ins. I guess I hadn't noticed."

"I heard the senior center is closed until after the New Year because of the flu."

"You got your flu vaccine, didn't you?" Sara tossed a quick look in her direction.

"Yes. Back in September. I didn't want to take any chances."

"Good girl but you may want to think about a second one after the first of the year. This is going to be a long flu season."

"I know. I don't like it, but I know."

"You inject all the time. Don't tell me a little flu shot bothers you."

"Insulin doesn't make me sore for days afterward like the flu shot does."

"Better than having the flu." Sara patted Margie's face and gave her a motherly grin.

"You're taking care of yourself, too, aren't you? Don't let yourself get run down. You need plenty of rest and proper nutrition."

"Tell that to the constant stream of patients through our waiting room, every one of them with a fever and sore throat." She prepared the sample and inserted it into the analyzer.

"You're still meeting us for dinner tonight, aren't you?" Margie plugged in the tiny Christmas tree perched on the shelf above the lab table.

"Oh, Margie. I forgot all about that." Sara groaned. "I wish I could but I'm not sure how late I'll be working. Two of the second-shift techs are out with the flu so we've had to shuffle everyone's hours around. I even had to ask Lucille to babysit Gypsy for a few days."

"But it's Christmas Eve."

"I know. And I wish I could promise to meet you, but I can't. Three new patients were just admitted and as soon as they're settled in their rooms I'll need to see them. And we're waiting on doctor's orders for a patient in ICU."

"You're needed in ER, Sara," Dr. Lesterbrook said on his way through to his office. "No time for visiting."

"Good afternoon, Dr. Lesterbrook," Margie called after him, grinning innocently. As soon as he closed the door, she turned to Sara and said, "Does he do anything useful? Why doesn't he help stick people when you're busy?"

Sara scowled then headed for the ER. Margie was right. Why didn't Dr. Lesterbrook help? A question Sara had wondered for the past two weeks as the patient load increased and the staffing dwindled. She assumed he knew how. Even if he hadn't used his lab skills recently he should still have them. After all, he had a master's degree in clinical laboratory science and a PhD in microbiology. Either his position as laboratory manager gave him the impression he was above working in the trenches, or he had risen to the peak of his own ineptitude. Whichever it was, Sara seriously considered saying something about it. But not today. Not when she had work backed up and patients waiting. The hospital didn't need her fired during a crisis.

She collected a nasal swab and blood sample from the patient in ER. By the time she returned to the lab, two more walk-ins were seated in the waiting room, both of them coughing and blowing their noses.

"Where's Trevor?" she asked Dr. Lesterbrook. "I need him to draw on the patients in the waiting room."

"I sent him home. He was coughing and has a fever. I told you everyone was to have a flu shot. Why didn't he get one?"

"I thought he did. He said he did."

"He's sick, so obviously he didn't get it."

Sara was tempted to point out he could have one of the other viral strains not protected by the flu vaccine, but she didn't want to open a can of worms she couldn't close.

"Can't human resources find us some help? Vacation personnel? Or temps?"

"I already called. They're working on it. They're bringing in additional nursing staff from other hospitals. We'll have to make do for now. It's just you and Tom. Edie is down in the ward, but she'll be back shortly."

"Dr. Lesterbrook," she started, but his telephone rang and he answered it.

"Anything else, Sara?" he said, covering the receiver with his hand.

"No." She closed the door and went back to work, ashamed she hadn't been able to say what was on her mind. "Just do your job," she muttered to herself. "Keep your mouth shut and do your job."

She wasn't the only hospital employee working overtime. Even though flu vaccines had been made available to all employees, the staff had been hit just as hard as the general public. This year's vaccine had not proven very effective. Tom and Edie agreed to stay a few extra hours. Tom was single and didn't mind, welcoming the overtime. But Edie grumbled about it.

"It's Christmas Eve, Sara," Edie whined. "My mom is having the whole family over. She always makes homemade oyster stew and my grandmother makes Italian Christmas cake and yeast rolls. It's tradition."

"I'm sure it's wonderful, Edie. But we're shorthanded." Sara picked two tubes out of the centrifuge and inserted two more before going to prepare a slide.

It was after six o'clock and the twinkle lights outside the window shimmered in the evening mist. Sara remembered Christmas with her parents when she was a child. Fairy lights and family gatherings. Gifts and the house smelling like a candy store. Her mother was a good cook. Sara wished she had paid more attention. She well understood Edie's disappointment and even felt envious. Edie had a loving family waiting for her. Sara didn't.

"Edie." Sara took the tray from her hand. "You go on home. I can handle things here."

"Really? Are you sure?" She looked toward Dr. Lesterbrook's office, but it was empty. "What's he going to say?"

"Don't worry about it. I'll take care of it. You go on now."

"Thank you, Sara. Merry Christmas." She wrapped Sara in a bear hug. "And thank you for the sweater. I love it."

"Merry Christmas to you too."

"Call me if you need me, okay?" Edie said as she hurried out the door.

The telephone next to the computer rang. It was the ward nurse. A patient had just been admitted directly from a doctor's office, an elderly man in respiratory distress with a low-grade fever, another flu patient who needed a workup right away. Sara ignored the urge to call Edie back to cover one more patient. She left Tom in the blood bank room, typing and cross-matching for an accident victim. She headed into the ward as she sucked on a Lifesaver. It would stave off hunger pangs since she probably wasn't getting dinner any time soon.

"Bed two," the nurse said, pointing to the patient behind the white curtain, pulled for privacy.

"Hello," she said, peeking around the curtain. Sara had scanned the printout for the tests ordered but she hadn't looked at the patient's name. "Batch?"

He looked pale, tired and old. He had dark circles around his eyes and was barking a weak but husky cough. Oxygen tubing ran from the wall to his nose. He looked up at her but didn't seem to recognize her.

"Batch, do you remember me? I'm Sara Patterson."

He didn't reply.

"I'm the napkin girl." Sara stood at his bedside, smiling down at him. She took his hand. It was warm, warmer than it should be. He indeed had a temperature.

"I remember," he finally said, but it was an effort.

"You're not feeling very well, are you?"

He shook his head.

"Well, you've come to the right place. We're going to get you fixed up and back on your feet. The doctor has ordered some tests so he'll know what kind of medicine you need. I'm going to take a little blood sample and a nasal swab. Is that okay with you?" She set the tray on his bedside table and began collecting what she needed.

"You do that stuff?"

"Yes," she said, securing the tourniquet around his arm. "Didn't Jessie tell you?"

"She said something about the hospital. I don't remember." He closed his eyes, his breathing labored.

"It doesn't matter. You rest while I do this."

He didn't flinch when she slipped the needle in his vein and drew the sample.

"I need to collect a nasal swab," she said gently.

He opened his eyes and nodded, allowing her to remove the oxygen tube and swab his nose.

"All finished," she said, adjusting the tubing and straightening his sheet. She wanted to ask if Jessie knew he was in the hospital, but it wasn't her place to ask. "Rest, Batch. Just rest. You'll feel better soon."

She was right. Batch had the flu, which lowered his defenses, allowing a bacterial infection to get a foothold. Batch had pneumonia. It was after ten when she entered the last result into the computer. She was famished. She had missed lunch and dinner. Two granola bars and a bag of nuts had her stomach growling like a rabid dog.

She stood at the row of vending machines just inside the cafeteria doors, considering the choices. Several of the slots were empty.

"Microwave macaroni and cheese. Cheetos. Peanut butter crackers. Jerky. Isn't there anything healthy in here? This is a hospital after all," she mumbled to herself.

"Pretzels and a box of raisins are about as healthy as you'll find." Dr. Lesterbrook said, standing behind her. She hadn't heard him come in and jumped at the sound of his voice. "The apples, bananas and V8 were the first things sold out." He dropped quarters in the slot and pushed the button for pretzels. "At least these are baked, not fried."

"Dr. Lesterbrook? I didn't know you were still here."

"Meetings with personnel. We're trying to find extra help. By the way, have you seen Edie?"

"I sent her home." Sara dropped coins into the machine and selected pretzels as well.

He scowled suspiciously.

"We don't need another sick tech in the lab," she added. She wondered if he was going to ask how sick Edie was. Her statement wasn't a lie: They didn't need sick employees spreading germs around the lab. But saying Edie was sick, would be a lie. But he seemed to accept Sara's explanation.

"Are we caught up for now?" he asked, slipping the unopened bag of pretzels into his lab coat pocket.

"Yes, for now. I heard the nursing home may be transferring a couple of patients sometime overnight."

"Pneumonia?"

"Probably."

Dr. Lesterbrook took a deep breath and shook his head.

"It's tough for the elderly. They can't fight it off. I hate to say it, but we're probably going to lose some of them." It was the first time Sara had ever heard him express compassion.

"I hope not," Sara said.

"Opportunistic infections claim more lives than the flu, Sara. Statistics don't lie." Dr. Lesterbrook strode out of the cafeteria, his hands in his pockets.

It was nearly midnight when the lab seemed quiet enough that Sara could take a break. She headed into the ward to check on Batch. He was sleeping as she tiptoed into his room. His breathing was strained in spite of the oxygen. Two bags hung from an IV pole. Their tubing was threaded through an infusion pump with its methodical beep, feeding the antibiotic into his vein. A catheter bag hung on the side of the bed. Sara assumed he was too weak to get out of bed or even call for a bedpan. He looked pale, paler than earlier. And that worried her.

"Has Mr. Singer had any visitors?" she asked the nurse making her rounds.

"Not that I've seen but they're being pretty strict with the visiting hours." She took Batch's vitals and checked his IV before turning out the overhead light and leaving the room.

Sara pulled up a chair next to his bed. He didn't know she was there, but it didn't matter. She wanted to be with him. She didn't want him to be alone. And perhaps she didn't either.

"Merry Christmas, Batch," she whispered, gently stroking his fingers as he slept. Outside the window a chilly mist had changed to a gentle snow. It didn't snow in Ilwaco. At least it didn't very often. But this Christmas it was. A beautiful snow. Sara lay her cheek against his hand and closed her eyes, listening to the click of the IV pump and the wheeze of his breathing. "Merry Christmas, Jessie."

Just after one a.m. Dr. Lesterbrook released Sara to go home and get some sleep. It was nearly two when she finally crawled into bed. She was exhausted but guilty she hadn't stayed a while longer with Batch. For a moment she considered contacting Jessie in Las Vegas to make sure she knew about her grandfather, but it was inappropriate for her to do that. Batch's doctor was responsible for initiating contact with next of kin. Sara couldn't stay awake long enough to place the call anyway.

CHAPTER SEVENTEEN

Jessie stretched out over the table, her pubic bone pressed hard against the railing.

"Corner pocket," she said, her eyes fixed and narrowed. She heard her opponent clear her throat, an old trick pool players used. But she had heard worse. Men hacking a wad of spit just as she was ready to shoot, or pacing the far side of the table as a distraction. Jessie had learned to tune it out, tune everything out. Noise, light, movement. Anything that stood between her and complete concentration. And this woman with the 1980s mullet haircut and the stench of cigarette breath was just another inconvenience. Jessie tuned her out and stroked the cue ball. The nine dropped into the corner. The game and match were hers. Jessie had her first quarterfinal victory. The woman offered a sweaty handshake then disappeared into the crowd.

"Ms. Singer, your next match will be at table sixteen and it starts at one thirty. We don't know who your opponent will be yet. They haven't finished their match." The tournament official wrote Jessie's name into the bracket. "You've got a couple hours if you want to get a bite to eat." She handed Jessie a meal coupon. "The casino is serving a Christmas brunch in the Bacchanal Buffet."

Jessie hadn't eaten there but she had served drinks in their bar. It was good but pricey. Caesar's Palace had fifteen restaurants and eight bars. She had served cocktails in six of them. But today was Christmas and, although it was a busy day for casinos and one where she could have made good tips, she made a point not to be working. This was her first big tournament. The Women's Mistletoe Classic.

Normally she spent Christmas with Batch, sometimes Ron as well. It was family time. But this year it was Jessie time. Tournament time. She still wanted to hear Batch's voice. She needed to hear it. The melancholy strains of "White Christmas" had her thinking of him and home and strangely, of Sara Patterson. She'd like to hear her voice as well. She pulled out her new cell phone and tapped in Batch's number. She didn't like this phone as well but it was an inexpensive replacement for the one stolen from her locker. She wondered how many messages she had missed and from whom. The call went directly to Batch's voice mail, the same as it had done yesterday. She tried the number at the bar. No one answered. She considered calling her father but went to eat instead. She filled a plate from the lavish choices. Some things she didn't recognize but tried them anyway and found a table. Halfway through her meal she tried Batch's number again. He should be either at home, burning toast and bacon for a late breakfast, or at the bar, eating a stale bagel and reading the newspaper.

"Answer the damn phone, old man," she said. "It's Christmas already."

Even if he was with Ron, he should answer his phone. He'd grumble and cuss about her being in Vegas, but he'd be glad to hear from her. She knew he would.

"What can I get you to drink, ma'am?" a polite waiter asked. "Coffee? Iced tea?"

"Perrier please." She smiled up at him. "With a cherry."

Jessie opened her wallet and took out a folded napkin. She smoothed it out on the table and stared at it a moment. Sara had written her name and number so legibly it looked like she had spent hours doing it, not just hastily scribbled. Jessie opened and closed her phone with her thumb as she stared at the phone number and Sara's message, "In case you reconsider." She finally put the napkin back in her wallet and finished her meal. She left a generous tip and returned to the conference room. Sara was probably with her friends or with Naomi, celebrating Christmas the way normal people do. Not crouched over a pool table, hoping to win a nineball tournament in Sin City.

The quarterfinal round meant it took seven games, not just five, to win the match and advance. It meant concentration had to be absolute. A blink, a stumble, a misread and her opponent could take the match. Jessie introduced herself to her opponent, a forty-something woman with biker tattoos and a weathered smile. But she had a reputation for being deadly accurate. She won the first game, sinking the nineball with the two. She won the second game when Jessie failed to sink anything on the break. The woman almost robotically moved around the table and dropped every ball. She had an explosive break, scattering the balls and dropping two. Jessie missed an easy shot on the next break, sending the woman back to the table. Before Jessie knew what happened she was down four games to nothing.

Jessie took a deep breath as she leaned against the stool. She hadn't played this badly since high school. She tried to remember what Batch had told her. Play smart. Play your game. Not theirs. At this level, players didn't go back and forth, trading shots, missing and hoping for another chance. If Jessie gave this woman the opportunity, she'd run the table on every game. Amazingly, the woman didn't leave herself a shot on the break. Jessie circled the table as she chalked her cue, calculating how much room she had. Could she sneak the cue ball behind the eight and not touch it but still tap the one? It was too close. She couldn't take a chance. But she wasn't going to let the woman run the table on her again.

Jessie circled again then leaned over the shot. She had one and only one chance. The table was hers if she could sink the one-ball. She aimed the cue ball in the opposite direction, bouncing it off three rails. She struck it hard but would it be hard enough? She watched, leaning to the side, as if her body language would help. The cue ball kissed the yellow ball and dropped it into the pocket. Jessie ran the rest of the table, winning the game. She finally found her concentration, blocking out everything and everyone, enough that she won the next six games and advanced to the semifinals. Finally she had done it. She would cash in her first Las Vegas tournament. Even if she didn't win, she would have a good check. But she wanted that trophy. She wanted to win. She had to know if she could do it.

She had two hours before her next match. Plenty of time to call Batch. And time to decide if she should call Sara too. But Batch still wasn't answering his phones. That wasn't like him. Jessie paced around the hotel, arguing with herself. Finally she tapped in Ron's phone number.

"Hey, Kid," he said with a cheerful voice.

Jessie didn't like him to call her Kid. That was what Batch called her. It was reserved for him and only him.

"Merry Christmas," she said. "Where's Batch? I've been trying to call him and he doesn't answer either phone. Is he there with you?"

"He's in the hospital. Didn't you hear? He's got pneumonia."

"What?" she demanded loud enough to turn heads in the lobby. "No, I didn't hear. When did this happen?"

"He's had the flu. Got all run down. You know how he gets. He wouldn't listen. I told him to take it easy. He started coughing real bad. The doctor put him in the hospital yesterday."

"How is he? What are they doing for him? Antibiotics?"

"I don't know," he argued. "I'm no damn doctor."

"What room is he in?"

"I don't remember."

"Have you been up to see him today?"

"Yes." But Jessie wasn't sure she believed him.

"Call me tonight after you go up there," Jessie said. "I want to know how he is."

"Okay, but I've got my hands full keeping the bar open."

"Then close it for a couple days. Put a sign in the window and close it."

"I told him I'd keep it open. And I am. He's sick. He ain't dead."

If Jessie was there, face-to-face with him, this was the remark that would bring her out of her seat. But she wasn't there. Maybe Ron was right. Maybe Batch needed him to keep the bar open and revenue coming in. It wasn't her decision to make. She ended the call with her father, neither of them exchanging words of endearment. But they seldom did.

Jessie placed a call to the hospital and asked for Batch's room but no one answered. She asked for the nurses station. No one answered there either. The switchboard operator explained the hospital was shortstaffed and very busy because of the flu and she should try again later. Jessie placed another call.

"Merry Christmas, Sara," she said to the voice on the other end of the line.

"Jessie, Merry Christmas." Sara sounded happy. "Where are you?"

"Vegas. Sara, my dad said Batch is in the hospital with pneumonia. I tried to call the nurses station but no one answered."

"The hospital is very busy right now. The flu is particularly rough this year. We're all working overtime. The nurses are probably with patients."

"What are they doing for him? How do I find out?"

"I saw him last night. He's resting comfortably and he's getting excellent care. Try not to worry, Jessie."

"Will you tell him I tried to call his room? Tell him Merry Christmas for me, will you, Sara? And yes, I'm worried. He's had pneumonia before."

"I'll tell him. I promise. I'm sorry, Jessie, but I'm at work and right in the middle of something I need to finish. Can we talk later?"

"Sure. And thanks, Sara. I shouldn't have bothered you but I didn't know who else to call."

"I'm very glad you did. I'm exactly the right person. I only wish I knew more."

Jessie closed her phone and walked back into the conference room to check on her next match but her heart wasn't in it. She wanted to be in Ilwaco at her grandfather's bedside. That's where she belonged. She stared at the bracket board. J. Singer was written on the line marked semifinal. She wished Batch was there to see it. He'd be proud. Gruff and sarcastic to hide his feelings, but proud. He'd slap her on the back and tease her about the games she had lost.

"What happens if I forfeit my next match?" she found herself asking the tournament official.

"You'd lose," she said with a chuckle, as if she couldn't imagine anyone coming that close to winning then quitting.

"Would I collect fourth-place money?"

"Yes, but it won't be near as much."

Jessie tossed her registration paper and ID on the table.

"Then do it. I'm out."

"Why?" the woman demanded with a critical set to her jaw.

"I have someplace else I need to be."

CHAPTER EIGHTEEN

"Merry Christmas, Sally," Sara said to the woman spooning gravy over her mashed potatoes.

"Merry Christmas. I love your bright red blouse. You look very festive. Would you like cranberry sauce?"

"Yes, please. And thank you. The turkey smells good."

"I'll give you a little extra. The cafeteria is about to close."

Two more patients were admitted Christmas morning, filling the hospital to capacity. Dr. Lesterbrook was able to convince a retired lab tech to work a few hours a day to relieve some of the pressure, although he still didn't get involved himself. Sara was working her seventh day in a row and all of them well past her normal eight hours. She didn't mind today. She wanted to be at the hospital to check on Batch, and Jessie's phone call had made her mission seem even more imperative.

Sara sat alone at the employee table, eating her Christmas dinner, when her phone rang. It was Jessie.

"Hello again," Sara said brightly. "I'm really sorry I had to cut our conversation short. I had a woman in the chair waiting to be drawn."

"No problem. I would have been disappointed in you had you not. Your patients come first."

Sara heard what sounded like announcements over a loudspeaker in the background.

"What's that? Casino announcements? By the way, how did you do in the tournament?"

"How did you know about that?"

"Batch told me. He said it was the Mistletoe Classic or something like that. Did you win?"

"I came in fourth."

"Wow, that's great. He'll be very proud when he hears."

"I hope so."

"Did I just hear someone say flight boarding?"

"Yes. I'm at the airport. I'll be in Portland just after midnight."

"You're coming home!" Sara said with a gasp.

"Yes. I wanted to get there this evening but I couldn't get a nonstop. Tell Batch I'll try to be in Ilwaco by breakfast."

"How are you getting here from the airport?"

"Taxi, I guess. There's a bus, but I'm not sure when it runs or where."

"That'll cost you a fortune. I'll pick you up, Jessie. What time is your flight?"

"You don't have to do that. That's not why I called."

"I want to. What time?"

"United flight forty-fourteen, arrives at twelve sixteen, just after midnight. Are you sure about this? That's awfully late."

"Absolutely, I am. I'll be in the cell phone parking lot. Call me when you touch down."

"Thank you, Sara. I really appreciate this."

"I'm glad you're coming home. Christmas wouldn't be the same without you. Batch will be happy to see you, I'm sure."

"They're calling my flight. I better go. See you later. Thanks again."

Sara suddenly wasn't hungry. Her stomach was doing flip-flops. Jessie was coming home. The tall woman with the radiant smile and sparkling eyes was returning to Ilwaco. Sara knew she was coming home to see her grandfather in the hospital. But it was hard for her not to imagine Jessie stepping off the plane with thoughts of seeing her as well.

Sara set up a last-minute throat culture before heading home to shower and change. She had worked a twelve-hour shift, the third in as many days. Thank heavens Lucille had Gypsy. She should have been exhausted. But she had a childish glee as she headed across the Lewis and Clark Bridge to Astoria then east on Highway 30. The traffic was light and the skies had cleared as she crossed the bridge at Portland and wound her way into the airport parking lot. She wanted to be there in plenty of time so Jessie wouldn't have to wait, but it was already after midnight when she pulled into a parking spot.

Twelve sixteen came and went with no call from Jessie. So did twelve thirty and twelve forty-five. Sara leaned her head back against the headrest, the long day finally catching up with her. She opened her eyes and noticed the dashboard clock said one twenty. She checked her cell phone. No messages. No missed calls. She wasn't angry at the delay. She was worried. What if something happened to Jessie? What if she missed her connection? What if the flight had mechanical trouble and had to turn back? She was working herself up to a disastrous imaginary scenario when her phone rang. It was Jessie.

"Hello," she gasped with relief.

"Did you give up on me and go home?" She chuckled.

"No. I'm here. Where are you?"

"I'm standing outside baggage claim, lower level, middle door."

"I'll be right there. Watch for a silver Honda Civic."

As soon as Sara rounded the corner into the terminal she could see Jessie standing on the sidewalk, a small suitcase in her hand. She was dressed in black slacks and a jacket. A few stray curls hung over her forehead. She looked tired, Sara thought. Jessie tossed her bag in the backseat and climbed in, a grin growing on her face.

"Merry day-after-Christmas," she said with a sparkle in her eye. "I really appreciate you doing this for me."

"It's what friends do." Sara reached over and gave her a hug. "How was your flight?" She pulled out into traffic and followed the signs to I-5 North.

"Delayed out of Vegas. Sorry I couldn't let you know. And I'm sorry you had to wait so long. How's Batch?" Jessie's face tightened.

"I checked on him before I left the hospital tonight. He was sleeping. The nurse said he ate a little soup this afternoon."

"I need to see him," she said with a catch in her throat.

"I know you do, Jessie." Sara took her hand and held it, resting it on the console between them. "He's going to be okay."

"I hope so." Jessie's eyes turned to the window, but she held tight to Sara's hand. "I bet he's been sick for days but too stubborn to go to the doctor. The last time he had pneumonia it almost killed him."

They rode along in silence. Jessie's furrowed brow and rippling jaw muscles spoke volumes about where her mind was. Sara continued to hold her hand, squeezing it gently when she noticed Jessie's breath quicken.

"Do you mind if I stop for a minute?" Sara said, pulling into a twenty-four-hour convenience store. "I need a cup of coffee before I doze off."

"Do you want me to drive?"

"Yes, please. I'm not used to driving at three in the morning."

Sara knew Jessie wanted to get to Ilwaco as soon as possible. She didn't want to watch her walk around a convenience store while she sipped coffee to wake up. Jessie climbed into the driver's seat and pulled back onto the highway.

"By the way, Jessie. Because of the flu epidemic, the hospital is being very strict about the visiting hours. They won't let you in until ten o'clock."

"You're kidding. I'm his next of kin."

"I know." Sara patted her hand. "We'll see what we can do."

Before Sara pulled her hand away, Jessie took it, once again intertwining their fingers. It was a comforting feeling. If Jessie needed the security of her hand, Sara would graciously oblige.

She leaned her head back and closed her eyes as Jessie steered them for home, content to have another hour with Jessie's hand in hers.

It seemed like only a few minutes later when Sara opened her eyes to downtown Ilwaco. There was no traffic in the predawn hours. The streetlights shone over the deserted sidewalks. The town's Christmas decorations suspended from lampposts were dark. Parking spaces, crowded just two days ago with Christmas Eve shoppers, were all empty. Jessie still cradled Sara's hand in hers, resting on the center console.

"That was a quick trip," Sara said then yawned.

Jessie smiled over at her.

"If you say so." She turned into a driveway, pointing the headlights at a two-story garage. "Will you be able to drive yourself home?"

"Sure. Can I give you a ride in the morning?" Sara realized what she said and laughed. "Okay, it's already morning. I meant later in the morning. I don't have to be in until nine. I can stop by and pick you up. Maybe we can get you in to see Batch a little early."

"Thanks, but I think I have a ride," Jessie said as she wrestled her suitcase out of the backseat.

"If you change your mind give me a call."

Sara was too tired for conversation pleasantries and Jessie seemed to know it.

"Thanks again, Sara. Goodnight."

Sara struggled to stay awake as she drove across town. Once home, she peeled back the covers and climbed into bed for a few precious hours of sleep. She hadn't moved a muscle when her alarm sounded. She showered and headed back to the hospital. She was thankful Dr. Lesterbrook had scheduled her for nine o'clock instead of seven. She wasn't sure she could have functioned accurately on two hours' sleep. She promised herself a full eight hours of uninterrupted sleep once the flu crisis was over and the work schedules were back to normal. She might even get to use a few of her vacation days. For now she'd grab a nap when she could and do her best to carry on.

She stood at the computer, reading orders from the ward as she pulled on her lab coat.

"Ms. Patterson," Dr. Lesterbrook bellowed from his office, his door standing open.

"Good morning, Dr. Lesterbrook," she said cheerfully, adjusting her collar.

"You're two hours late," He glared up at her. "We've got doctors on rounds waiting for test results. ER needs blood chemistries and a sed rate on a transfer patient. And ICU is waiting for two units of whole blood. I thought you were more responsible than this."

Sara felt her stomach drop.

"Dr. Lesterbrook, I was scheduled to come in at nine. Not seven. You filled out the schedule." Sara's juvenile insecurity had her wondering if she had misread the schedule even though she had checked it both online and the one taped to the wall before she left last night.

"You're wrong. Why would I schedule you for nine o'clock when we're shorthanded?"

"I have no idea. I was not asked to fill out the schedule," she snapped defensively. She snatched the printout off the wall and thrust it at him. It had been crossed out and scribbled over so many times it looked like a child's doodling. "Right here." She stabbed her finger at the initials wedged between two names with red lines drawn through them. "S.P. Nine a.m. With all due respect, Dr. Lesterbrook, I'm not wrong. I was here fourteen hours yesterday. I know when I was to be here today."

"Are you sure that's S.P.? Looks more like G.D." He still sounded combative.

"Who is G.D.? We don't have anyone with those initials."

He squinted at the paper as if he wore glasses but didn't have them on.

"You know we've got an emergency here in the hospital, Ms. Patterson. I need to be able to count on you to step up."

"Yes sir. I'm happy to do whatever I'm asked to do. You know that. That's why I came in at nine. You asked me to. And I assume I'm working late again tonight."

"We'll consider this a miscommunication and move on." He handed her the paper and turned back for his desk. "If you have time perhaps you should generate a new schedule printout."

"Yes sir." She taped the schedule to the wall and headed to the ER.

"Hey," Margie called, hurrying to catch up with her. She had a stack of folders under her arm. "How was your Christmas?"

"Busy."

"How late did you work?"

"You don't want to know." Sara was still trying to quell her anger with Dr. Lesterbrook. She was in the right, but that didn't make it any easier to deal with.

"I drove by your house last night. I was going to drag you out for a little holiday merriment, but you weren't home. And you weren't here either. So where were you? Who were you out with?" Margie giggled.

"I wasn't out with anybody. I had to run down to the Portland airport for a midnight arrival."

"Wow, Christmas arrival. Must have been important."

"It was Jessie Singer. Her grandfather is in the hospital."

"We'll talk about it later, okay? I want to know every detail." Margie grinned, then turned and hurried down the hall.

Sara threw herself into her work, more determined than ever to show Dr. Lesterbrook she was capable. She wanted to know how Batch was doing and if Jessie had found a ride to the hospital, but she barely had time for a quick trip to the ladies' room. As soon as one patient was discharged from the hospital another was processed through admissions.

Dr. Lesterbrook took over duties such as refilling solution bottles and running quality control, more supervisory than hands-on patient care, but at least he was out of his office and helping. Nothing more was said about the scheduling mix-up. As soon as Sara had a few spare minutes she printed out a new roster and taped it prominently for all to see.

"I'll be down the hall if anyone needs me," Sara announced, and retrieved a phlebotomy tray from the shelf.

"Are you going to room one-eighteen?" Dr. Lesterbrook asked, passing her in the doorway.

"Yes, Mrs. Rollins."

"FYI, she may be on her way to X-ray. You may have to wait."

Sara expected him to suggest she wait for word that Mrs. Rollins was back in her room instead of wasting time walking down there, but he didn't. He stepped out of the way, nodding her through the door. Just as she turned the corner at the nurses station an orderly from X-ray was pushing a female patient in a wheelchair out of room one-eighteen. Dr. Lesterbrook was right. She'd have to wait or return to the lab. Or she could use the twenty minutes to check on Batch, something she hadn't had time to do yet today. Sara could hear the rhythmic beeping of the IV pump as she entered his room. The curtain was drawn around his bed and the light was out. She assumed he was alone and sleeping when she stepped around the curtain.

"Hi," Jessie said quietly from a chair next to Batch's bed. She looked like she had been napping. Her head was back against the cushion and her arm resting on his bed. Batch was asleep.

"How is he doing?" Sara asked, reading the label on the IV bags then checking the oxygen sensor clipped to his finger. Eighty-six percent. Exactly what she'd expect from a pneumonia patient.

"Tired. He ate some oatmeal this morning and some chicken broth a little while ago. The doctor said the flu made his system weak and he couldn't fight off the pneumonia. Pneumo-something or other."

"Pneumococcal pneumonia. It's a bacterial infection. That's why the heavy-duty antibiotics." She smoothed her hand down the sheet. "Rest is the best thing for him."

"That's what the doctor said. That's why the…" Jessie nodded toward the catheter bag attached to the bottom rung of the bed. "They don't want him to get up if he doesn't have to. He's got a bad knee and they're afraid he'll fall."

"How long have you been here?"

"Since six," Jessie confessed sheepishly.

"Six o'clock this morning? And they let you in?"

"The nurse was too busy to say much. I told her I'd take care of feeding him. Besides, I think I know her from the bar. I may have had a date with her a couple years ago. She drinks rum and Diet Coke." She grinned. "It pays to know people." Jessie sat up and looked over at Batch, a worried look on her face.

"You've been here all day?"

"Yep. You were right. The food in the cafeteria isn't too bad. I had linguini for lunch."

Sara didn't ask how she got to the hospital. She didn't want to know which of her girlfriends was taxiing her around town.

"Sara, Mrs. Rollins is back in her room," the nurse said from the doorway.

"Thank you, Diane. I'll be right there." She picked up the tray and headed for the door. Jessie followed her out into the hall.

"Thanks for being here, Sara," Jessie said and gave her a hug. "You're a good friend."

Sara smiled, hoping to soothe the fear in Jessie's eyes. "I'll be in the lab if you need anything."

Sara dealt with Mrs. Rollins and returned to the lab. The tests confirmed it: She was another elderly pneumonia patient.

"Sara." Dr. Lesterbrook stared down at the computer screen, a cup of coffee in his hand. "Are we caught up in the wards?"

"Yes. And unless someone just walked into the waiting room, we're caught up with the walk-ins, too."

"Cripes, don't say that and jinx it," he grumbled, but she saw a slight curl at the corner of his mouth. "We've got coverage for tonight. Why don't you clock out?"

"It's only seven o'clock. I thought you needed me here until at least eight."

"Ten hours is long enough. It won't help the cause if you get sick too." He looked over at her. "Seven o'clock tomorrow morning, right?"

"Yes sir. Seven o'clock."

Sara hurried out to the parking lot. She planned on picking up Gypsy then heading home. Lucille had been gracious about doggie-sitting during the flu crisis, insisting Gypsy was no trouble. But it was time for Sara to reclaim her dog and spend some quality time with her. She missed Gypsy. And Sara needed to catch up on laundry. The last day she had off was so long ago that the towels in the hamper were starting to smell.

A gentle mist had fallen throughout the day, freezing on the windshield once the sun went down. She turned on the defroster and sat waiting for it to melt, mad at herself for not putting the scraper back in the car. Traffic in and out of the parking lot was unusually busy. She attributed it to the inordinate number of patients and their visitors. She wiped her sleeve across the condensation on the side window just in time to see Jessie emerge from the front door of the hospital and head down a row of cars. She sat watching, wondering who had come to pick her up. But Jessie didn't climb into a car. Instead, she swung her leg over the seat of the red motor scooter and rocked it off the kickstand. Before Sara could put her window down and yell, she was gone, pulled out into traffic and heading downtown.

"Sorry, Gypsy. Momma's going to be a little late."

Sara followed, peering through the small dome of melted ice at the bottom of the windshield. Jessie pulled up in front of Batch's Bar and Grill. The lights were out. She unlocked the door and went inside as Sara eased into the parking spot behind the scooter. Sara sat, waiting and watching for the Open sign to light up or the neon beer signs to flicker. But the bar remained dark behind the tinted windows. Sara's curiosity got the best of her and she went to the door. It was locked. She knocked, wondering if she was being too nosy. What if Jessie was meeting a woman at the bar? What if she had plans for a romantic rendezvous with one of her girlfriends? A little wine. A little music. A little sex. What better way to forget her worries?

The door opened and Jessie stood eating a handful of popcorn.

"Hello. Am I interrupting something?" Sara asked.

"Heck no. Come on in. How did you know I was here?"

"I followed you from the hospital parking lot. You're riding the scooter."

"Yeah. I didn't sell it. Remember?" Jessie relocked the front door and led the way into the kitchen where the light was on.

"It's wintertime. It's cold."

"It's not too bad if you dress for it. Have you had dinner?" She opened the big stainless steel refrigerator and peered inside.

"I haven't. And I'm hungry. I decided I didn't want leftover hot turkey sandwich from the cafeteria."

"I was going to eat leftover whatever's in my fridge."

"My fridge in the apartment is empty. I haven't had time to go to the store. I had a tray of ice and six bottles of condiments."

"The bar's closed because of the holiday?" Sara asked as she untied her scarf and slipped off her coat.

"The bar's closed because Ron can't run it by himself without screwing things up. Batch ordered it closed for a couple days. Ron argued, but thank God he didn't win." Jessie pulled a stack of hamburger patties from the freezer. "Batch woke up right after you left. He sure has a husky cough."

"I'm not surprised. But that's good. That means his body is breaking up the congestion. It's gross to think about, but he needs to cough up all that phlegm and get it out. They'll probably encourage him to do that."

"You're right," Jessie said, looking around the edge of the refrigerator door. "It's gross."

"Don't you have something you could fix that doesn't require a big production? You'll have to heat up the whole grill, won't you?"

"I don't mind." Jessie said it but her face didn't agree.

"Peanut butter and jelly?"

"That's not very culinary."

"But it's easy. I'm the queen of easy cooking." Sara boosted herself onto the counter and sat watching.

"You're kidding. I took you for a great cook. Sauces and glazes and casseroles full of healthy ingredients."

"Only in my dreams. I never had the time to learn to cook. I was either working or going to school. Or both. Who has time to create in the kitchen, especially when it's just for one?"

"But you're so smart with science and medicine and stuff in the laboratory."

"No correlation," Sara said with a chuckle. "I can boil water though."

"So if I lined up all the ingredients for cinnamon rolls on that counter you couldn't make them?"

"Nope. Well, if I had a detailed recipe I might. Maybe. But I could run a fasting blood sugar on you the morning after."

"You need cooking lessons." Jessie had been spreading peanut butter and blackberry jam on bread. She cut the sandwiches in half, added a handful of chips to the plate and handed one to Sara. "It's not a cheeseburger with grilled onions but it's filling."

"It's perfect. Thank you, Chef Singer."

They carried their plates to the bar and sat on the high stools.

"I haven't had a peanut butter sandwich in a long time," Jessie said, the peanut butter sticking to the roof of her mouth.

"Me either. Do you mind?" Sara asked, pointing behind the bar.

"Sure. Go ahead. I'm sorry. I should have offered something to drink."

"What can I get you to drink, ma'am? Tap water or water from the tap?" Sara picked two glasses from the shelf behind the bar.

"How about Perrier over ice?" Jessie said with a twinkle in her eye. She pointed to the small refrigerator under the counter.

"We can do that." Sara traded the two glasses for two stemmed goblets and set them on the rubber mat. "Ice?"

"Stainless steel bin next to the sink. Open the lid. And there's probably a jar of maraschino cherries in the little fridge." Jessie continued to eat her sandwich, amused by Sara's bartending.

"Here you are. One fizzy water, on the rocks."

"Here's to bartending." Jessie held up the glass then sipped. "And to Batch Singer, may he recover quickly and be back home before the New Year."

"I will definitely drink to that." Sara took a sip as well. "Oh, look. Limes." Sara picked three from a dish, holding them as if she was ready to juggle them. "How do I do this?" She tossed one in the air but struggled to trap it against her chest. "Not like that, I'm sure."

"Let me show you." Jessie came around the bar and stood behind her. "Imagine a big X in front of you. Aim for the tops of the crossbars with alternating tosses." She took control of Sara's hands, tossing the limes in the air and trying to catch them.

Sara giggled, feeling like a puppet within Jessie's arms.

"Catch it, catch it," Jessie teased, continuing to make tosses.

"I got it. No, I don't."

Finally all three limes were on the floor. Sara and Jessie laughed hysterically, Jessie still guiding Sara's hands as if she had limes to toss. Sara leaned back into her, laughing so hard tears were streaming down her face.

"Don't quit your day job, slick," Jessie teased. She picked up the limes and tossed them into the sink then took her seat at the bar.

"You have to promise to teach me how to do that someday."

"Right after I teach you billiards, cooking and how to ride a motor scooter."

"I hope I do better at scootering than I did juggling or I'll be in big trouble. Can Batch and your father juggle? Is it a bartender thing?"

"I doubt Ron can." Jessie scowled at the thought.

"Can I ask you a personal question?"

"Yes. And the answer is, when I was fifteen in the backseat of my grandmother's Buick." Jessie mused.

"Thanks for sharing, but that's not what I was going to ask." She dropped cherries in their glasses then poured the rest of the Perrier.

"Okay, shoot."

"Your father. Ron. I get the feeling something is strained between the two of you. Lord knows I'm certainly not the standard bearer for parental relationships, so I'm not being judgmental. It's just when you mention him there's a little crease that runs right down between your eyes, right here." She touched the spot on the bridge of Jessie's nose.

Jessie frowned deeply.

"Yes, just like that."

"My *dad* and I don't have a great relationship, you're right. Batch is more of a dad than Ron ever was."

"Your grandparents raised you after your mother passed away?"

Jessie nodded as she fished a cherry out of her glass.

"But he was there, helping, wasn't he?"

Jessie's nod changed to a headshake.

"Only occasionally. He worked on a cruise ship then as a long-haul trucker. Any job that took him out of town. My grandparents always told me where he was and what he was doing. They tried to make it sound like he was some great explorer, conquering the wilderness. They'd show me postcards and pictures of places he had been. The Grand Canyon, Canada, Gulf of Mexico." She chuckled. "I was ten or twelve before I realized the postcards didn't have any writing or postage on them. He hadn't sent them. It was just their way of defending him."

"Or protecting you."

"My grandmother did the best she could. I was in junior high when my father was home for a visit. He was working at the bar. I think he was home because he needed money. I overheard my grandmother tell him she was planning my birthday party. She wanted to know what he had gotten me." Jessie took a slow sip.

Sara watched without interrupting. She had her own parental demons to deal with and could well sympathize.

"He told her he didn't get me a present. I think his exact words were, 'Hell no, I'm not buying her anything. She's got enough shit.'"

"That's terrible. He's your father."

"I don't think he ever thought of me that way."

"Maybe he was jealous of the attention your grandparents gave you. After all, he was their son."

"I think he somehow blamed me for my mother's death. I don't think he has ever gotten over losing her."

"How in the world could he do that? You were not responsible for that."

"They say I look like her."

"She must have been a gorgeous woman then," Sara said softly.

Jessie looked up at her and smiled.

"Thank you."

"Did you tell Batch about the tournament? I'm sure he's proud of you. He seems very devoted to everything you do."

"I haven't yet, but I will." Jessie lowered her eyes as if hiding something.

"Fourth place. Isn't that good in a big tournament like that?"

"Yeah, well."

"I sense there's more to this story." Sara took a sip then stared at Jessie over the rim of the glass. "What aren't you telling me?"

"I quit. I pulled out of the tournament right before the semifinals."

"Why, for heaven's sake? Couldn't you have won?"

"I'll never know. I cashed, that's the main thing. I knew if I stayed until the end of the tournament I'd be distracted. I'd feel guilty I wasn't here, with Batch." She quickly looked up and pointed a finger at Sara. "You can't tell him anything about this. He's not to know. I'd never hear the end of it."

"You did it for him. I think that's wonderful."

"I did it for myself. I wasn't going to stay in Vegas and feel like an ungrateful granddaughter."

"But you were so looking forward to playing in a Las Vegas tournament. It was your dream. You're going back aren't you? There'll be other tournaments, won't there?"

"I don't know. I haven't decided." She downed the last of her Perrier and set the glass on the bar.

"Jessie, you have to. You can't quit now. You'll never forgive yourself."

"That's what Ballard Cues said. They'd have offered me a sponsorship if I had won."

"If this is what you really want to do, you have to go back and try again." Even as Sara spoke the words she felt a lump rise in her throat. Once again she was pushing Jessie to leave. And she hated herself for it.

"You think I should?"

"Absolutely, I do. You don't want to look back someday and say I had a chance and didn't take it."

Jessie walked to the end of the bar and snapped on a light over the first pool table. She pulled a cue from the rack and began indiscriminately shooting at the color balls on the table. Her brow was furrowed as if she was wrestling with her choices.

"What would Batch tell you to do?"

"He wasn't happy I was going in the first place. Now that I'm back he'd probably tell me to stay." She stroked the cue ball, sending it around the table, dropping two balls before coming to rest right in front of her.

"What's in all these boxes?" Sara peeked into one of the boxes stacked on an adjacent pool table. "They're all marked with X's."

"They're for the Christmas decorations. Batch wants the decorations down and packed away ASAP after Christmas. I think Ron brought them out but that's as far as he got." Jessie looked up at the tinsel garland draped from the ceiling and light fixtures. "I'll get them packed up before he gets home or he'll climb the ladder and try to do it himself." She went back to shooting.

"Where's the ladder?"

"Storeroom," she said while lining up a long shot across the table. As soon as it dropped Jessie turned with a scowl. "Oh, no. You are not doing that."

"Why?" Sara was already heading for the storeroom to find the ladder.

"Because it's not your job. Don't you have someplace you need to be?" Jessie put the cue back in the rack and hurried to catch up with Sara. "I'll do this later."

"This is a two-person job. Why can't I help?" Sara flipped on the light and scanned the storeroom for a ladder. "We can have it done in no time if we work together. Wow, there's sure a lot of booze in here."

"Is this what you're looking for?" Jessie said, pulling the door back to reveal a stepladder standing behind it.

"Yes." Sara grinned and reached for it.

"I've got it."

Jessie carried it into the bar and set it up then climbed to the top. She released the end of a tinsel garland and let it fall. Sara coiled it and dropped it in a box. She followed Jessie around the room as she took down garlands, snowflakes and wreaths. Sara stood at the bottom of the ladder, boxing whatever she was handed.

"Be careful," Sara said, grabbing the sides of the ladder as Jessie extended herself to reach a small wad of foliage taped to the ceiling. "Use a stick or something to get that. You're going to fall."

Jessie made a lunge at it, knocking it free.

"I got it," she said, and descended the ladder. "I think that's the last of it."

"What is that?"

"Mistletoe."

"That's mistletoe?"

"Sure." Jessie held the crumpled wad of twigs at arm's distance and stared at it. "Vintage mistletoe."

"I thought mistletoe is supposed to be green with little white berries on it."

"This has some green leaves. A few. Okay, two leaves. Batch bought it at the farmers market years ago and he insists it's still good. So, I'm not throwing it out."

"Remind me to buy him a new sprig of mistletoe next year," Sara said.

"I know what he's going to say. This isn't used up yet. It still works."

"How does mistletoe work? It's a parasitic plant."

Jessie stepped closer and held the mistletoe over Sara's head.

"Like this," she said, and kissed her on the cheek. "See? It still works."

"Yes, I guess so. But I don't think that's the way it's supposed to be used."

Jessie's playful grin dissolved into a tender smile.

"You're right." Jessie held it up again and gently pulled Sara to her, kissing her full on the mouth. It was a long kiss. But for Sara, it ended too soon. She held the pose, her mouth turned up to Jessie's and her eyes closed, languishing in the memory of it. She felt Jessie's lips return to hers, softly at first. Then demanding and hot. Jessie's tongue pushed its way inside and lapped at the roof of Sara's mouth. Jessie's arms folded around her with a kiss like no other Sara had ever felt. It was soft yet commanding, sweet yet mature. It was perfect and she didn't want to give it up. She slipped her arms around Jessie's neck, giving herself to the kiss.

Jessie backed her against a pool table, their lips still locked together as she leaned Sara's back onto the felt. She cradled Sara's head in her hands as she continued to devour her mouth, licking, sucking, probing. Jessie had released some eager animal in Sara. Jessie's breasts and hips pressed against hers. Her mouth was hot and commanding. It was hard not to want even more.

"Sara," Jessie whispered, gasping for breath. "I have to stop. I have to stop or I won't be able to stop."

"Yes. I think so too." Sara pulled herself off the table, embarrassed that she had allowed things to go so far. And embarrassed that she wished Jessie hadn't stopped. "I need to get home. It's late." She collected her coat and scarf.

"I'm sorry, Sara. I didn't mean to let that happen," Jessie said, taking her arm. "Are you okay? Are you mad at me?"

Sara touched Jessie's face.

"No, I'm not mad. If I didn't want you to kiss me, I would have stopped you."

Jessie followed her to the front door. She inserted the key and turned the latch, but held the door closed.

"Are we still friends, Sara?"

"Yes. Of course."

"Then why are you leaving?"

"Because if I stay we're going to do something we're not ready for."

Jessie stared into her eyes for a long moment. She draped Sara's scarf around her neck, her fingertips gently sliding down folds of the fabric.

"You're right. We're not."

Sara pulled the door open and walked out into the darkness, her heart still pounding furiously. Something else deep inside was reminding her she was a woman with needs. Needs that wouldn't be satisfied tonight. Needs that only Jessie could satisfy.

CHAPTER NINETEEN

It had been two days since The Kiss, a kiss even the frantic pace at the hospital couldn't diminish. The hospital was filled to overflowing. Private rooms were converted to hold two patients. Even surgical recovery rooms were used for flu patients. Batch was still in the hospital on antibiotics and oxygen. He was improving and able to sit up, but his white count and temperature indicated he wasn't ready to be at home. Sara saw Jessie briefly, passing her in the hall or in the cafeteria. Sara was too busy to linger. She wasn't sure where the conversation would lead anyway. What her heart increasingly wanted to say wasn't what she knew Jessie needed to hear. Sara couldn't ask her to stay in Ilwaco. To give up Las Vegas and her dream. To settle for anything less than the happiness she deserved.

"Hey, Sara, did you see who's in the hospital?" Margie asked, sliding her tray onto the table.

"Big Bird and Cookie Monster." Sara took a bite of ravioli.

"What?" She chuckled. "No."

"Yes, they are. Down in the pediatric ward. The fire department is doing it for the kids."

"That's great, but that's not who I meant." Margie squirted ketchup on her plate then dipped a tater tot in it. "I saw Jessie going into her grandfather's room." She leaned in and whispered, "So, tell me all about it. You picked her up at the airport. And?"

"She came home to see Batch."

"Speak of the devil," Margie said, elbowing Sara and nodding toward the drink station. Jessie was filling a glass. "She's coming over here."

"Hello, Margie," Jessie said with a polite smile, then turned a soft gaze at Sara. "Hi. The doctor said Batch can go home tomorrow if his lab work is better."

"I'm so glad he's improving, Jessie." She patted the vacant spot next to her at the table. "Sit down. Eat with us. Tell me how he's doing."

"Thanks, but I can't. I told Batch I'd be right back. This is for him," she said, lifting the tray. "I know he's better. He's complaining about the food."

"I'm sure he's ready to go home. I'll get his CBC run as soon as the orders come through."

"I'd like to get him settled before I leave tomorrow evening."

"You're leaving? When?"

"Yes. I've got a red-eye out of Portland. I start back to work at Caesar's Saturday. I'm meeting with a potential sponsor on Tuesday."

"I'll take you," Sara offered eagerly.

"Jimmy's going to take me after she closes the kitchen. Batch agreed to let Ron reopen tomorrow. Besides, that's too late for you to have to drive back alone. Jimmy's staying in Portland with her sister." She looked down at the tray. "I better get this down there before he rings the nurse and asks what happened to me."

"I'll see you before you go, won't I?" Sara asked.

"Sure."

Sara stared down at her ravioli, swallowing back her disappointment.

"What was that all about?" Margie asked, once Jessie had disappeared into the hall. "And no, I don't mean the hospital stuff. What is going on with you and Jessie?"

"Nothing."

Margie turned her head sideways and leaned down to see Sara's face.

"Yes, there is. What?"

"It's nothing. Jessie is going back to Las Vegas now that Batch is going home. That's all."

"And you're upset about this why?"

"I'm not upset. I think it's great. Jessie wants to go back and I'm happy for her. She isn't a small-town girl. What she wants she won't find here." Sara dropped her fork on the tray, her appetite gone.

"Did you think she was going to stay in Ilwaco? Is that what this is about?"

"I thought she might. Maybe," Sara said with a shrug.

"Have you told her how you feel?"

"No. And I don't plan to."

"Why not?"

"She wants to go. Besides, I'm not sure she'd stay even if I asked."

"So, you love her?" Margie asked solemnly.

Sara frowned at her, surprised she had come to that conclusion.

"Well, do you?"

"Yes. I think so," she finally confessed.

Margie stared in silence, a dumbstruck look on her face as Sara stood and carried her tray to the cart.

Sara returned to the lab, eager for the distraction of work.

"I hope these are the influenza A ninety-six-well plates," Dr. Lesterbrook said, hurrying into his office with a FedEx box in his hands.

"Let's hope so. There's only one left in the box," Sara said, escorting a patient into the drawing station. She had just slipped the butterfly needle into the back of the woman's hand when she heard a loud cuss word. Dr. Lesterbrook rushed out of his office, holding a handkerchief around his wrist.

"Ms. Patterson," he bellowed. "Bring me four by fours and a surgical dressing. Hurry."

No one else was in the lab to help, but Sara wasn't going to pull out the needle and have to do it again.

"One minute, please. I'm in the middle of a draw." She finished collecting the tube of blood, attached a bandage and ushered the woman out.

"Hurry up!" He stood at the sink and watched blood run down his hand from a gash on the back of his wrist. Sara quickly gathered bandages, tape and surgical dressings from the cabinet.

"What happened?"

"Goddamn box cutter slipped." He didn't seem to be in pain. Rather more aggravated he had done it. "I'll do it." He took the gauze from her, pushing her away with his elbow.

"Let me help, Dr. Lesterbrook." She reached for his arm, but he blocked her.

"I can do this. You go on back to work." He had a harsh set to his jaw, as if mad at her intrusion.

Dr. Lesterbrook couldn't bandage his wrist without help. Sara could see that. But his male stubbornness or his managerial dominance wouldn't allow it. She needed to convince him to let her help before he lost enough blood down the sink to need a transfusion.

She handed him several gauze squares.

"Apply pressure," she declared and unwrapped a surgical adhesive dressing. "Do you need stitches? That looks pretty deep."

"No. Just a dressing." He pressed hard enough to turn his fingers white.

"Trade me for fresh ones." She handed him clean gauze squares when the others became saturated with blood. When she reached for the bloodied ones in the bottom of the sink he stopped her with an elbow.

"Leave them. I'll get them. Just apply the damn bandage."

Sara started the edge of the dressing above the wound on his forearm. She planned to smooth it down over the gauze, sealing it around the gash to prevent infection. But Dr. Lesterbrook pulled his arm away once it was started, as if he knew best how to dress a wound.

"I'll finish it."

"Let me do that. It needs to be straight and tight."

"I said I've got it." He smoothed it down his arm. It wasn't perfect but it was done.

"Dr. Lesterbrook, I know how to attach bandages. Why don't you let me help?" She turned on the hot water, ready to clean out the sink.

"Ms. Patterson, please get back to work. You've got patients waiting. I'll take care of this."

Sara didn't say a word. She washed her hands and went back to work. She escorted the next patient to the drawing station. When she finished and led her out, the waiting room was filled to capacity. Edie returned from the ward where she had taken throat swabs on two children in pediatrics.

"Can you take one of the walk-ins?" Sara asked.

"As soon as I get back from ER. They need a blood chemistry drawn stat." Edie labeled her swabs and sat them in the fridge to be processed then headed to ER.

Sara could hear a chorus of coughing and sneezing from the waiting room. She knew the longer the patients had to sit and wait, the worse they felt. If anyone out there didn't already have the flu, they were being exposed to it. But she could only do so much. One patient at a time. She couldn't keep up with the needle sticks on the patients, let alone running the tests. No one else was in the lab to help, except…

"Dr. Lesterbrook," she called, labeling a tube.

"Yes?" he said, striding out of his office with a stack of paperwork.

"I've got six walk-ins out there waiting. Francis doesn't come in until four. We've got three out with the flu. I'm worried we're getting too far behind."

"Where's Edie?"

"She's been called down to ER."

"When she gets back have her do the draws while you process."

"Dr. Lesterbrook, I've got nurses calling for results. I don't have anything to tell them. I need more help than that."

"I've got a call into three labs, asking for temporary help. Some of our people should be back in a couple days. For now, we'll have to do the best we can."

"Could you help with a few of these, just until I get caught up?"

He furrowed his brow.

"I'm busy right now, Ms. Patterson. You'll have to take care of it. I trust you can do that, can't you?" It wasn't so much a question as a demand. He rotated his forearm as if reminding her of his wound.

"I'll run the tests if you'll just draw a couple of these for me, please?"

"Ms. Patterson, that's what we pay you to do. If you can't do it, let me know and I'll see about replacing you."

"Yes sir. I'm sorry. I'm just a little tired."

"We all are. Take a deep breath. When you have a minute, get yourself an energy drink." He walked out and disappeared up the hall.

With Edie's help, Sara finally finished the last draw, labeled the tubes and placed them on the rotator. She peeled off her latex gloves and stuffed them in the biohazard bucket on her way out the door. She headed down the hall to the ladies' room, her teeth clenched and her fists deep in the pockets of her lab coat. She closed and latched a stall door and leaned back against it, releasing a sigh. She didn't need to use the ladies' room. What she needed was a moment alone to collect herself. Events were starting to back up on her and she didn't like the feeling. She was furious. Jessie was leaving. Dr. Lesterbrook was acting like a distrusting prima donna. She hadn't taken time for so much as a coffee break in three weeks yet more was expected of her.

She took a deep breath and tried to compose herself. It didn't help. Hard as she tried, she couldn't stop the tears welling up. She buried her face in her hands as she began to cry. She slid down the door until she was squatting, hugging her knees as she sobbed.

She was a good medical technologist. She knew she was. She took pride in her work. This was the job she always wanted. Someday she too might become a laboratory manager. She was not about to let Dr. Lesterbrook intimidate her. Whatever his problem was with her, she knew she was more than capable. She blew her nose, dabbed water on her face to wash away the tearstains and returned to the lab to let him know that as well.

"Dr. Lesterbrook," she said, standing in the open doorway to his office. He was perusing an online catalog of laboratory equipment.

"Are we caught up?" he asked, without looking away from the screen.

"Yes. For now anyway." She closed the door and sat down in the chair at the edge of his desk. "Dr. Lesterbrook, I am concerned with the work atmosphere and I think we need to discuss it."

He tossed her a sideways glance then went back to his search.

"I'm listening."

"I realize there are some extraordinary conditions in the hospital right now. They're no one's fault but I think they have contributed to an unhealthy, even acrimonious situation. I'm sure you've noticed it."

"Acrimonious. That's a hefty description. Are you saying there's discord in the ranks?" He continued to read supply prices.

"Yes." She sat waiting for attention, however long that took. He finally closed the laptop and swirled his chair to face her.

"And how do you suggest we resolve this?"

"If you had asked me that a year ago I probably would have said I quit. But that isn't the resolution I'm seeking."

He tipped his head slightly, as if evaluating her answer.

"Dr. Lesterbrook, I don't want to quit. I like my job, most of the time. This is what I've always wanted to do. But I feel like I'm swimming against the current here."

"Because I can't find you additional help?"

"Because you wouldn't offer help," she said firmly. "I know my job description. But we were in a crisis today. I asked for assistance so the walk-in patients, a room full of them, didn't have such a long wait. You refused. I am concerned you put the patients' health in jeopardy. Every one of them was presenting with flu symptoms, more than half with bronchitis and or pneumonia. Yes, you are an administrator now, but patient care should have taken precedence. With all due respect, sir, I think you should have helped."

He lowered his eyes and rocked back and forth in his desk chair as if contemplating his reply. It was a long time in coming.

"Ms. Patterson, Sara, I'm sorry you think I neglected my duties today. It was not my intent." He heaved a heavy sigh then glanced out the window in the door, as if checking to see if anyone was in the lab. It was empty. "Sara, the patients *are* my first concern. Never dispute that fact. First. Always." He held up a stern finger. "Choices I make, I make in their best interest. Not yours. Theirs. You are my second in command and you should know that. I would expect the same from you."

"Yes sir. Absolutely. I'm just not sure I understand your reasoning for the choices you made."

He stared at her as if challenging her right to know. He could have summarily ended the conversation and sent her back to work. She wouldn't have been surprised had he done so. Instead, he opened the top drawer of his desk and took out a folder marked Standards and Controls. He flipped through several pages of reports and printouts until he seemed to find what he wanted. He read down the page then took it out of the folder and handed it to Sara.

"Fourteen months ago," he said, "white count, six thousand. Lymphs, thirty percent. Both within normal range." He handed her the next page from the folder. "Seven months ago. White count, fifty-two hundred. Lymphs, twenty-five percent. Low to normal range." He handed her the last page from the folder. "This month. White count, four thousand. Lymphs, twenty percent. Both below normal."

"These are yours?" she asked as she studied the test results.

"Yes."

"What about your red count?"

"It's normal."

"So no anemia?"

"That's right." He watched her, as if allowing her to come to her own decision.

"My first thought is an immunodeficiency." Sara looked up at him. "Have you been tested for HIV?"

"Four years ago the Red Cross set up their bloodmobile in the parking lot. I stopped in during my lunch break. I'm AB positive, so a little rare and they always need it. I hadn't donated in years. Two days later I got a letter. They couldn't use my blood and suggested I contact them as soon as possible." He swallowed. "I was HIV-positive." Their eyes met. His, glistening with his admission.

"Your doctor has you on antivirals?"

"Yes. And we're trying out a new one, hoping for some better results. Like all other medical tests, Sara, this information is private and privileged. You are the only other person in the lab who knows."

"Does the hospital know?"

"Yes, of course. I told them immediately. It was agreed that I could remain on staff so long as I was capable, and with obvious restrictions to my hands-on patient care."

"What was your last T-helper cell count?" Sara slowly drew her eyes up to his, knowing she had just ask him if he was no longer just HIV-positive, but had full-blown AIDS.

"It was below two hundred."

"And the most recent?" she asked, knowing he was already at risk for infection, an infection which could prove life threatening, an infection like pneumonia.

"Sent off last Tuesday," he replied with a catch in his throat.

Sara looked down at the printouts, summoning her courage. "I understand why you didn't want to help with the flu patients. I am truly sorry. I wish I had known." She had a new understanding of the man, but it had come at a high cost. She knew the waiting for his test results would be pure agony. And there was nothing she could do to help him ease that burden.

CHAPTER TWENTY

Sara was busy the next morning when Edie went into the ward to draw from various patients, including Batch. Sara ran the CBC herself. Batch was well enough to go home. She processed a walk-in patient then headed down to Batch's room to wish him well. She also wanted to visit with Jessie before she flew back to Las Vegas. But he had already been discharged. Sara planned to stop by Batch's after work but that idea was squashed when she received a text from Jessie just after three.

Found an earlier flight. Jimmy and I are on the way to Portland. Sorry I missed you. ttyl. J.

Sara decided it was probably for the best. Jessie's electrifying kiss had taken control of her practicality. She could have easily been just another notch on Jessie's cue stick. She was glad she wasn't. Lovemaking wasn't something Sara did just for the thrill of it. It took three days and no further word from her before Sara finally deleted Jessie's text. She needed to do it, if only for her sanity.

"Are you being a brave little soldier?" Margie strode into the lab with her test kit in hand. She perched on a stool and opened the kit.

"About what?" Sara pushed the buttons on the analyzer and watched the tray of tubes advance through the machine.

Margie stuck her finger and touched the test strip to the droplet of blood before replying.

"Jessie, of course. She went back to Las Vegas, didn't she?"

"Yes. What's your number?" Sara looked over Margie's shoulder to see the meter reading. "Three ten?"

"Glazed doughnut." Margie grinned. She took out a syringe and injected herself. "Have you heard from her?"

"Jessie? No. I'm sure she's busy."

"If you had let her know you were interested I bet she'd call or at least text once in a while." She studied Sara a moment. "What's that frown all about? You told her, didn't you? You told her you loved her and she went anyway."

"No, I didn't tell her anything. I'm not even sure myself. Maybe it was just circumstances." She prepared a slide for the microscope, hoping to divert the conversation.

"What circumstances? You're far too practical to fall in love with a bartender without good reason. What is it? Keep in mind we are best friends so I'm licensed to ask such questions."

"We kissed."

"Really?" Margie's eyes lit up.

"Yes. But that's all we did. Just kissed." Sara wanted to add it was an incredible kiss, but she didn't. That was for only her to know.

"Where?"

"At Batch's, on a pool table."

"Really? Horizontal on a pool table? I can certainly picture that. Wow. On a pool table."

"Oh, stop it."

"Where were her hands?"

"On the ends of her arms, Margie. Don't you have accounts to process?"

"Okay, I'll go. But I have to know one last thing. Did you kiss her back?"

"It was a standard, four-lip kiss. She kissed me and I kissed her."

Sara's eyes drifted past Margie's grinning face to see Dr. Lesterbrook staring back at her. He had obviously heard at least some of the conversation and didn't look pleased. Margie collected her paraphernalia and strode out of the lab, leaving Sara to face him alone. But he didn't wait for an explanation. He went into his office and closed the door.

"Okay, so now there's no doubt about it. He knows I'm gay," Sara whispered to herself and returned to work.

What Sara hadn't confessed to Margie was the text she composed two days ago and had waiting to be sent to Jessie. She had tinkered with it, rewritten it several times, added cute little icons, even added a picture of Gypsy extending her paw, but she hadn't had the courage to send it.

Sara did the next best thing. She went to Batch's for dinner. She ordered a mushroom spinach pizza and a Perrier, and sat at a table near the front window and imagined Jessie's smile and bright eyes as she tended bar. Batch wandered around the room, refilling water glasses and chatting with his customers. When he saw Sara he made a beeline for her table, grinning happily.

"Hey there, missy. How's the pizza?" He snatched her check off the table and crumpled it into his pocket before she could stop him.

"It's wonderful. I love thin-crust pizza."

"That's Jessie's idea. I thought pizza had to be thick crust."

"How is she doing?"

"I thought you'd know."

"No, I haven't heard from her. What makes you think I would have?"

"She mentioned your name a couple times. All I know is she's bartending at Caesar's and she beat the pants off some yahoo wearing silver-tipped cowboy boots." He chuckled mischievously. "She said he had a big stick."

"Batch, the Coke canister is empty," Ron called, holding up the nozzle.

"Damn, always something," he grumbled and walked away, but not before giving her a wide smile.

Sara checked her phone for messages. There was nothing important or at least nothing that needed an immediate reply. Nothing from Jessie. She opened the draft of the text she had been working on. She didn't plan to send it but she began tweaking the contents. She finally gave up, deleted it and started new.

> *Just checking on you. How's Vegas? Is the world's best bartender juggling limes for the customers? I'm at Batch's for dinner. No one here to give me cooking lessons so I'm enjoying mushroom spinach pizza. And fizzy water. Batch looks good, back to his jolly old self, I'm glad to say. But I think he misses his granddaughter, big-time. Me too. I miss the mistletoe. Take care of yourself. Luv, S.P.*

She rearranged the words, added a smiley face and played with the phrasing as if it was mindless doodling. She was ready to delete the text when someone bumped the back of her chair. She accidentally touched the send button and in an instant it was gone, sent on its way to Jessie.

"NOOOOOO," she gasped. "No no no no no. I don't want to send that. Stop." She quickly stuffed her phone in her jacket pocket, as if hiding the evidence. She sat silently for a minute, listening for the phone to chime. It didn't, and she went back to her pizza, relieved the text seemed to have fallen on deaf ears. She took a bite, trailing a long string of cheese from her mouth to the slice when the phone did chime. It was a text from Jessie.

Thin crust?

Sara grinned and replied.

Of course.

She sat chewing pizza and waiting for another text. A few more minutes passed, raising her angst. Finally, a reply.

Hello, by the way.

Hello. How's Las Vegas?

Best bartender in the world, eh? I don't know about that.

Sara tapped out a reply, but Jessie sent another text before she could finish.

You miss me? Is that true?
Sara cleared the screen and typed an answer.
Yes. No one's here to serve my fizzy water in a goblet.
LOLOLOL I'll have to let Ron know he's doing it wrong.
Jessie immediately sent another text.
Do you really miss me? At least a little.
Yes.

Sara stared at the phone, waiting for Jessie's reaction. She finished the pizza and her Perrier but no reply. She waved a thank-you to Batch and walked out into the cold January mist. Whether by fate or accident, Jessie now knew how she felt. Sara would have to deal with it. She was happy living in a small town, working in a small-town hospital and having a small circle of close friends. She liked its stability, boring as it was. She wouldn't ask Jessie to give up her wanderlust or her quest for bright lights to settle for that. But the thought that Jessie finally knew how she felt brought a smile to her face.

Sara headed home. Gypsy was waiting for her at the door, wagging her joy.

"Hello, baby. Yes. Momma's home." She gave the pup a smile and a pat. "Did you and Lucille have fun today playing with Buster?"

She dropped her keys on the table and pulled her cell phone from her jacket pocket. Still no reply from Jessie. She sorted through her junk mail, refilled Gypsy's dishes and gave her a treat, made a cup of ginger peach tea and started a load of laundry, but still no reply. She put on her pajamas and slipped into bed just after ten, her cell phone at her side, but Jessie hadn't replied and Sara wondered why. Maybe she should have explained herself. Maybe she should have said yes, she missed her and looked forward to her next trip home. Or yes, she missed her and hoped she was having a good time. Or yes, she missed her like she misses all her friends when they are away. Sara turned out the light and had just placed it on the bed table when the phone chimed. It was from Jessie. It was just a smiley face. Nothing else.

Sometime during the night three more texts arrived, but Sara hadn't heard them. Next morning she hungrily opened them.

Sorry it took so long to reply. It's nuts down here. Three weddings and four conventions all at once. You'd think computer geeks and investment bankers wouldn't be heavy drinkers. FYI, no one ordered Perrier in a goblet. I would have noticed. J.

So, it's okay if I text occasionally? When I'm not schlepping drinks and juggling limes, that is. J.

And thanks, it's nice to be missed. Batch never says anything like that. I've got a tournament in Reno coming up. It's small but if I can cash, I'll have a sponsor. Nothing huge, but it's a start. At least it's better than Ernie's Quick Lube in Ilwaco. I've given a couple private lessons. Rich gals pay well if you admire the way they lean over the table. Hi to Gypsy. Give her a pat for me. J.

Sara couldn't decide if she was envious or jealous of those women. She knew what Jessie's body felt like pressed against hers. She showered, dressed and stood at the kitchen window, eating a cup of yogurt while she mentally composed a reply. Gypsy sat staring up at her, wagging her tail, as if she wanted to know why Sara was grinning happily at the rainy Washington morning.

"Jessie says hi, Gypsy." The dog held up a paw. "And you're going with Lucille today to the assisted living center in Longview so you have to be on your best behavior. Where's your vest?" Gypsy cocked her head and perked her ears. "Go get your vest." The dog trotted down the hall and returned with a tennis ball in her mouth. "Well, that's almost a vest. We'll need to work on that one."

Sara finished her breakfast and leaned against the counter as she tapped out her text reply.

Sure, it's okay to text. If I'm busy or you're busy, they'll wait. I'm glad to hear about the sponsor. Let me know how you do at the tournament. I'm sure you'll be victorious. Why wouldn't you? I've seen that killer look in your eyes. :) I'm still working extra hours but the flu crisis seems to be ebbing. I hope you got a flu shot. It's not too late. btw…if I'm not mistaken, these little text machines can also be used to make phone calls. Take care. Luv, S.P.

She sent the text and loaded Gypsy in the car. She just pulled into the hospital parking lot when Jessie replied.

They make calls too!!!! Who'd've thunk it? I'll have to try that. Have a great day. J.

Sara smiled as she reread the text on her way across the parking lot. Gypsy trotted along, her leash looped around Sara's wrist.

"Gypsy, why did Momma wait so long to text Jessie?" she said, holding the door. "Can you say dimwitted?"

"I beg your pardon?" Dr. Lesterbrook said, passing them in the hall.

"Good morning, Dr. Lesterbrook. I was just talking to myself." She grinned.

"How long will the dog be here?"

"I'm not sure. Lucille is taking her to Longview today. She should be here any time."

He looked down at Gypsy, raising an eyebrow at the dog's enthusiastic tail wag.

"Gypsy, say good morning to Dr. Lesterbrook." Sara gave the signal and the dog barked then sat down and offered a paw.

"Does she fetch?"

"Yes, if I ask her to bring me her therapy vest, she brings me her ball."

He chuckled and started up the hall.

"You'll keep her out of the way, won't you, Sara?"

"Yes sir. I will."

Sara slipped on her lab coat and checked the computer. The lab was finally back to full staff. Sara moved Gypsy to an out-of-the-way corner while she worked at the microscope.

"Is that dog still here?" Dr. Lesterbrook said on his way through to his office to answer the phone.

"She'll be out of here shortly, sir."

Sara pulled out her phone to check with Lucille's office to see if she had left yet, but Dr. Lesterbrook called from his doorway before she could call.

"Sara, ER needs a blood chemistry, stat," he said.

"I'll be right there. Gypsy, sit. Stay." She grabbed the phlebotomy tray and headed out the door, trusting Gypsy would stay put for a few minutes. When Sara returned to the lab Gypsy wasn't in the corner. "Gypsy?" she said quietly, checking the other corners of the room. "Gypsy?"

Edie caught her eye and nodded toward Dr. Lesterbrook's office and his open door. He was sitting at his desk, typing on his keyboard. Gypsy was between his feet, curled up in a little ball and apparently asleep.

"Sara," he bellowed. He didn't move or look up, but held up a folded piece of paper. "This was delivered ten minutes ago."

Sara opened it and read the message.

Sara, Sorry but Gypsy and I will have to reschedule our outing. I've got a cold and just can't face it today. Talk with you soon, Lucille.

"Dr. Lesterbrook, I'm so sorry about Gypsy. I truly thought she'd be gone by now. If you can spare me for thirty minutes or so, I'll take her home."

"Nope. Leave her. She's out of the way. Run that blood chemistry."

"Are you sure? I can hurry."

"She's fine. Run the test."

Sara ran the test and entered the results. She processed two walk-ins and did a workup in the blood bank for ICU. When she went back to Dr. Lesterbrook's office, he was leaned back in his desk chair reading a report in one hand while his other was draped over the side, stroking Gypsy's head as she slept. Sara went about her work without disturbing him. She planned to take Gypsy outside during her coffee break, but he had already done it and was walking her back into his office.

"I would have never believed that," Edie said softly. "The old fart actually has a heart."

"Edie!"

"Well, when have you ever seen him that nice to any living creature? No wonder he's single."

Sara glanced through the window of his closed door. If only Edie knew what he was facing maybe she wouldn't be so hard on him. It was five thirty when Sara hung her lab coat on the hook and went to collect Gypsy. Dr. Lesterbrook had his feet propped up on the corner of his desk and Gypsy was on his lap. He was adjusting her therapy vest.

"Gypsy, are you ready to go home?" she said. The pup immediately hopped down and came to her side.

"She needs a new vest. That one spins around and comes loose because it's too big."

"I was wondering if that was the problem. I'm sorry if she was a nuisance today. I wouldn't have brought her to the hospital if I'd known Lucille wasn't up to taking her."

"It's done. Good night, Sara." He offered the feeblest of smiles but it was a smile, nonetheless.

"Good night, sir."

"By the way, I'll start interviewing for a new assistant next month. I just wanted to let you know." His phone rang before she could ask for details. She assumed he'd tell her on a need-to-know basis. If he was replacing her, he'd tell her that too. She'd just have to wait. She was too tired tonight to worry about it.

January bled into February then March with typical cold rainy Washington weather. Sara and Jessie texted and occasionally called each other, but both had busy work schedules. Jessie announced she was working double shifts, insisting the money was too good to pass up. The midnight shift tipped better than the day shift and the women were hotter looking, she had confessed with a chuckle. Bartenders were no longer allowed to use their cell phones while on duty so their communication time was limited to the daytime, when Sara was busy at work, or very late at night. When she wasn't bartending Jessie was either playing in tournaments or practicing. She cashed in four tournaments since Christmas, boosting her popularity with potential sponsors. She sent Sara a picture of herself as she worked the bar at a reception for the cast of a movie being filmed in Las Vegas.

Sara waited until she was alone in the lab before tapping out a reply.

Who's the good-looking woman in the red tuxedo vest? Is she in the movie too? S.P.

LOL You're biased. J.

GUILTY!! I'm going to Batch's tonight. I want a good hamburger. S.P.

I'm jealous. Burgers here are greasy and overpriced. Gotta go. I'm giving a private lesson. The woman doesn't know a cue stick from a lipstick but hey, it's money. Let me know how the burger was. Lv J.

Sara grinned at the *Lv*. That was as close to *Love* as Jessie had used in any of her texts. She'd take it.

* * *

"Good evening, Sara," one of the waitresses said with a welcoming grin. Sara had become a regular, eating at Batch's once a week, sometimes twice, depending on her leftovers at home. She threatened not to come back if Batch didn't allow her to pay. He snarled and grumbled but agreed, although she suspected he altered the amount she was charged. Hamburgers weren't supposed to be two dollars. Sara tried to strike up a conversation with Ron, but he seemed distant and disinterested.

"What are you going to have, missy?" Batch asked, bringing her customary glass of Perrier with two cherries. She could easily ask for it in a stemmed goblet, but that was Jessie's province.

"What's good, Batch? Surprise me." Sara was in a strange mood. Giddy, for lack of a better word. It was fun texting with Jessie. It was even more fun lying in bed, talking to her late at night while she was on break, the noise of the casino in the background. She felt like a teenager passing notes in study hall.

"Navy beans and ham soup," he suggested. "With corn bread."

"Sounds good."

"You coming for the party?" he asked.

"Party for what? Birthday?"

"I'm going to retire. I'm sixty-eight. I've saved a little and it's time to give it up. I've been doing this long enough."

"Does Jessie know you're retiring?"

"Yep. She said she'd be here. She's not happy about it, but she said she'd come."

"I'm sure she doesn't expect you to run the bar forever," Sara teased.

"That's not why she's mad. She thinks I shouldn't give it to Ron."

"You're giving Batch's Bar and Grill to Ron?" It came out of Sara's mouth before she could filter it and she knew it sounded judgmental. "I'm sorry, Batch. That's none of my business."

"Jessie's got her own life. She's moved on. She doesn't need a bar hanging around her neck like a millstone." He nodded toward Ron behind the bar. "He ain't got shit. He needs it more than she does."

Sara looked down at her phone as tears welled up in her eyes. If he gave the bar to Ron, Jessie would have no reason to come back to Ilwaco. At least, no reason to stay.

"Batch, I'm sorry. There's something I forgot to do." She left money on the table and hurried out into the night air as tears rolled down her face.

It was fifteen minutes before she brought her emotions under control enough to send a text. She knew she couldn't call without crying at the sound of Jessie's voice.

Why didn't you tell me Batch is retiring? S.P.

Jessie replied almost immediately.

I guess I thought you knew. I'm sorry, Sara. I suppose you know he's giving the bar to Ron. J.

Yes. Batch told me. S.P.

Sara's phone rang. It was Jessie, but she didn't answer it. She sent a text instead.

I can't talk right now. I'm sorry, Jessie. I'm a little upset. S.P.

Why are you upset? I'm the one he's screwing over. Ron Singer is nothing but a giant puddle of stupid. If Batch thinks I'm ever going to work for him, he's nuts. My father will run that place into the ground in six months. Maybe less. J.

I wish you had told me, Jessie.

My shift starts in ten minutes. I have to go. Can we talk later? J.

Sure.

Sara sent the text but her heart wasn't in it. She felt betrayed. She wasn't sure if she was mad at Batch for destroying her hopes that Jessie would eventually come home to work in the bar, or mad at Jessie for being so far away when she needed someone to comfort her. But Jessie didn't call later that day or the next.

Sara's phone finally rang, waking Gypsy asleep at the foot of the bed.

"Hello," Sara said sleepily.

"Oh, crap. I woke you up."

"Jessie? What time is it?"

"Seven twenty-three. I thought you'd be up. You said you were an early riser."

"It's Sunday."

Gypsy crawled up the comforter and curled up next to Sara, as if she heard distress in her voice and came to console her.

"It's been four days. I need to know if you're still upset with me."

"I'm not upset. I'm more disappointed," Sara replied.

"Judge, can I have the court clerk read back Ms. Patterson's testimony from last week?"

"Okay, I said upset. But it was a shock."

"No kidding. There's going to be nothing gradual about it. Batch is deeding the place over to Ron on the twentieth."

"That's less than three weeks. How can he make such a big decision in just three weeks?" When Jessie didn't reply, Sara said, "It's been more than three weeks, hasn't it? You've known about this?"

"Yes."

"How long have you known, Jessie?"

"A while."

"How long?"

"I knew he had been thinking about retiring last summer. I didn't know he planned to transfer ownership to Ron until Christmas. He told me while he was in the hospital. I didn't know it meant that much to you, Sara."

"How could you not know? We're friends. I thought you'd at least tell me when things happen in your life that could change that friendship."

"Mistletoe friends who kiss?" Jessie's voice softened.

"Yes."

"Do you kiss all your friends like that?"

"No. I only kiss special friends. Very special friends."

"So, I'm a very special friend?"

"You know you are, Jessie."

"Special enough to ask you out on a date?"

"It's a little geographically challenging, don't you think?"

"I'm driving back. Would you go to Batch's retirement party with me, Sara?"

"Yes."

"You will?" Jessie gasped. "You'll go out with me?"

"Yes. I'll go out with you, Jessie Singer." Sara snuggled beneath the covers, grinning at the thought. "So long as it's not on the back of your motor scooter."

"I think you need scooter lessons."

"Will you teach me?"

"Okay, but your first lesson will be on the beach, with no traffic around."

"Are you saying you expect me to fall off?"

"I didn't say that. But I'm taking no chances. I don't want you to get road rash. I don't want anything about you hurt."

"Oh, goodie. I get to learn to ride a motorcycle."

"Motor scooter," Jessie corrected.

"Hush. Don't spoil this. It's a motorcycle."

"Fine. Motorcycle lessons on the beach."

"And a date with a bartender," Sara added softly.

"Absolutely," she said with quiet satisfaction. "I have to go, Sara. I'm playing in a private tournament today. It's a bunch of guys with money in their pockets and a buzz on. Wish me luck."

"Good luck, Jessie. And yes, I miss you."

"Good. I like that. I miss you too," Jessie whispered then ended the call.

Sara placed the phone on the pillow next to her and smiled contentedly.

"Gypsy, Momma's got a date with Jessie."

Sara had just stepped out of the shower, the glow of excitement still fluttering around her, when an incoming text chimed on her phone. It was from Dr. Lesterbrook.

I need to see you in my office Monday morning, seven o'clock, sharp.

CHAPTER TWENTY-ONE

Monday was a bright sunshiny morning. Sara stood under the shower, fighting her mixed emotions, each dueling for superiority. A date with Jessie made her feel giddy all over. But a meeting with Dr. Lesterbrook could be career-altering. He had never sent her a text before demanding a meeting so this was obviously important. Over the past few weeks she had watched a parade of men and women through Dr. Lesterbrook's office, their résumés in hand, knowing he was interviewing job candidates. If he planned to replace her and had found his choice, so be it. If he expected her to train a new co-worker then answer to them, she'd deal with that as well, at least for now. Practicality and reason said the meeting with Dr. Lesterbrook should take precedence. She could soon be among the unemployed. But her heart wouldn't hear of it. Jessie was on her mind. Jessie's smile and delectable kiss.

She arrived at the hospital early. Dr. Lesterbrook was already in his office. She donned her lab coat, checked the computer for orders then knocked on his door.

"Come in," he said, without looking up from his work.

"I'm ten minutes early. I hope that's okay." She closed the door and placed her hands in her lab coat pockets to hide their nervous fidgeting.

"Sit down, Sara." He finished reading a page then looked over at her. "Do you know Shawn Breck?"

"No sir. I'm sorry, I don't. Should I?"

"Not necessarily." He handed her a page from the folder.

"Wow, this is a very impressive curriculum vitae. Graduated magna. Curator's scholarship." She read down the page. "I don't see any work experience, but his educational background is solid. Bachelor's in medical technology. Master's in clinical laboratory science. Very impressive." She handed the paper back.

"Mr. Breck will join our team the first of the month. This will be his first actual job experience. I'm sure he'll be nervous."

"Excuse me, sir. I'm not sure why you are telling me this. Am I supposed to train him to take my job? Am I being replaced?"

"Yes, to both. Mr. Breck has the educational background to be well qualified, but he has only limited on-the-job training. He'll need a couple months to get up to speed on how things are done here at Ocean Side. That's up to you to decide."

"I'm supposed to train him so I can be fired?" She asked defiantly. "Is this because I'm gay?"

"What makes you think you're being fired? I said nothing about firing you, Sara. Mr. Breck is being trained to take your job because you are being promoted to take mine. The hospital asked me to find and train my own replacement and I have. I recommended you for the job. We now need to get you a capable assistant. I think Shawn has the credentials you'll need. If you don't agree, we'll reevaluate in a couple months." He leaned back in his chair. "And why is homosexuality an issue?"

"Dr. Lesterbrook, are you stepping down?" she asked, stunned at his revelation.

"Yes. July first. Sooner, if things change."

"Does this have anything to do with your test results?"

"Yes. It's time for me to rethink my treatment options." Dr. Lesterbrook had, in not so many words, just admitted he had

AIDS and he had done it without so much as a crack in his voice. But the glisten in his eyes belied his stoic exterior.

"I am so, so sorry. Is there anything I can do?" Sara wished she had his strength. She was on the verge of tears, but knew that wouldn't help.

"Sara, have I ever given you the slightest indication I had a problem with you being gay? Have I said anything?"

"No sir."

"And I never will. I don't believe in throwing stones."

Sara gave him a curious look.

"As in living in glass houses?" she asked carefully.

"Yes." He sat staring at her, as if waiting for her next question. "Go ahead. You may ask."

"Dr. Lesterbrook, are you gay?"

"Yes. Since even before it was cool to admit it. I lost my partner to cancer years ago. I've never met anyone good enough to take his place. And now, well," he said with a small resigned smile on his face. "I have his memory." He stood up, as if putting that thought to rest. "Shall we get to work?"

"Yes sir. Thank you. I really appreciate you giving me this opportunity." She stood and extended her hand to him. "Thank you for your confidence in me, sir. I'll do my very best."

"I know you will, Sara. I've been hard on you for a reason. I knew you had potential, but this job comes with lots of headaches. I had to know if you could handle it. You've overcome every obstacle I've thrown your way. I think you'll do fine. Just don't let the job get to you. Have a life outside this lab."

"I plan to."

* * *

Sara worked overtime, rode miles on her exercycle and went on long walks with Gypsy, anything to pass the time as she waited for Jessie's return to Ilwaco. Their occasional texts and phone calls only heightened her anticipation. It didn't help that Jessie chuckled when she mentioned how excited she felt. But

Sara suspected Jessie was just as anxious, something her jokes and chitchat couldn't hide.

"Are you sick?" Margie asked.

"No, why?" Sara pushed her nearly uneaten lunch back on the tray.

"You haven't eaten a complete lunch all week. You've wasted more food than I eat, and I'm a piglet."

"I have not. And you're skinny. Here, eat mine. Mashed potatoes and gravy are good for you." Sara sipped her coffee.

"Are you okay, Sara? You sure spend a lot of time staring off into space and humming. That's not normal."

"Jessie's coming back for Batch's retirement party. And she's asked me out on a date."

"A date with the bartender?"

"She's not just a bartender. She's also a professional pool player. And a chef. And a restaurant manager, or was."

"But, honey, she moved to Las Vegas. You're having a date with a woman who drifts into town every few months then leaves again. That's like trying to rope the wind. You can't fall in love with someone like that."

"It's too late. I already have. I can't help it. Even if we never have a future I'm going to enjoy it while I can. Even if it's only one date, one time."

"When does she get here?"

"Tomorrow. Batch's retirement party is at eight. She invited me to go with her."

"You have that stars-in-your-eyes, across-a-crowded-room look on your face."

"If you mean being with her makes me feel contented, yes."

"Then I have to say I'm envious. I wish I had someone who made me feel like that," Margie said dreamily.

"You'll find someone. Don't give up. You're wonderful and caring."

"Don't get me wrong. I still believe she's out there, somewhere. That someone who'll rock my world and make me walk funny." Margie gave Sara a hug, carried her tray to the cart and went back to work.

Sara considered working overtime, but she was too excited to sit. The next day was worse. Jessie was on her way home and Sara couldn't wait.

"Sara," Dr. Lesterbrook said with a scowl.

"Yes sir?" Sara had left the water running in the sink and had turned on the centrifuge with nothing in it. "Oh, sorry. I forgot." She grinned sheepishly.

"Where is your mind today?" He didn't wait for an answer.

The hours and minutes couldn't pass quickly enough. She rushed home after work and showered to get the lab smell off her skin and out of her hair. Gypsy sat on the bed, watching as Sara sifted through her closet, looking for the perfect retirement party outfit. This was to be a celebration. At least it was for Batch and Ron. And she would dress appropriately.

Sara pulled out a white pantsuit. It was tailored and expensive and not suited for anyplace she had been in Ilwaco so far. She had always wanted one so she had splurged and bought it with her first paycheck. It had an elegant collar, one that accented the silk blouse she had bought to go with it, a collar that also framed her cleavage surprisingly well if she chose not to wear a blouse. "Blouse or no blouse," she asked Gypsy. "Let's try no blouse."

She dressed and stood at the mirror. She didn't remember the placket of the jacket revealing quite so much cleavage.

"Definitely needs a blouse." She went back to the closet to find it, but the doorbell rang first. Sara stepped into her white pumps and went to answer it. Jessie wasn't due to pick her up for nearly two hours so she expected it to be a salesman or an evangelist, neither of whom she would give even a minute of her time. But it was Jessie, dressed in black slacks and a white tuxedo shirt, the sleeves rolled back to the elbow.

"Wow," Jessie said with a wide grin. "You look incredible."

"Wow, yourself. I didn't expect you until later." Sara pulled her inside and threw her arms around Jessie's neck, hugging her warmly. "It's wonderful to have you back in Ilwaco. I thought the party was at eight."

"It is. Shall I go and come back later?" Jessie raised an eyebrow then turned for the door.

"No," Sara gasped, grabbing her arm. "Don't be silly. I'm not ready is all."

"You look pretty good to me." Jessie's gaze drifted down Sara's cleavage.

"I wanted this evening to be special. After all, Batch only retires once."

"You'll be the best-dressed woman there. I guarantee it."

"You look pretty good yourself. I like the tuxedo look. Very sexy. Kind of casual chic."

"I wish I could say I planned it, but the truth is this is the result of poor time management. It's the only thing I have clean."

"Well, I like it. You look sexy." Sara straightened her collar.

Gypsy scampered across the living room and jumped up against Jessie's leg, wagging and pawing for attention.

"Hello there, Gypsy. Yes, I missed you too. I brought you a present but you'll have to fight your mommy for it." Jessie reached down and ruffled the dog's ears.

"That's sweet of you. What do I get? A rubber ball or a rawhide chew?" Sara teased, smiling at Gypsy's acceptance of Jessie.

"Neither." Jessie fished in her pocket and pulled out a wad of crumpled leaves.

"What is it? Dandelion greens?"

"This is hand-picked and brought to you directly from the Sonoran Desert. It's mistletoe. I picked it myself when I was in Phoenix last month for a tournament. It grows in the tops of the trees. Big clumps of it. You said you missed the mistletoe. So I brought you some. Fresh, sort of."

"Oh, Jessie. What a sweet, wonderful present. Thank you." She reached for it but Jessie pulled it away.

"That isn't the present. This is." She held the mistletoe over Sara's head and kissed her.

Sara moaned contentedly.

"I like this present better," she whispered, and kissed Jessie back.

Jessie wrapped her arms around Sara and devoured her mouth hungrily. Sara fell into her embrace as Jessie's tongue slipped in and out of her mouth and her hands stroked her back.

"Should I stop?" Jessie whispered. "I know we said we weren't ready before. But I love you, Sara. And if I kiss you again, I don't know that I could stop. So, tell me." She drew a fingertip down Sara's cheek and across her lips. "What do you want me to do?"

"I love you too. And always will."

"I don't want to have sex with you. I want to make love to you. Over and over again." Jessie pushed her fingers through Sara's hair. "But only if you're ready."

Sara knew she couldn't walk away from Jessie, not this time, even if it meant months of heartache waiting for their fleeting moments together. There was only one answer she could offer. Sara kissed her. With all her love, she kissed her. She closed her eyes, pressed her body against Jessie and felt her arms fold around her. There would be no regrets.

Jessie unbuttoned the white jacket and let it slip to the floor as her hands caressed Sara's firm breasts, then removed her bra. Sara peeled Jessie's shirt off her shoulders. She wasn't wearing a bra and her nipples were already erect and hard. Sara guided Jessie onto the sofa, pulling her down on top of her. Jessie's nipples gently kissed Sara's, brushing back and forth against them until Sara groaned in delight. Then Jessie's lips formed around Sara's erect nipples, sucking and licking at them. Jessie unzipped Sara's slacks, gently slipping them down over her hips. She unzipped her own slacks and placed herself against Sara's eager wetness. Jessie repeatedly brought Sara to climax with a gentle passion Sara had never known. When they could take no more, they showered, standing together under the water.

"Can I fix you something to eat?" Sara leaned back into Jessie's strong arms as the water cascaded over them.

"I don't want dinner," Jessie said, kissing Sara's neck.

"You're not hungry?"

"I didn't say that."

Sara turned within Jessie's arms to face her, smiling up at her.

"Show me."

Jessie turned off the shower and knelt, taking Sara's hot sweetness in her mouth. Sara closed her eyes and leaned back into the corner as a volcanic eruption exploded through her. When she was finished she reached for Jessie's sweet spot, coaxing her to an orgasm as well. Jessie shuddered and released a deep sigh then pulled Sara into her arms.

"What did this bartender ever do to deserve you?" Jessie whispered.

Sara didn't like the joke. It reminded her Jessie would soon return to Las Vegas and her hectic world of bartending and billiards.

"We need to get dressed or we're going to be late." Sara climbed out of the shower and dried off then went to dress. They hurriedly dressed and headed into town. Sara couldn't bring herself to ask when Jessie was going back to Vegas. For tonight, she didn't want to know or even think about it. She'd have plenty of time to worry over that news.

It was after eight when they came through the door to Batch's. It was crowded. It wasn't a private party. Batch said he wouldn't have been a successful businessman if it hadn't been for his customers so the doors were open to all. A banquet table with platters of pizza, chips and hot wings as well as a chocolate fudge cake that read "Happy Retirement" treated the customers. The jukebox was playing country music. Some of the tables had been moved, cleared away for dancing. Several couples were two-stepping around the floor. Ron and another woman were behind the bar, pouring drinks. Jimmy was in the kitchen keeping the banquet table restocked.

Jessie held tight to Sara's hand as they moved through the crowd, greeting everyone with a smile and a nod.

"Do you know all these people?" Sara asked, staying close.

"Only about half of them. But they're customers so you smile. Batch's rule."

Batch saw them coming through the crowd and grinned broadly. He was wearing a bright red shirt and a black bow tie. He gave them each a hug, adding a handshake and slap on the back to Jessie.

"You did the right thing, Kid. I'm proud of you. Your grandmother would be proud of you too. You won't be sorry. You'll see."

He turned to Sara.

"Can you two-step, missy?"

"I don't know. Maybe." Sara hadn't danced since her ballroom dancing class in college, a class she took in no small part because she had a crush on the instructor.

"Good, 'cause I can't." He laughed out loud and led her into the middle of the dance floor. He wrapped an arm around her and began to dance, shuffling them both in a big circle. It wasn't graceful but it didn't have to be. They were having fun, loud, raucous, exuberant fun. Sara did her best to keep up as they went around and around. Jessie watched from the edge of the dance floor, smiling proudly. The song ended and changed to a slow one. A man in cowboy boots and tight jeans cut in on Batch, a gleam in his eye at the chance to dance with the attractive blonde in the white pantsuit. Batch nodded and backed away, but Jessie had other ideas. She set her glass on a table and crossed the floor, tapping on the cowboy's shoulder.

"May I have this dance?" Jessie asked.

Sara stepped into her arms.

"Yes, you may, good lookin'. And thank you for rescuing me." Sara rested her head on Jessie's shoulder as they danced around the floor. "Batch is a sweet man. You're very lucky to have family like him."

"He thinks you're sweet too. He told me so."

"Is he going to miss this?"

"Probably, for a while. He's not as young as he'd like to be. He'll probably want to help out once in a while, but the stress of running things has gotten to him. He hasn't taken a vacation in years. He said there's nowhere he wants to go. I couldn't get him to come down to Las Vegas for even a weekend." Jessie turned and twirled in time to the music as Sara held on to her.

"You'll be back this summer to give me scooter lessons, right? You promised. I know, I know. Your schedule may get busy, what with work and tournaments and travel for your sponsor. It just doesn't seem fair you have to be gone so long."

"I bought it."

"As soon as you go back to Las Vegas we'll be texting and talking again like it's no big deal. Like there was never anything between us. Like it was just a one-night stand."

"I bought it," Jessie repeated softly.

"One-night stands don't work for me. They never have. You bought what?"

"I bought the bar. I bought out Ron. I worked double shifts and saved all my tournament money so I'd have enough. I talked it over with Batch and I bought him out. I didn't say anything because I wasn't sure he'd accept my offer. I thought he might turn me down just out of cussedness. But as they say, I made him an offer he couldn't refuse. As of midnight tonight, it's mine. I'm sure Ron will be here from time to time. He may need a job now and then. But I think we can work that out."

"You bought Batch's Bar and Grill? You own it?"

"Yes, I do. I even own the name. I wanted a place of permanence."

"You own Batch's and you're staying in Ilwaco?" Sara asked, as she held her breath, still trying to process Jessie's news.

"Yes. I am."

"I thought you wanted to follow your dreams. I thought you wanted to become a professional pool player."

"I got to do all that. I followed my dreams. I played pool and won tournaments and made money. But that life isn't all it's cracked up to be. If I want to play pool, I can do it here. I want roots and stability and I want to be practical. I want to hold on to something that is real. I want you in my life, now and always."

Tears began to roll down Sara's face. And she couldn't stop them. Jessie wiped her thumbs across Sara's cheeks.

"And to think I would have never found you if I hadn't come to your lab that day to have tests run," Jessie said softly as they continued to sway to the music.

Sara placed her hand on Jessie's chest and held it there.

"It may be your breasts that brought us together but it's these two hearts that will keep us together."

"So, how about a long-term relationship with a bartender?"

"I thought you'd never ask." Sara slipped her arms around Jessie's neck and kissed her as they stood in the middle of the dance floor, Jessie's dance floor. Their dance floor.

THIS COULDN'T POSSIBLY BE THE END

Bella Books, Inc.

Women. Books. Even Better Together.

P.O. Box 10543
Tallahassee, FL 32302

Phone: 800-729-4992
www.bellabooks.com